"LUKE, I CAN'T,"
CAROLINE MURMURED.

"I can't let my feelings get in the way of what's important to me. There can't be any *us*, not while you're trying to ruin Granbury with your darn theme park."

"Caroline, I—" Oh, hell! What was the use of more talk? Taking her in his arms, he lowered his lips to hers and summoned a kiss from her soul.

She felt breathless when, finally, he released her.

"Caroline," he whispered. Drawing her hand to his chest, he pressed it to his thundering heart. "Feel that?"

When she nodded, he took her other hand and pressed it to the curve of her breast. "And this, do you feel this?"

She nodded again, feeling her own heart racing even faster.

"*That's* what's important, sweet thing."

ABOUT THE AUTHOR

When asked if Granbury, Texas, the small-town setting of *Midnight Blue*, was a real place, Nancy Landon was mildly outraged. "Of course it's a real place!" said Nancy. "I spent my vacation there. And let me tell you—you can't find a prettier place, with nicer people." Nancy makes her home in Oklahoma City with her husband, Mike, and their son, Greg. Her two older children, Lisa and Robert, both live in Texas.

Nancy Landon

MIDNIGHT BLUE

Harlequin Books

TORONTO • NEW YORK • LONDON
AMSTERDAM • PARIS • SYDNEY • HAMBURG
STOCKHOLM • ATHENS • TOKYO • MILAN

Published June 1989

First printing April 1989

ISBN 0-373-70358-9

To Harold and Wilma Pickens:
How rich my life has been
because of you, my dear parents,
who kindled my dream and said,
"You can do it."

To Mike, my husband,
who shared the struggles,
as well as the joy of success;

And to Greg, my younger son,
my toughest critic,
who said, "Mom, this one's going to sell."

CHAPTER ONE

"Hop in my bed, sweet thing, and I'll take you for a ride."

Caroline McAlester shielded her eyes against the piercing rays of the north Texas sun and squinted up. Way up. "Am I supposed to know you?"

A man with broad shoulders and coal-black hair knocked the brim of his white cowboy hat upward with his knuckle and hooked his thumbs into the waistband of his button-up jeans. "I never invite a woman into my bed unless I know her."

Then, sidling up to Caroline, he squeezed her elbow and spoke in a husky voice that sent a shiver down her spine. "And I do know you. Maybe not well, but I've wanted to get to know you better for a long time. Now hop on into my bed," he said, and without another word, he grasped Caroline by the waist with both hands and lifted her onto the twin mattress as if she weighed no more than a twenty-pound sack of potatoes.

"Grab those bedposts, sweet thing. With your tiny frame and my long legs we'll win hands down."

Caroline hesitated, glancing first at the rotund mayor in the official's booth on the near corner, then at the appealing stranger who'd plopped her into his bed. He stood behind the brass footrails, his fists on his slim hips and a smile curling the corners of his mouth.

The mayor's right arm stretched high over his head, the sun glinting off the chrome-barreled pistol clutched in his hand. As he tested the microphone, Fourth of July revelers jockeyed for good viewing positions for the annual bed race around the Granbury Town Square.

"Ladies and gents, get on your mark!" the mayor announced.

Caroline swatted a fly buzzing her wheat-blond curls, then flattened herself onto her stomach on the lumpy mattress. The moment she grasped the bedposts, the sound of male laughter rippled through the crowd. When her fingers slipped from the shiny brass, she knew why. Vaseline! A glance down the row of beds told her the other women contestants were equally dismayed, and she couldn't help chuckling herself.

"Get set!"

She stole a quick glimpse at her attractive bed partner, who was leaning forward, his hands grasping the footrails, his tall body tensed, waiting. She cupped her mouth and yelled over the din of the crowd, "But who are—?"

A pistol shot cracked the air, obliterating Caroline's question. Her head snapped back as the bed raced forward and she tightened her grip on the bedposts. No doubt about it. Whoever this guy was, he had his heart set on crossing the finish line first.

Cheering onlookers pressed against the red, white and blue plastic ribbons that cordoned off the quaint town square. Youngsters waved United States flags and threw colored confetti at the six teams as they raced by.

The bedposts vibrated violently in her hands, as the bed jolted around the Square on its metal wheels. Caroline watched helplessly as her fingers slowly slipped from the posts again. Determined to win, she gripped the mattress with her hands and with the narrow toes of her red cowboy boots, inching her way up the black-and-white ticking crab-style. As she regained her grip on the bedposts, she collapsed onto the mattress. Her heart pounded furiously beneath the bright red shirt she'd knotted at her midriff.

"You okay, Caroline? Caroline?"

At the sound of her name, she lifted her head and nodded, wondering if her partner's eyes or the sun were responsible for the warm feeling that spread across the bare skin above her jeans. She wanted to look into those eyes again. God, they were gorgeous! Midnight blue, with an intriguing, mysterious glint. But who was the man, and how did he know her?

"Hang on. Watch out for your feet!" she heard him yell.

She braced herself as their bed bumped into the one on their right. But her partner deftly avoided a three-bed collision, and they emerged from the first turn a length ahead of the pack. The crowds that lined the sidewalks cheered, and somewhere a bugle played "Charge."

Caroline turned her head and signaled her partner thumbs up. His face broke into a broad grin, and he wiggled his brows, then ducked his head and shoved the bed even harder.

What Caroline could see of his jet black hair contrasted sharply with the stark white of his cowboy shirt. Through that shirt she could see his muscles flexing, and she caught her breath as another pearlized button snapped open, exposing more of his chest. Someone in the crowd gave a wolf whistle. Caroline whipped her head around and caught a quick glimpse of a woman in the crowd, her fingers still at her lips.

As they rounded the corner by the Opera House, Caroline scanned the faces in front of her store, hoping Ellie had managed to sneak out long enough to watch the race. Sure enough, there she was, her orange-red curls bobbing in the noonday sun. Caroline caught Ellie's attention, shrugged and cocked her head in an effort to tell the buxom widow she was as much in the dark about the man whose bed she was in as Ellie probably was.

Wouldn't Granbury's first ladies have frowned if they could have seen her spread-eagled on a bed, racing around the Square like some dance hall hussy? That was probably the only aspect of Granbury's colorful history Caroline wasn't anxious to preserve—the insistence that ladies of fine upbringing behave with propriety. Give her the raucous, wild and woolly pioneering spirit any day, and propriety be hanged.

With a sudden surge, the young couple in the bed to the far left stole the lead. Caroline recognized them as the couple who'd married that morning in the gazebo on the Square. She thought of the two hundred dollars in prize money and wished she could signal her leggy teammate to slack off enough to give the newlyweds the edge.

As if he'd read her thoughts, her partner backed off on his speed, but so slightly that only she could sense it, and they sailed across the finish line by McNutt Brothers Hotel a close second to the newlyweds.

Crowds mobbed the winners, hoisting them gaily onto shoulders and parading them to the gazebo. Caroline smiled at her partner. Surrounded by a crowd of admiring young ladies, he tipped his hat and smiled back.

Feeling a slight twinge of envy, Caroline blew him a triumphant kiss, then stood up on the mattress to watch the procession. The boisterous, friendly crowd and the distinctive aroma of a Texas barbecue reminded her of other parades on the Square she'd viewed from her granddaddy's shoulders.

This year's winners were the kind of good sports the crowd loved. As two stocky young men carried the newlyweds on their shoulders to the gazebo, the bride and groom strained toward each other until they could wrap their arms around each other's neck. When they kissed as if they hadn't seen each other in weeks, Caroline clapped wildly. Then, as she pursed her lips to whistle, she felt the bed move beneath her and dropped to all fours to steady herself.

Her partner was tugging their bed backward around the corner, away from the crowded Square. She turned around on her hands and knees, crawled to the end of the bed and grabbed the top brass footrail. "What do you think you're doing?" she asked him.

With a devilish twinkle in his eyes, he winked at her and continued to back slowly away from the Square. "Running off with the prettiest little filly in town."

Caroline laughed and shoved a stiff forefinger into his taut stomach. "Oh, you think so?"

He halted his backward steps and folded his arms over his chest. "If you were a man and had a pretty little blonde in your bed, what would you do?"

Caroline smiled and shook her head, enjoying her partner's sparkling eyes and sense of humor. Even as she laughed, she realized there was something about his appealing cleft chin that bothered her, that tugged at her memory.

She crawled off the bed and wiped the Vaseline from her hands onto the seat of her jeans. "Fortunately I'm not a man."

His eyes took in the full length of her petite frame, slowing their perusal where her jeans hugged the curves of her hips. "No kidding."

Caroline lowered her gaze beneath his penetrating stare and kicked a dirt clod with her boot, hoping she wasn't about to hurt his feelings. "I wish I could remember your name."

The glimmer of excitement faded from his eyes. "I should've known you wouldn't remember me."

It seemed she had hurt his feelings. Maybe he had been in one of her classes at the University of Texas. Had she met him on spring break in Cancún? If she could get him to talk about himself, perhaps she could solve the mystery. "Are you from around here?"

He plucked his hat from his head and stared down into her eyes. "The name Luke O'Connor ring a bell?"

It didn't. "You look familiar...in a way, but I'm afraid..."

"Granbury High, Class of '76. Does that help?"

Caroline felt a flush on her cheeks. He was from Granbury, and she didn't remember him? "I'm sorry. But you graduated—what—five years before me? It's been a long time. I've been away, and—"

"I know. So have I." He shrugged, stroking the indentation in the crown of his hat between his thumb and forefinger. His fingers were long and tan, with a smattering of crinkly black hair on top.

Suddenly his eyes riveted to Caroline's, and he smiled again, almost as if he'd forgotten she didn't remember him. "I could sure use a glass of lemonade. How about you?"

"Sounds great."

"Rinky-Tink's okay?"

She nodded, relieved to see a smile on his face again. As they turned toward the Square, Luke cupped her elbow in his hand. His warm fingers brushed the tender bare skin above the curve of her waist, and in spite of the stifling summer heat, she felt herself shiver. When she glanced up, she found Luke smiling down at her.

They worked their way through the crowds, the smell of hot dogs and mustard mingling with the sweeter aroma of crape myrtle blossoms. People drifted in and out of the restored turn-of-the-century shops, some buying, some looking, some seeking a respite from temperatures in the high nineties. The old limestone courthouse, gleaming in the afternoon sun, sat in the center of the Square, like a sentry guarding the holiday festivities.

Curious looks from townsfolk warned Caroline she and Luke would probably be the topic of hot gossip on the Square in a couple of days when the holiday excitement died down. The ornery part of her briefly entertained the thought of giving the purveyors of local gossip something substantial to talk about.

Her temptation grew at Rinky-Tink's. Two young boys, sons of the man who owned an antique shop on the Square, sat at the table next to her and Luke, taunting her unrelentingly with a chant of "Caroline's got a boyfriend."

"So, you're still popular with the men about town," Luke observed.

Caroline took a sip of ice-cold lemonade and wrinkled her nose at the two kids. "They drop by my store every day and tease me."

"Can't say I blame them."

Caroline's fingers poised motionless on her straw as she felt the warmth of Luke's gaze. She smiled, tugged nervously on the red print bandanna around her neck and changed the subject. "That, uh, was a nice thing you did out there." She nodded in the direction of the street.

"What thing?"

"We could have won," she whispered, leaning forward. "I felt you slow down just before the finish."

A sheepish grin spread across his tanned face. "Nah, got tired, that's all."

"No way." Her eyes flicked to his broad chest and back to his eyes. "You hardly broke a sweat."

"Pushing you was easy. You're still a little thing."

She smiled, pleased by his compliment, and again tried to place him. But no matter how hard she tried, Caroline couldn't conjure up a younger version of Luke.

She was also sure he hadn't been in Granbury in the six months she'd been back in town. There was no way Caroline could have overlooked Luke—not with those eyes of his and...and everything else. She couldn't wait to ask Ellie what she knew about him.

The thought of her sales clerk reminded Caroline she had to get back to her shop. "I've got to go, Luke. I've got a store on the Square, and today's the busiest day of the year. I only stepped out to watch the race. My girls probably have their hands full with this holiday crowd."

Luke stood up and stuck two dollars under his lemonade glass. "Come on. I'll walk you over. I'd heard you'd restored the Emporium. I'd like to see what you've done with the place."

Caroline led him back across the Square and through the front door of Cain's Emporium.

Throughout the store, shoppers were eagerly examining the handcrafted items from Granbury she made it her business to stock. She noted that a lot of items were almost sold out.

Ellie stood behind the antique cash register, peering over Ben Franklin glasses while she poked the numbered buttons with a pencil. Her eyes darted from Caroline to Luke and back. She nodded toward the back room and gave Caroline one of her "I can handle it" looks.

Caroline glanced around the store again and decided she could wait a few minutes to restock it. Waving her thanks to Ellie, she pulled Luke through the blue-and-white gingham curtains that separated the shop from her back room.

Luke's gaze swept the well-stocked storeroom, and he whistled his approval. "I never dreamed you'd do something like this."

"Like what?"

"Run a store. I pictured you—" he narrowed his eyes and stroked his chin "—on the stage, as a model, maybe."

"Me, a model? I'm afraid I'm a half-dozen inches too short. As for the stage, I'll admit I had dreams of stardom when I was a kid taking dance lessons three or four days a week, but along about high school I got more practical with my dreams."

She frowned, then continued. "I just can't understand why you say this—" she gestured around the room "—doesn't fit me."

"I guess I never pictured the mayor's granddaughter doing anything ordinary."

"Ordinary?" Caroline echoed Luke's last word, but her thoughts snagged on the sarcasm in his voice when he referred to her position in the community.

"Don't take offense. I meant it as a compliment."

He sure had a strange way of complimenting her, she thought. She motioned to a small wooden table in the corner and sat down across from him.

"When we were kids we used to sneak in this old place and pretend it was haunted," Luke said.

"Some say the whole Square is haunted."

He snorted. "You don't believe that nonsense?"

"Well . . ." she hedged.

"Come on, the only ghosts in this town are in people's minds."

Caroline propped her elbows on the table and rested her chin on her palms. "Wouldn't it be neat if a ghost from the nineteenth century lived around here and could talk to us? Make us feel what it was like back then?"

"If it's all the same with you, I'll stay in the here and now. I like it right where I am."

"A man of today—a modern man—is that what you are?"

"Oh, not really," Luke said. "I just don't like to dwell on the past."

"That's how I felt until I remodeled this place. I never shared my mother's and grandfather's excitement about preserving this, preserving that. But something strange happened while I painted, while I sanded the floors. Why, I could close my eyes and almost feel what it was like when my great-granddaddy first opened the store."

Luke slapped his palms on the table. "You remodeled this place? All by yourself?"

She sat up straight and arched one brow. "Why does that surprise you?"

He squirmed in his chair and tugged on his earlobe, chancing a quick glance at her from beneath lowered lashes. "How can I say this without offending you? Oh, hell, Caroline," he blurted out. "I just never pictured you ... working."

If that was another one of his compliments, she didn't appreciate it. She reflected for a moment on her upbringing and felt her anger ebb. By most people's standards perhaps she had been spoiled—spoiled, indulged and pampered. "I guess I can see how you'd think that," she said. "But I've changed since I was a little girl." She ran her thumb back and forth over the persistent calluses on her fingertips. "For one thing, I've learned to put these to good use."

Luke glanced at her hands and did a poor job of smothering a grin. "Why don't you tell me how you got this place looking so good."

"It was a bigger job than I imagined. As it turned out, I did just about everything except the plumbing and electrical work. I'm a little disappointed with the paint."

She stood up, crossed the room and ran her fingers over a rectangular spot on the wall. "I found this patch behind an old cabinet. I think it's the original paint. But I gave up trying to match it."

Luke walked to the gingham curtain, took a quick look out front, then sauntered over to stand directly behind her. "Let me know if you ever paint again. I think I can help you match that."

She turned around, finding herself staring at a pearlized button on Luke's shirt. Springy black chest hair curled over it onto the white fabric. Caroline swallowed over a lump in her throat, remembering the way his chest had glistened in the sun. What was it they'd been talking about? Paint? She lifted her lashes and found him smiling at her. "You know paint?"

"You could say I do."

The seductive rumble of his voice made the hair at her nape stand up. "Ninety-year-old paint?" Her words came out squeaky, as if they'd been said by a lovestruck adolescent.

He grinned again. Damn the man! He knew exactly what effect he had on her. She sidestepped out of the narrow space between him and the wall, sure he could hear the telltale beat of her heart.

"My daddy painted lots of old houses around here before he retired," Luke said. "At one time or another he did every store on the Square—the ones that managed to stay open during the hard times, that is. After school and on weekends, I'd help."

"Strange, I don't think I ever met your dad."

A flicker of pain, or discomfort, or some other emotion Caroline couldn't define clouded Luke's eyes.

He shrugged and stared at his ostrich-skin boots. "Not so strange. You and I grew up in different worlds."

Her world. How it had changed in the past six months. For the umpteenth time since she'd returned to care for her mother, Caroline sighed and let sweet, golden memories of her childhood flood her mind. She glanced out the window on the back door and remembered skipping about the empty store as a child while her mother and grandfather rambled on about plans for reopening Cain's Emporium someday. ''We never knew how easy we had it when we were kids, did we?''

With a sweet smile of remembrance she turned to Luke. ''I sure miss them. I miss them all—Mother, Daddy and Granddaddy. He was so good to me.''

Luke's mouth clamped shut resolutely, and his nostrils flared. Without speaking, he returned to the table, shoved back the chair and sank into it. A cold stare froze his eyes to a pacific blue as he draped his elbow over the cane back and balanced his weight on the chair's two back legs.

Suddenly the front two legs of the chair hit the floor, and Luke snapped his gaze back to Caroline. ''Being the mayor's granddaughter had its advantages, didn't it?''

Caroline wondered what strange force had transformed Luke into the brooding, ill-tempered individual who glared at her from across the room. Whatever the cause for his change in attitude, she didn't appreciate his surly tone of voice when he'd mentioned her grandfather.

She dug her heels into the polished boards as she crossed the room. Stopping abruptly in front of him, she planted her fists on her hips. ''What do you mean by that?''

His eyes seemed to bore straight through hers for a moment. Then he glanced away. ''Nothing. Forget I said it.''

She tapped him on the shoulder, narrowing her gaze. ''You have something against my grandfather?''

Luke pursed his lips and looked at her with a cold stare. "Don't get in a huff. I just meant not every kid in Granbury remembers his childhood as you do."

Frowning, she tilted her head and tried to sift the intended meaning from his words. Granted, a painter's family had probably had it a lot rougher than hers. He was right. She'd been lucky to be Barron McAlester's granddaughter, to grow up in his spacious Victorian home, never wanting for anything.

"Being the mayor's granddaughter did have its advantages," she admitted. "But he's gone now." She glanced away and sighed. "They're all gone."

"I'm sorry, Caroline. I didn't mean to be rude. It's just that—well, as a kid, I was a bit envious of you."

Realizing that must have been hard for Luke to admit, Caroline sat down with him again. "Are your parents alive?"

"My father is."

"Then you're the lucky one now. All I have left is the house and this place and memories."

Absently she rubbed a spot on the table. "My daddy died when I was ten. Granddaddy was wonderful. He kept me busy until I got over the hurt. He used to bring me down here to the Square. He and his friends made me feel so...loved, so special."

Suddenly she remembered her manners. "Are you as hungry as I am?"

"Me?" He laughed and patted his stomach. "I'm always hungry."

From her back-room provisions, she produced apple slices, crackers, peanut butter and mint tea.

Luke spread peanut butter on two crackers and handed one to Caroline. She felt him study her as she devoured hers, then watched him as he ate his with deliberation.

Luke broke the silence. "Why did you come back, Caroline? For this?" His gaze swept the room and returned to her.

"Not really. Momma was sick." She managed a thin smile.

"She'd had a stroke, hadn't she?"

"You knew?"

"I've kept track of you—and your family—over the years."

Wondering why, she decided to pursue answers to her own questions. "You haven't been back for long, have you?"

"Uh-huh. Drove in from Arkansas last night."

"For the Fourth?"

"Nope, other reasons. Family. Business."

"Does your dad still live around here?"

"Sure does. Couldn't get him out of the old house with a crowbar."

"Is his health good?"

"Can't paint anymore. Has arthritis pretty bad in his hips and knees. But he does okay. Except he misses Mom. We lost her three years ago. Heart attack."

"I'm sorry."

"At least she didn't suffer. Dad's found a hobby that helps him pass the time now that she's gone."

"A hobby, you say?"

"Wood carving. Makes swell nutcrackers and toy soldiers."

"What does he do with them?" Caroline asked with more than casual interest. She'd had several requests lately for nutcrackers.

"Sticks them around the house mostly. Sent my brother in Maryland a couple for his kids."

"I'd like to see them sometime. In fact, I'd like to meet your father."

Luke glanced down at the table and fingered an apple slice. "I'll . . . see about that when I talk to him tomorrow." He looked up again. "What about you? Do you plan to stick around? From the looks of things, you've invested quite a lot of time and money here."

Caroline noticed how abruptly he'd changed the subject when she'd mentioned his father. "Momma always dreamed of restoring this place. When she realized she'd never get to do it herself, she asked me to do it for her. She died three months before my grand opening in May. Stick around? I don't know. I might stay."

The look in Luke's eyes hinted he understood the intensity of her pain. "You've done a good job. She'd be proud, I'm sure."

"You want to know something funny? My daddy would have had a fit."

"Why?"

"He said his little princess—that's what he called me, his princess—should spend her time in the arts. Every day after school I had lessons—dancing, singing, acting. I did plays and shows in the summer. Until I took this on, I'd never done a lick of manual labor in my life."

"I used to sneak into play rehearsals at the Opera House, pretend I was one of the cast," Luke confessed. "If my dad had caught me, he would have skinned me alive."

"You like to sing?"

He shrugged. "I sing some. Dance a little, too."

Caroline's gaze shifted to Luke's thick, black hair, styled in the latest cut. He didn't look like a man who made his living with his hands, and somehow the cowboy shirt and hat didn't fit the image of him she had built in her mind. She pictured him in a sweater, sleeves pushed up his forearms, and a button-down shirt, open at the neck. She wondered how it would feel to sift her fingers through his dark hair, to feel his arms about her.

She cleared her throat and pulled her hands into her lap, wondering what had evoked such images of intimacy with a man who was almost a stranger. "You never told me why you came back."

Her question prompted a boyish grin that slowly faded while Luke studied her face for a long moment. Then the corners of his mouth turned up again. "Can you keep a secret?"

Caroline nodded, eager to hear it.

Luke stood and paced the floor in front of the table, his boot heels clicking rhythmically on the oak floors. He paused before her, leaned on the table with both hands and held her attention with eyes that danced with excitement. "I've put together a project that's going to put Granbury on the international tourism map."

Caroline swiveled toward him in her chair. So Luke shared her interest in tourism. Perhaps they could work together. There were still buildings in Granbury that needed restoration. She liked the prospect of spending long hours working beside him. "Tell me about it."

"You know that vacant stretch south of town, with the good view of Comanche Peak?"

"Yes." Her mother had made sure she memorized her granddaddy's stories about that land. How the Indians had swept down from the double mesa, attacked the settlers to keep the white man from taking the land west of the Brazos River. Someday she'd tell the same stories to her grandchildren.

He slapped his fingertips on the table lightly and stood tall. "I bought it."

"Bought it? That must have cost a pretty penny." She hadn't been aware that the land was for sale and wondered how the transaction had escaped the town gossip. "What do you plan to do with it?"

"Have you been to Dinosaur State Park?" he asked.

"The place on the Patuxey River over by Glen Rose? The place with the dinosaur tracks? Sure."

"That's where I got my idea."

"What idea?"

He drew back his shoulders and puffed out his chest. His eyes danced like fireflies, his entire face a big, infectious grin. "I'm going to call it O'Connor's Dino-Land."

Caroline blinked and widened her eyes. "Dino what?"

"Dino-Land. A huge theme park, like Disney World, only everything will be dinosaurs. We've designed a replica of each kind of dinosaur—a couple are fifty feet high, just like the real ones were millions of years ago. They'll be spread across Dino-Land and be lit up with blinking lights. I haven't decided whether to use neon or incandescents. We'll have Dino-Burgers, a Dino-Dipper ride, a Dino-Go-Round. I've even designed a ride where the kids can sit in a spiked tail that whips from side to side."

Caroline heard Luke speak, but the words didn't register. Feelings of disbelief surged through her. Did he honestly plan to desecrate that historical land with a—what did he call it—a Dino-Land? Even worse, did he plan to turn beautiful little Granbury into a big, bustling tourist town?

She grabbed his arm and interrupted his description of the Dino-Swamp. "Tell me this is a joke."

Luke's gaze fell to Caroline's hand, then snapped to her eyes. "What do you mean a joke? I'm dead serious."

After taking a deep breath to steady herself, she asked, "When do you plan to run this by the city council?"

He looked at her cautiously. "I'm on the agenda for Tuesday. Why?"

"You don't seriously think they'll approve it?"

"Why not? It'll be great for Granbury—lots of jobs, sales tax revenue and—" he tapped the tip of her nose with his finger "—it sure won't hurt your shop any."

She pushed his finger aside. Although she didn't want to offend him, she was unable to control her repulsion at his idea. "Look, I don't want to hurt your feelings, but I don't think fifty-foot dinosaurs fit the reputation of an authentic, restored 1880s Western town that we've worked hard to establish. Now you want to ruin it by sticking up…tacky dinosaurs on the highway."

Luke snorted and shook a finger in her face. "What makes you think you know what's good for Granbury?" he asked, beginning to pace, the midnight blue of his eyes now almost black. "I should have listened to Dad."

By then Caroline's face felt as hot as the first bite of a chili pepper. "What does your father have to do with this?"

Luke stopped pacing and narrowed his gaze as he spoke. "He always told me to steer clear of you. He said, 'Never trust a McAlester.' I thought you were different, but you're just like the rest of your pack."

Caroline knotted her fists at her sides and resisted the urge to plant one in Luke's cleft chin.

That chin. It reminded her of someone her grandfather had talked about in a hushed voice when he thought she wasn't listening. Suddenly the realization of who Luke was and why she hadn't know his family swept over her. "Now I remember you! You're Old George's grandson."

Luke glared down at her with an icy stare. "So what if I am?"

"Talk about family! At least everyone in my family could stand up at the end of the day!"

As soon as the words were out, she regretted them. But Luke shouldn't have attacked her family, not the McAlesters.

It took him two steps to reach the table. He swept his hat from the scarred maple surface, planted it on his head and tugged the brim low over his eyes. His nostrils flared as he spoke. "At least my family..." he began, but he paused, the moment of silence as telling as the unspoken words.

Caroline waited for him to finish the snap of his verbal whip. Instead of completing his sentence, he pursed his lips into a slash and shook his head slowly.

Caroline jabbed her forefinger straight at the floor. "You got anything to say about my family, go ahead. Say it. Right here."

His eyes blazed down at her with the fury of a forest fire, his square jaw a determined block. Then, turning on his heel, he took three resounding steps to the back door, shoved it open with both hands and slammed it shut so hard a glass figurine toppled from a shelf. As glass shards skittered across the hardwood floor, the burglar alarm pulsed its frantic warning in Caroline's ears, through the store and out onto the Square.

CHAPTER TWO

CAROLINE WAVED a curious Ellie back to the customers up front and reset the burglar alarm. Through the back window, she watched Luke's tall, lean form retreat from her store. He reminded her of a coiled spring, with his hands tightened into hard fists at his sides, his boot heels digging into the dirt, his legs taking long, purposeful strides in the direction of Lake Granbury.

For not the first time in her life, Caroline wished she had her mother's knack for diplomacy. If she'd kept a tighter rein on her temper, she could have conveyed her opposition to Luke's Dino-Land without attacking his family. What she'd said to him about his grandfather had been deplorable.

With a frown she acknowledged that Luke had had his own diatribe against the McAlesters on the tip of his tongue. But he'd had the good sense to catch himself before he'd blurted it out.

She couldn't help wondering what resentments the O'Connors harbored against the McAlesters. That there was some deep-seated antagonism against her family was all too clear. How deep the resentment ran Caroline could only guess, but Luke had apparently been willing to consider his family's hostility to hers as their problem, not his. Now that she'd thrown her little temper tantrum, he was probably convinced his family was right about her and about all the Mc-Alesters. Remembering his hurt look, she prayed she'd have a chance to apologize.

There wasn't much she knew about the O'Connors, other than what she'd heard her grandfather say about the man he'd called "Old George." Luke's family must have had a rough time of it, since George had been the town drunk for as long as Caroline could remember.

Thoughts of George and his problem reminded her of Amrod and his. Amrod was an old man who lived in a cottage on the grounds of her home. He tended her garden and did odd jobs about town. He was also a notorious drunk. She wondered if poor Amrod could manage to stay sober during the Fourth festivities. The old family friend wouldn't have to look far for a beer or a shot of whiskey, judging from the bottles she'd seen tucked into boots on the Square.

This holiday would be especially hard for Amrod, now that her mother was gone. Before Caroline had left home that morning, she'd found Amrod tinkering with the lawn mower behind the house. Knowing he had no family to celebrate the Fourth of July with, she'd encouraged him to come with her to the store. She could have kept him busy restocking the shelves and greeting customers.

He'd insisted he needed to do some repairs to the cottage behind her family's house, where he'd lived since he'd quit his job as postmaster many years ago. Because there was no one at home to keep an eye on him now, Caroline worried about him, as her mother and grandmother had worried before her.

It had been two weeks since Amrod's last binge, a record since she'd taken over the family responsibility of watching out for him. It was only a matter of time until he gave in and went on another binge. She didn't like it, but she didn't know what she could do to change a pattern he'd established long before she was born.

The gingham curtains parted as Ellie came into the back room. The older woman smiled, her skin soft from the years and lined as only a face could be that had smiled often and fully.

"What're you doing back here, child? It isn't like you to lollygag when we're this busy."

Caroline sank into a chair. "I—I have a couple of things to tend to. I'll be with you in a minute."

Ellie ambled over to Caroline's chair, squeezed her shoulder and said gently, "Things or people, child?"

Caroline forced a smile, then let the corners of her mouth droop. She couldn't fool Ellie. Ellie had been able to see right through her ever since Caroline was five years old and Ellie had caught her stealing purple irises in her garden between their two houses.

Ellie's willingness to work in Caroline's store weekends and holidays was one of life's blessings. Not only was Ellie cheerful help, she was like a grandmother to Caroline at a time when she desperately needed family.

Caroline turned in her chair and stared at the back door. When Luke had stormed out, she'd caught herself reaching for the doorknob, tempted to run after him and apologize for behaving so badly. But sorry or not, she couldn't lie about her reaction to his project. She couldn't lie period.

That's why she needed a few more minutes before she could express sincere friendliness to her customers—a few minutes to overcome her disappointment and clear the vision of an angry Luke O'Connor from her mind.

"You know me too well, Ellie. I just blew my top...at Luke O'Connor." The last two words came out as if it hurt her to say them.

Ellie raised her brows and sighed. "Thought so. I heard voices. Couldn't make out the words, but it was clear you two weren't happy with one another."

Caroline closed her eyes and let out a deep sigh. "I made a mess of things."

Ellie patted her shoulder softly. "There, there, child. Don't worry. These things have a way of working out the way they're supposed to. He'll call again. Give the man some time. We'll cover up front until you pull yourself together."

Caroline squeezed Ellie's hand. "Thanks. I won't be long."

Ellie headed for the storefront, then paused and said, "I remember that young man when he was just a boy. Always thought there was something special about him."

After Ellie disappeared through the curtains, Caroline attempted to sort through her feelings. She knew she wanted to make amends for her angry words, to resolve the argument she'd started with Luke.

What she didn't know was what to say about Luke's theme park idea. If she hadn't been such a hothead, she could have pointed out to him Granbury wasn't the choice location for Dino-Land. The area around Squaw Creek Reservoir, south of the nearby town of Glen Rose, was the logical place. Near Dinosaur State Park, the Glen Rose area, which already had a drive-through wildlife ranch called Fossil Rim, would lend itself more favorably to the Dino-Land concept than Granbury. She'd approach Luke with her relocation idea—after she apologized.

There was only one thing wrong with her relocation idea. Luke had said he'd already purchased the land for his park in Granbury. That meant she needed to persuade him the land could be put to a more tasteful use than a theme park. Maybe houses for those who had tired of the big city rat race in nearby Dallas and Fort Worth.

Caroline pursed her lips and shook her head. That wasn't what she wanted, either. If she had her way, Luke wouldn't do anything with that land that might make Granbury into a more populous, more impersonal place to live.

It was Saturday. She had three days to persuade Luke to change his mind before his presentation to the city council Tuesday evening. If she talked as a reasonable person and kept her temper, she knew she could make a good case for relocating Dino-Land.

She could invite him to dinner at her house Sunday. Caroline grimaced. That would be the supreme sacrifice. She was as allergic to cooking as she was to poison ivy. But if a home-cooked meal would make up for her rudeness and help her accomplish her goals, she'd try it.

Thoughts of the influx of holiday visitors made her frown. She'd never have time to cook unless she could persuade Ellie to manage the store during tomorrow's afternoon rush. The older woman usually baked pies Sundays after church, but it wouldn't hurt to ask.

Right now Caroline felt a mess. She wrinkled her nose and felt the sunburned tightness of her fair skin. Riding in Luke's bed had taken its toll on her appearance. If she'd known she was going to compete in the bed races, she would have applied sunscreen to her sensitive skin. Now she would probably peel. And get more freckles on her nose.

Caroline smiled as she relived the race around the Square, picturing again Luke's muscular thighs with the denim stretched taut across them.

She retrieved her lipstick from her purse and applied a bright red, creamy line to her lips. Luke O'Connor was no average, run-of-the-mill man, and certainly no pushover. He presented a challenge worthy of her best effort.

LUKE UNROLLED the architect's plans and weighted down the corners. For the first time in two years he felt something besides euphoria at the sight of the drawings.

Frustration, that's what it was. Anger? That, too. And disappointment. Deep disappointment that Caroline McAlester had put the quietus on his plans before she'd heard him out.

He'd always considered himself a good judge of character. Before Caroline had exploded like a Fourth of July firecracker, he would have bet his hard-earned, five-hundred-dollar boots she would have listened to his dreams, shared his excitement, judged his ideas fairly.

Now he realized he'd been dreaming. She was a McAlester, all right. And as his father had said, McAlesters and O'Connors didn't see eye to eye on anything.

He replayed Caroline's words in his mind, and winced as he remembered her holier-than-thou attitude when she referred to his grandfather's reputation as the town drunk.

His gaze dropped to the lower right-hand corner of the blueprint and the name "O'Connor." So few people had known the George O'Connor he'd known, the man with a touch so gentle that a person forgot the rough texture of his carpenter's hands. A man who'd never been too busy to listen to a grandson who felt like an outcast. It hadn't been Luke's fault he'd had to help his dad paint and hadn't the time for children's games. When Luke couldn't stand the kids' taunting and teasing any longer, his grandfather had listened to him and helped ease the hurt.

I promise they'll respect you, Grandpa. Before long the O'Connor name will mean as much in Granbury as anyone else's. Maybe more.

More than the McAlesters'? Luke lifted the weights from the corners and rolled up the plans tightly. He smacked the roll smartly against the palm of his left hand.

Maybe even more than the McAlesters'.

After he slipped the roll into a white cardboard tube, Luke put the plans in the small closet of his second-floor room at the McNutt Brothers Hotel.

Hearing the folderol from the watermelon seed-spitting contest out front on the Square, he walked to the window, sank down on the bed and drew the lace curtains aside. To think he'd actually entertained the thought of enjoying the day's festivities with Caroline at his side.

Strange. He still felt drawn to her, even after she'd treated him so rudely. About as rudely, he recalled, as her grandfather had treated his Grandpa O'Connor.

A knock at the door interrupted his thoughts. He crossed the room in two strides and, opening the door, found the hotel clerk—someone new in town since

Luke had moved away thirteen years ago. "Yes, what is it?"

"Phone downstairs for you, Mr. O'Connor. A lady." The young man smiled. "If I'm any judge of women, I'd say she sounds mighty nice."

I hope you're a better judge of women than me, Luke thought as he followed the clerk downstairs.

In the restored dining room, hungry guests were attacking platefuls of home-style cooking. The scent of honey-glazed ham and corn bread teased Luke's nostrils as he picked up the telephone on the antique oak registration desk adjacent to the door to the Square.

"O'Connor here." The only reply was the sound of someone breathing. "Hello? Is someone there?"

"I was rude, inconsiderate, obnoxious and unfair."

Luke grinned. "Caroline?"

"You guessed."

"It was the 'unfair' that did it."

"I'm sorry. Truly I am."

Luke pictured the petite blonde as he'd last seen her, the flush of anger on her cheeks. He'd say one thing for her. She wasn't wishy-washy. A fellow knew where he stood with her. That was a welcome relief from the women who became oh-so-attentive once they discovered he was a successful land developer hooked up with the famous Conway Carriker. "No damage done."

"I want to make it up to you."

Luke's heartbeat quickened perceptibly. "What do you have in mind?"

"Dinner. Tomorrow night. At my house."

"Your house?"

"I moved back into my family's old place. Listen, I'm not a gourmet cook, but I can do justice to fried chicken."

Dinner in the McAlester house? Ten years ago Luke would have been awed at the prospect. But after years of fantasizing about this moment, all he could do now that it had almost arrived was regret that tomorrow night was a full twenty-four hours away. He wanted to see Caroline, and he wanted to see her now. "Can't we get together before then? When do you close the store?"

"Six. We have tickets to see *Pal Joey* at the Opera House before the fireworks." There was a muffled sound; then Caroline spoke again. "Wait a minute. Ellie begged off so she could see the Texas Rangers on TV, so I've got an extra ticket. Would you like to join me?"

"Sounds great. I'll pick you up at six. We'll go to Carmichael's for a bite to eat, take in Joey and the fireworks—then maybe we'll walk over to the lake and go for a ride on the *Granbury Queen*."

"I'd like that, but I'm not dressed for Carmichael's, and I'll be too busy this afternoon to go home and change."

Luke caressed her soft curves in his mind, thinking he'd never seen a pair of blue jeans so appealingly filled. If he owned a restaurant, she could come dressed in those jeans any day of the week. But in the past few years he'd come to understand how women from families like Caroline's felt about dressing appropriately. "Let's keep it simple," he said. "Maybe grab a buffalo burger on the Square. We can go to Carmichael's another night."

CAROLINE'S FINGERS lingered on the receiver as she replaced it in its cradle. So he wanted to see her now.

She smiled. Apparently Luke felt the attraction between them, too.

Her smile persisted as she restocked an antique rocking chair with a half-dozen Raggedy Ann and Andy dolls. It took some effort to remember that while she enjoyed Luke's company, she had a mission to accomplish—and only three days in which to do it.

"Things better with the O'Connor boy?"

It was Ellie with her omniscient eyes...and ears. Caroline nodded, knowing that her face betrayed her excitement.

"What did I tell you?"

"You were right, as usual. Only he didn't call. I called him."

Ellie sighed. "Womenfolk calling men. Couldn't have done it in my day. I expect the change is for the better. By the way, is Luke back to stay, or here to visit? Did he say?" Ellie rounded the counter and smiled at the customer waiting to pay for an armload of handcrafted items.

Caroline frowned and remembered her oath. Even if she did think Luke's theme park idea was half-baked, she had promised to keep it a secret. Ellie would simply have to understand she couldn't betray a confidence. Besides, with a little luck, Luke's project might be altogether different by the time anyone else in Granbury heard about it. Caroline settled for telling Ellie a half-truth. "Business, I think."

While Ellie added up the customer's purchases, Caroline's thoughts turned to the job the city council had offered her a month ago: director of historic preservation—a fancy title with a meager four-figure salary. Of course she couldn't take it. It wouldn't bring anything close to the compensation that went with her accountant's job in Fort Worth.

Her job. How much longer would Baker and Ramsey hold it open for her? When she took a leave of absence in January to be with her mother, she'd told her boss she wasn't sure how long she'd be needed. He'd been understanding, continued to be every Monday when he called and she begged for a little more time. She was lucky she'd stayed with the international accounting firm that had hired her out of college. With four steady years of public accounting experience, she was in demand, if not at Baker and Ramsey, then at any number of other excellent accounting firms.

Heading for the storeroom, she pressed her palm to her abdomen, trying to will away the knot forming in her stomach. It was the same knot, the same acrid taste in her mouth she had every time she thought about returning to her job...and that apartment.

She sank into her desk chair and tried to make sense of the panic that had begun to sweep over her...again. When she had decided to reopen the Emporium, she'd planned to hire a manager to run it for her once the grand opening was behind her.

So why couldn't she follow through with her plans? She ran her damp palms up and down her denim-covered thighs and stared at her scuffed-up boots. *Admit it. You don't really want to go back to your job in Fort Worth. You don't want to go back to Forth Worth period.*

Strange. When she'd left Granbury at the age of eighteen Caroline had never thought she'd entertain thoughts of settling down here. She gripped her knees and sighed. *But that's exactly what I'm doing, isn't it?*

She heard Ellie chattering away out front with someone who sounded familiar, and suddenly it seemed clear to her. Ever since she'd returned to Granbury, the town had seemed like a sanctuary, not a place to escape from. It was comfortable living among people who cared about her. People like Ellie. Maybe she should quit her accounting job, stay on in Granbury and in her spare time work on historical preservation.

That thought reminded her of a job she needed to do. So she left her desk and grabbed a half-dozen tiny frames from a shelf in her stock area. Each frame housed a nail used in 1886 to build the Granbury Opera House.

With the window cleaner she spritzed the protective glass on one frame, then buffed it with a paper towel. Her reflection in the glass made her pause. She sure didn't look like a woman who'd fancy the old days, not with her curly, windblown look.

On her way out front with the frames, she smiled as she thought of her supervisor at Baker and Ramsey. He'd suggested she adopt what he called "a more professional hairstyle" in order to fit the mold of the conservative young accountant. Caroline had pointed to the bottom line on her job performance—and a stack of letters from clients raving about her ability to do her job amiably and efficiently.

Her supervisor had never said another word about her hair. Flamboyant? Maybe. But Caroline didn't let her appearance interfere with her determination to achieve her goals.

Like now, she thought wryly, skimming back to the challenge Luke presented to her. On the town payroll or not, she'd have to function as Granbury's historical preservationist, and that meant figuring out a nice way to persuade Luke to develop his Dino-Land dream elsewhere. Briefly she wondered how her grandfather would have handled the challenge.

How she missed all of them—Momma, Daddy and Granddaddy. Right now, she especially missed Granddaddy. He would've loved this year's Fourth of July festivities. Bigger, better, drawing more tourists, more dollars than ever before to Granbury—to *his* town, he'd always called it.

The only thing he wouldn't have liked was her consorting with the likes of Luke O'Connor. She wondered why her grandfather had insisted on pigeonholing Luke's family as disreputables, yet had served as Amrod Brewster's benevolent protector for years. Hadn't Amrod and George O'Connor been plagued with the same problem?

None of that mattered now. All her relatives were gone. No one was left to raise a stink at her seeing George O'Connor's grandson. Caroline shook her head. She could almost see what her mother's face would have looked like if she'd lived to hear of her daughter dating Luke O'Connor. Never mind that Caroline was a mature, self-supporting woman of twenty-six. Her mother would have expressly forbidden her to see him.

But Caroline was going to see him, and she was going to make it up to him for being such an insensitive little snip.

A smile curled the corners of her mouth. And in the process, she just might have the most memorable Fourth of July she'd ever had.

THE WATER behind the *Granbury Queen* churned as the riverboat's paddles rhythmically flap-flapped in a weird cadence that matched the song strummed by the banjo player on the deck below. The musician whipped the large crowd into a last-stanza frenzy of "Old MacDonald Had a Farm." Hands clapped, feet stomped and voices boomed the lyrics across the water and onto the shore, where someone swept sparklers in a night tribute to the Fourth.

Tiny blue balls volleyed across the sky and exploded into thousands of glittering stars that drifted eastward, then faded into the night.

"They look like falling stars, don't they?" Caroline said, remembering lazy nights long ago when she had lain on a quilt in her backyard and stared at the summer sky. She leaned against the second-deck railing of the *Granbury Queen* and looked higher into the sky above the lake. As another meteoric shower burst forth in the sky, she felt the curls on the back of her head brush lightly against Luke's chest.

He was silent for a moment, as if the nearness of her hadn't affected him as it had her. Then he slid his fingers across her shoulders and squeezed her gently. "When I was a kid I used to dream about . . . this."

Caroline turned around and felt Luke's hands settle on the curves of her shoulders. Her gaze drifted slowly over the swells of his chest, then rose to the shadowed cleft in his chin, to lips that glistened, to his eyes. There she saw golden stars reflected in their night-dark depths. "You dreamed about . . . the fireworks?"

She wondered what he could have been thinking for his eyes to soften so. His gaze lingered on her face for a moment before drifting over her head and fixing on some distant point across the water. Caroline saw the muscles on either side of his jaw flex, then relax.

"I dreamed about lots of things...." He looked at her and smiled. "I always wondered what it'd be like to do this...watch the fireworks from the lake, that is."

"Is it all you dreamed it would be?"

His Adam's apple rose and fell. "More. Much more."

"So, you're a...a dreamer. I like that."

A muscle in his jaw twitched. "Sometimes a man's dreams are all that keep him going."

His voice was so full of emotion that Caroline couldn't help responding to it. She rested her hands lightly on his chest and felt the erratic cadence of his heart against her fingertips. Closing her eyes, she inhaled the humid lake air and caught the woodsy scent of him.

The rhythmic slapping of the paddle wheels punctuated the musical sounds of laughter and glasses tinkling on the deck below. Caroline heard the strum of a banjo and a crystal clear alto voice singing a lively version of "Me and My Gal."

Her eyes closed, she felt Luke's knuckle beneath her chin. As she lifted her lashes, he tilted her face so her eyes met his. "Do you want to go downstairs with the others and sing, now that the fireworks are over?"

She moistened her lips with her tongue. "Are they...over?"

He stared at her for a long moment, so close that she felt his breath feather across her face. "Not...really."

The apology that had been on her conscience all evening sprang to her lips. "Luke, I'm sorry I didn't recognize you. I'm sorry I—"

"Sshh," he said, locking his hands loosely behind her back at her waist. "I won't have you ruin tonight with an apology."

As she felt the weight of his hands settle against the small of her back, she thought how long it had been since she'd felt the warmth of a man's touch, since she'd wanted a man to kiss her.

"With the moonlight in your hair, you look like...like a fairy princess."

She gave in to the impulse to touch the ebony hair that waved behind his ears. "If I'm a fairy princess, you're a—"

Luke jerked his head to the side. "Did you hear that?" His body tensed like a trained pointer's, he turned one ear to the water.

"Hear what?" All Caroline could hear was the disappointment in her voice, as if she'd been awakened from a dream.

"There it is again. Did you hear it?"

Caroline shook her head. "All I hear is music and laughter and a bunch of half-drunk people downstairs. Is that what you mean?"

"It sounded like...like a man...or an animal, maybe. A sick animal." He walked the length of the deck, then leaned over the rail and stared into the darkness of the waters below.

She giggled. "Maybe it was that ghost they talk about on the Square."

"I'm not joking, Caroline."

"I'm sorry. Really, I didn't hear a th— Wait a minute! I heard something."

"Where?" he asked. "Show me."

She pointed to the stern of the boat. "Back there, I think."

Luke grabbed her hand and pulled her with him to the back of the boat, where they stood at the aft rail and listened.

"Help! Help meeeeeee!"

Caroline shivered at the eerie sound of the plea. She grabbed Luke's arm and pointed to something floundering in the water behind the boat. "Over there. I think it's a man." Panic tore through her as she saw arms flop aimlessly in the water like a rag doll's.

"You're right," he said, a steely edge to his voice. "And whoever he is, he's headed right for the paddle wheels."

CHAPTER THREE

LUKE GRASPED Caroline's shoulders firmly in his hands, feeling her shiver beneath his fingers, as if the light breeze off the lake had brought a midwinter chill instead of balmy summer air.

He swallowed hard and bent his knees until his eyes were level with hers. "Get downstairs and find the captain. Tell him to shut off those engines. Now, Caroline!"

But Caroline's gaze seemed transfixed on the figure floundering in the water. "He—he can't swim," she said.

Luke saw what she saw—hands sinking below the surface in the moonlight. He eased his hips onto the railing and swept both feet over it in a fluid motion. There was barely room for his boots on the narrow ledge on the other side.

"What are you doing?" Caroline gasped.

Luke grasped the railing on either side of him and hooked his heel beneath the lower wooden bar. Using the bar as a bootjack, he tugged off one boot, handed it to Caroline, then removed the other boot. "There isn't much time. Do as I told you. Please, Caroline."

Narrowing his gaze, Luke searched the rectangle of water faintly illuminated behind the boat by the first deck lights. Nothing. He saw nothing.

"You aren't going to jump! Not from here! The sand bars—remember the sand bars. The water might be only a few feet deep!"

"If the boat made it, so can I. Now go. Get the captain."

Caroline bolted for the stairway to the first deck, while Luke scanned the water's surface once more. Flexing his knees, he prayed and dived into the churning water to the left of the paddle wheels.

The water was warm, like a tepid bath, and blessedly deep. Luke arched his back to reverse his descent, then thrust his hands high above him and whooshed his arms straight to his sides to propel himself up to the surface.

His jeans, soaked with water, tugged on his body like weights. He kicked his burdened legs frantically, turning in a full circle as he treaded water. Where had the guy gone? *Oh, God,* Luke prayed silently. *Please don't let me be too late this time.*

A sharp shake of his head cleared the water from his eyes, but fresh droplets fell on his face as the paddle wheels continued their counterclockwise swing only a few feet away.

He could make out Caroline standing on the first deck leaning over the railing. She pointed at him, and a crewman hefted a large white ring into the water. But the paddle wheels continued their incessant slapping. Why hadn't the captain turned off the engines?

As if the captain had heard Luke's thoughts, the boat's engines sputtered to a stop. Mayhem erupted on board as passengers crowded along the stern railings, some climbing onto the backs of benches for a better view.

Panic churned Luke's stomach when still he saw no signs of the poor soul in the water. He cupped his hand to his mouth and yelled over the din. "Caroline, where is he? I can't see—"

Something struck Luke's head from behind, and he heard an animallike moan. Hands clawed at his head, and Luke gasped for air as he was shoved beneath the surface. Arms, encased in something scratchy like denim, grabbed him around the neck, while legs locked about his waist.

Luke felt himself sinking lower and lower as he grasped the gripping legs and tore them from his body. What was it he'd learned about lifesaving when he'd turned sixteen? Subdue the drowning swimmer if necessary in order to save him?

Before he could react, a knee stabbed his kidney, sending white-hot pain searing through his backside. Luke moaned, exhaling precious air, while yet another blow struck his back.

His lungs screamed for air as his feet sank into the mucky bottom. He tried to push himself up, but the man who clung frantically around his neck pressed him deeper into the muddy ooze.

Luke's head was getting light. If he didn't act quickly, he'd give in to the urge to suck water into his lungs. A vision of a fiery blue-eyed blonde flashed through his mind, giving him that extra surge of adrenaline he needed to get the frantic man off his back.

With one quick jab back of his elbow, Luke connected with the soft stomach of the man whose legs hooked around his hips, and dear God, it worked.

The man's body went limp with an underwater moan and an outrush of bubbles. At last Luke was free of him!

So he wouldn't lose him in the dark waters, Luke grabbed the man with one hand, then slipped his forearm under his own thigh and jerked upward frantically to free his feet from the sucking lake bottom.

But he felt so dizzy! And his chest—he clutched it, fighting the mad urge to take a deep breath. *Come on, just a few seconds more. Must save him. Must get him to the surface.* His strong legs, conditioned by jogging, propelled Luke upward, with the man held stiff armed over his head. Just as Luke thought he had no more reserves, they broke the surface.

Luke gasped the air in great precious gulps. God, it was sweet to breathe again!

The weight of the man was lifted from his arms, and Luke fell back blindly into the water. He felt an arm confidently sweep beneath him, elevating him into a back-float position. A hand curved about his chin and pulled him through the water.

Luke was still gulping lungfuls of air, when his head bumped something hard. Half dazed, he felt arms drag him from the water and lay him on his back on the boat deck. Two small hands with callused fingertips stroked his hair from his forehead, and he was vaguely aware of a voice, a familiar voice, calling his name.

He opened his eyes and grabbed a handful of curly blond hair that dripped lake water onto his face. "Caroline—?"

"Sshh, it's okay. You're safe now."

Luke coughed and felt hands roll him onto his stomach. "No. Stop. Is he—is he okay?" Luke asked, and rising to his knees, he tried to stand, but his legs collapsed beneath him.

"Please, Luke. Just lie here for a few minutes. We'll go over to see him when you have your strength back. They say he's going to live, thanks to you. The captain's taking us into shore so they can take the guy to the hospital."

Luke closed his eyes and relaxed against the weathered wooden deck. So he hadn't been too late, after all. The thought comforted him as he rolled to his back and slung his wrist across his eyes. God, he was tired!

He wasn't too tired to realize who it was who lifted his head and cradled it in her lap. Slowly he opened his eyes, and saw Caroline smiling down at him. In the moonlight he could also see that her red shirt was wet and clung to her softly rounded breasts.

"It was you?" he said incredulously, half asking, half stating it. Caroline McAlester had dragged him from the lake? All one hundred pounds of her?

Her fingers fussed with his shirt collar. "I was afraid. The others . . . well, most of them had been drinking, and . . ."

He stilled her hands in his. "Something tells me you're capable of a lot more than I ever thought."

Someone draped a blanket over him, and Caroline tucked it beneath his chin. His gaze followed her fingers as she secured the soft folds about his chest, his waist, his hips. He had just begun to appreciate her ministrations, when he noticed a bunch of people crouched in a circle on the far side of the deck. Two feet stuck out from the crowd, toes pointed out, legs relaxed. They looked too relaxed for Luke. "That must be him."

Caroline brushed another lock of hair from his forehead. "He's safe, thanks to you."

Luke looked at the still figure, needing to see the man move, even a little. "Is he *really* going to make it?"

"That's what they told me. I don't know. I—I haven't been over there. I wanted to stay here with you."

Luke shook his head. "He was like a crazy man down there." Luke threw back the blanket, rose to his feet and offered a hand to Caroline. "Let's go see how he's doing."

"Miss Caroline, you okay now?" a whiskered crewman asked, and draped a blanket around her shoulders as she stood up. She clutched it to her chest and smiled appreciatively, instantly recognizing him as the man who'd been the custodian at her elementary school.

She nodded but realized she was trembling. "I'll be fine. Thanks for the blanket. I didn't realize how cold I was." Her eyes darted to the man stretched out on the deck. "What about him?"

The crewman stepped between her and the people clustered around the man Luke had saved. She strained to look around the crewman's shoulder, but he moved over, obscuring her view. "He isn't—"

"He'll be fine. Just leave him to us. You and your boyfriend there best go inside."

She couldn't contain her smile. *Boyfriend?* She glanced up quickly at Luke. He winked at her and grinned.

Reluctantly she tore her gaze from Luke and gestured toward the man Luke had saved from drowning. "Who is he? Do you know him?" Luke draped his arm around her shoulder, and she leaned into the comforting warmth of his chest.

"Uh, yes'm, I do," the crewman said.

A moment of silence ensued. Caroline frowned. "Well, who is he?" She tilted her head up, feeling both admiration and pride for the man who had risked his life for another. "I think Luke would like to know."

Her old acquaintance stuck his hands into his pockets. "Aw, Miss Caroline, don't do this to me."

"Do what?"

The old man shuffled his feet and kicked the wet rope on the deck. "Make me be the one to tell you."

She grabbed the crewman's arms. "Don't tell me it's—"

He wrinkled his brow into deep furrows and ran a dry, cracked hand through his hair. "Stewed like a prune. The guy who gave him mouth-to-mouth almost gagged."

Caroline shoved her way through the crowd and knelt beside Amrod. Except for the slight rise and fall of his chest, the old family friend who lived behind her house seemed lifeless. She picked up his weathered hand and squeezed it, fighting back the tears.

His face, ruddy as usual, was all that showed above a tan blanket. Caroline shut her eyes and sighed. He'd almost done it this time—served himself up to whatever demon it was that had been eating at him most of his life.

She felt a slight pressure in her hand and bent over to kiss his cheek. The unmistakable odor of alcohol—lots of it—assailed her. "Oh, Amrod," she whispered into his ear. "Why do you do this to yourself?"

Luke knelt beside her and ran his hands up and down his wet denim-covered thighs. "I had no idea. I couldn't see—"

"I couldn't, either," she interrupted. "But I've been worried about him since Momma died. She used to watch out for him, keep him busy so he wouldn't have time to think about drinking. I've tried, but I've had so much to do with the holiday and the store...." She looked up and saw the muscles in Luke's jaw flex.

"How often does he do this?"

"Six, seven, maybe eight times since I came back home in January." She ran her fingers lovingly over Amrod's face. "I should've known this would happen today. It's my fault. I should've insisted he come with me, instead of—"

"No!" Luke said insistently. "This isn't your fault. We'll talk about it later."

LATER came way past midnight, after Caroline and Luke had accompanied the rescue vehicle to the hospital. Amrod's lungs had been X-rayed to make sure they'd sustained no permanent damage. Then Caroline and Luke had signed for the old man's release and taken him to his cottage behind her house.

Caroline opened the cottage door and stumbled over something as she stepped into Amrod's living room. "What in the world?"

Luke flicked on the light switch with his elbow and waded across the cluttered room, with the snoring Amrod in his arms. "You want to clear a place for him there on the couch? He may be a small man, but it feels like he weighs a ton."

Caroline brushed several layers of newspapers and magazines from the couch and stepped aside while

Luke lowered Amrod onto it. She glanced around the room, pressing a hand to her chest. Like the couch, the carpet and other pieces of furniture were all but obscured by newspapers, crumpled clothing, mail and a good number of empty beer cans and bottles.

Amrod's bedroom was as messy as his living room. On his chest of drawers a portable television set hissed a snowy pattern.

Caroline shut her eyes and let her shoulders droop. "I—I haven't been back here since Momma died. He always comes to the house when he needs to discuss a repair job. I should have helped him . . . with this."

"It isn't your fault he chooses to treat his home like a garbage dump."

"But if I—"

"Caroline," Luke said, his jaw set in a determined line, "I know what I'm talking about."

She supposed Luke had had his share of experiences like this with his grandfather. The thought made her embarrassment over Amrod's behavior a little easier to bear. Even though Amrod wasn't officially part of her family, he'd lived on McAlester property so long she felt responsible for him, as she was sure her mother and grandmother had when they'd looked after him.

"Tell you what. Amrod's snoring away on the couch over there," Luke said. "I'm not sure he knows what happened. Why don't you go on up to the house and change into some clean clothes. Shower, if you like. I'll start cleaning up this place. When you get back, I'll help Amrod shower. He'll be too shaky to do it by himself."

"I'll stay and help. I can shower later. If you can stand me, I can stand myself."

They tackled the bedroom first. Caroline stepped over the debris to one side of the bed; Luke, to the other. She gestured toward the bed. "You want to start here?"

He sucked in his cheeks, sending the dimple deeper into his chin. "What do you have in mind?"

She had to pull her gaze from the devilish twinkle in his eyes. Smiling at his audacity, she went to the closet in search of clean linens. Her heart was still thumping in response to his teasing when she spotted a clean set of sheets on a shelf above the clothes bar.

A smile crossed Caroline's face, as she noticed the hand-embroidered *M* that graced the broad cuff of the pillowcase. That was dear Grandma Lydia's work. Lydia—who was her grandmother on her father's side—had tried several times, unsuccessfully, to get Caroline to sit still long enough to learn the tedious handwork. The gentle woman had died in her early sixties, when Caroline was still a child. Caroline had regretted ever since not having taken the time to learn embroidery from her grandmother, to get closer to the sweet woman.

Luke's concerned voice interrupted Caroline's reverie. "Hey, are you okay?"

Turning around, she found him close, a nearness that comforted her. "I was just thinking about my grandmother."

His gaze followed hers back to the embroidered pillowcase. "She was a special woman, your grandmother."

"You knew her?"

His eyes searched hers for a moment. He opened his mouth as if to answer her, then shut it again. "I'm afraid I never had the pleasure." He dropped his hands to his sides, turned on his heel and strode to the far side of the bed.

Caroline walked slowly to the opposite side of the bed and laid the sheets on the mattress Luke had stripped. "If you didn't know her, why did you say—?"

"Sshh. Did you hear that?" Luke cocked his head, then stepped through the doorway into Amrod's living room.

Caroline followed him. "Hear what?"

"That strange little shuffling noise."

"Did anybody ever tell you you have the ears of a watchdog?"

Luke scanned the living room, where Amrod lay snoring on the couch. "I know I heard something move in here."

Caroline glanced at the form on the couch. "It was probably just Amrod. Maybe he's beginning to come around."

"No, it wasn't him. Listen, I think I heard it again."

She stood perfectly still and heard a faint rustle, then traced the peculiar sound to the kitchen. What she saw there made her grin and motion for Luke to join her. "Come here. I think I found your sound."

Luke stood behind her, his fingers lightly touching either side of her waist. "Well, I'll be darned."

"Isn't he cute?" Caroline squatted beside a rectangular aquarium tank on the floor and watched a little furry animal licking water from a watering device with rapid strokes of its tiny tongue.

Luke squatted beside her and tapped the glass lightly with his fingernail. The snowy white creature stopped drinking, sat motionless for a moment, then darted to the far corner of its cage. It climbed onto a metal wheel and raced it into a spin.

"Notice anything, Caroline?"

"Sure. The little guy's full of energy. I could sure use some of it."

"Look again. What do you see?"

She curled her fingers over the edge of the aquarium and peered in from the top. "I see a hamster, a wheel, a watering device and a food dish. Am I missing something?"

"Look how neat this little guy's cage is. Amrod takes good care of him—" Luke perused the room "—even if he doesn't take care of himself."

"What are you trying to make of all this?"

"I just thought it ironic that a person would not take care of himself, yet pamper a pet."

Caroline thought about Luke's observation and reached in to touch the animal's soft fur. "It's too bad Amrod never had a family. Maybe he would've been different if he'd had some children to love, some kids to love him back."

"We'll never know, will we?"

"I guess not," she said softly.

"You know you're the only family he has now."

Caroline nodded, feeling the weight of the responsibility.

"It's up to you to help him solve his problem."

"I never knew how much of a problem he had. Momma always took care of him. I'm not sure I know what to do."

"I'll help you all I can," Luke offered.

AN HOUR LATER they had completed the cleanup. In another thirty minutes Amrod was snoring between crisp, clean sheets, apparently oblivious to the fact his home had been transformed into a vision of tidiness, probably for the first time in weeks or months.

Caroline kissed his wrinkled cheek and smoothed his curly white hair from his forehead. The poor man needed someone to look after him, and she would have to be that someone. She took a lingering look at him before she clicked off the lamp by his bed.

Satisfied Amrod was resting peacefully, she joined Luke on the broad veranda her mother had extended to the back of the house during her last renovation of the old Victorian dwelling. Caroline had been a freshman in college when she'd come home one semester break and found workmen in the backyard, putting on the last bits of gingerbread trim.

She was so tired! With her palms on either side of her spine, she arched her back. What a day it had been! She frowned and lowered herself onto the glider, smelling the lingering odor of fireworks in the air. "I wonder how we missed seeing Amrod on that boat."

Luke watched as Caroline stretched like a cat, the fabric in her red blouse molding to her firm breasts. Had she asked him a question? Oh, yes. The boat and Amrod. "The captain said he'd found Amrod asleep on the *Queen* a number of times lately. He was probably asleep on the edge of the deck outside the railing when we all got on, and nobody noticed him."

Caroline closed her eyes and leaned her head back on the glider pad. "What am I going to do with him?"

Luke shifted in the swing to face her. He picked up her hands and squeezed them lightly, running his thumbs over her knuckles. "You could start by making him face his problem. It is *his* problem, you know."

"I'm afraid it's too late for that. He's eighty, a little old to change his ways. He's been drinking for as long as I can remember, although I never saw this side of his problem before. Maybe if I spend more time with him, let him know I care, he won't go on these terrible binges."

"Uh-uh," Luke insisted. "No matter what you do, he still has the problem. He has to face it. If you really care for him, you'll confront him with it."

"So what do I say? 'Amrod, dear, I love you, but you're a lush—let's sit down and talk this over'?" Her words sounded snippy, and again Caroline found herself wishing she hadn't let her temper color her words.

"That would do for a start."

"I can't be that cruel."

Luke stared at her for a long moment. "You want to know what's cruel? Cruel is continuing to let him drink himself to death."

She drew her hands away from his and backed into the corner of the swing. "Let him? You think I want him to drink himself into a stupor the way he did tonight?"

"Of course not. But in effect, that's what you and your family have been doing for years."

Caroline closed her eyes and pressed her throbbing temples with her fingertips, willing herself patience and forbearance in the face of yet another attack on her family. "Let's not talk about it now, Luke. We're so tired we're both saying things we'll regret later. I don't want to make that mistake again."

Luke stood up, hooked his thumbs in his front jeans pockets and strode to the far side of the veranda. In the moonlight Caroline could tell from the expression on his face that he was struggling with something, a memory, maybe.

He turned to her. "I'll let it go tonight, but we will talk about it. I have to talk about it. I made myself a promise a long time ago, a promise I intend to keep."

Caroline sensed that his promise had something to do with his grandfather, but she thought it improper to question Luke about George O'Connor after the shameful comment she'd made about the man earlier in the day. Still, the way Luke stood there on the veranda, as if he were waiting for her to ask questions about his grandfather, about the mysterious promise he'd mentioned, made her feel she needed to say something.

"You miss him as much as I miss my grandfather, don't you?" she finally said, joining him at the railing. She wondered if his insides still ached from the loss, if the pain of losing a loved one ever went away.

His eyes flashed some indescribable emotion, then he looked out over the yard. "I think of him every day of my life. He was my friend. He understood me. I could tell him anything, and he would accept what I was, what I'd done. I accepted him for what he was, too. The trouble was, I understood too late that what I should have done was try to help him with his drinking problem. I should have helped him face whatever it was that drove him to drink."

"Surely you don't blame yourself for his problem."

"No, I can't do that any more than you should accept the blame for Amrod's problem. But a man can't help looking back, wishing he'd done things differently."

Caroline didn't know what to say, but she felt that in some small way she was sharing Luke's grief with him, and she needed to touch him to let him know she understood the pain. She patted his upper arm, then wrapped her fingers around the tensed muscles and squeezed gently. "Luke, I'm sorry about your grandfather."

His eyes holding her gaze, he covered her hand with his, brought it to his lips and gentled a kiss on her fingertips. Then, releasing her hand, he placed his hands at her waist, drew her close and kissed her forehead, almost reverently.

Caroline's insides did flip-flops. Instinctively she placed her hands on his chest and felt the runaway beat of his heart—a heart that ached, that needed consoling, a heart that had nearly burst in his efforts to save Amrod.

She could still smell the odor of lake water on his clothes, but it was the clean scent of soap that pleasured her nostrils, the soap from Amrod's shower.

"You look bone tired," he told her, twisting her body gently from side to side with his hands.

"I'm so tired I could go to sleep standing up. But speaking of sleep, that reminds me of something that's been puzzling me."

He tugged on a curl on the side of her face and watched it spring back into place. "What's that?"

"How'd you get in the bed race today? I thought the lineup had been set for weeks."

"Just lucky I guess."

She boxed his chest playfully. "Really. I mean it."

"I finished lunch at the hotel and came outside to watch them get ready for the race. Some young guy—looked to be about eighteen—got a phone call from his fiancée. Seems she had a little accident with her car—nothing serious, nobody hurt—but she couldn't drive it. Her fiancé left to help her with it. I offered to take his place."

Caroline smiled. "How'd you know you'd find someone to be your partner at the last minute?" Then she remembered the women who'd flocked around him after the race and was sorry she'd asked the question. He could have had any one of a dozen women in his bed.

Luke cradled her chin in his hands. "I didn't want just anybody, Caroline. I wanted you."

Caroline felt a lightness spread through her limbs. She turned her head until her lips brushed the pad of his thumb. Her eyes fixed on his face, she lightly kissed his thumb, closed her eyes and longed to feel the touch of his lips on hers.

"I'm glad you picked up the phone," Luke said, his voice a husky whisper.

"I had to apologize. The minute you left, I regretted the way I'd behaved. I started to go after you, but . . . but you seemed so angry."

"None of that matters now," he said, gathering her to his chest. His breath sifted through her hair. "Now that we've settled our differences, we can be friends. I'd like to think we might be more than friends."

That prospect sent her pulse soaring, but his words triggered a question in her mind. "What do you mean, 'Now that we've settled our differences'?"

He drew back and kissed the tip of her nose. "You know—that business about Dino-Land. I can't tell you how much it means to me that you've changed your mind about my project."

She pressed her palms against his chest. "What do you mean, changed my mind?"

A cautious look crossed his face. "You did call and apologize. I remember your exact words."

She shook her head and took a deep breath, determined not to lose her temper this time. "What you heard was an apology. My apology for being so unkind about your grandfather—for acting like a spoiled two-year-old instead of telling you how I felt, like a rational adult."

Luke dropped his hands to his sides. "You mean you haven't changed your mind about my project?"

"I have not. In fact, I wanted to talk to you about it tonight. I've been doing some thinking since we had our little disagreement this afternoon."

He rubbed the back of his neck with his palm. "Somehow I think it'd be better if we ended this conversation now. If we talked about this tomorrow."

"There's no use putting it off. We have an honest difference of opinion. But I think I've found a solution to our problem—some common ground, so to speak."

He smiled. "I like it when you call it *our* problem."

She caught his finger as he was about to touch the curve of her chin. "It won't do you any good to try to distract me."

His eyes twinkling, Luke backed her against a molded support post of the veranda and planted his forearm against the post, just above her head. He grinned at her, looking like a possum eating possum grapes. "So I distract you, do I?"

Caroline ducked under his arm and crossed the porch, wishing he'd listen to what she had to say. She wanted them to be able to compromise. Maybe then they could be—as Luke had said—more than friends. She held out her palms like a traffic cop. "Listen."

He smiled. "Okay, boss."

She wrinkled her nose at him, thankful that his playful attitude had lightened the tension between them. "After you left the store this afternoon I got to thinking about the inspiration for your project—the Dinosaur State Park near Glen Rose."

He crossed his arms and gave her a studied look. "So, what about it?"

Caroline paced the wooden porch, her cowboy boots thudding rhythmically on the oak boards. "That's where Dino-Land belongs, Luke—smack dab in the middle of that state park, right next to the dinosaur tracks."

"Caroline, I don't *want* to build my project in Glen Rose. I want it here, in Granbury. I've already bought the land, which cost, as you put it, a pretty penny."

Caroline detected the cool edge to his words. She spoke in her calmest, most controlled voice, the one Ellie called her kindergarten teacher voice. "You could sell it, or turn it into a wildlife preserve, let it go back to nature, as it was when the Indians were here."

"I paid a lot of money for that land. Besides, I have other reasons for wanting to build Dino-Land in Granbury."

She paused. "Other reasons? What other reasons?"

Luke glanced away. "Just reasons, that's all."

She stepped in front of him and demanded his attention by her presence. "I can't support you on this project of yours. I honestly believe it's wrong for Granbury."

"Why, Caroline? Why are you so all-fired opposed to a project that'll mean more tourists, more revenue, more jobs for folks around here?"

"You make it sound like I'm against all that's right and good."

"Seems like it to me."

"Luke," she said, heaving a deep sigh, "I don't think you understand what your project would do to Granbury. To this beautiful small town."

Luke slowly shook his head. "You can't stand in the way of progress out of some misplaced desire to plunge Granbury into the past."

Caroline stuck her balled-up fists on her hips, knowing she was losing control of her temper and not caring if she did. "Misplaced desire? Is that what you call it?"

"I don't mean to hurt your feelings. I know you think you're doing what's best for Granbury. But the way I see it, you're trying to make up for the fact you don't have any—well, any family now. You want to turn back the clock to a time when your parents and grandparents were alive and well—and..."

"And?" she demanded, shaking her head officiously.

"And damn well ran this town—that's what!"

Caroline narrowed her gaze and jabbed a finger into his chest. "I'll fight you on this. I'll fight you every step of the way."

Luke grabbed her finger and held it tightly before him. "You do that, Miss McAlester. And while you're doing it, pay close attention, because I *will* get my project approved for Granbury."

Her heart pounding in her chest, she jerked her finger from his grasp and stomped to the door that led to the kitchen. Leveling one last glance at him, she lifted her chin defiantly. "You want to bet, buster?"

CHAPTER FOUR

"WHAT HAPPENED to Amrod last night?"

The familiar voice permeated Caroline's subconscious and lured her back to the present. She lifted her head from the wooden table in the back room of the Emporium, squinted into the sunlight streaming through the back door and made out Ellie's distinctive profile.

Ellie was here? Already? What time was it, anyway?

Cupping her hand over her eyes, Caroline focused on the neon clock above the gingham curtains. It was...noon.

Noon? How could it be noon? Only a few minutes ago she'd laid her head atop her folded arms for a short rest after arriving at the store at eight sharp.

Her eyeballs ached. Her head felt as if she'd been kicked by a mule. She rubbed the back of her neck and stretched her arms high over her head, feeling her body complain in a zillion little muscles for giving it only four hours' rest. And those four hours had been punctuated by visions of dinosaurs chasing cowboys and Indians and McAlesters.

Ellie's question about Amrod tugged at the edges of Caroline's consciousness.

For the first time since her mother had died, Caroline almost wished she were back in her Fort Worth apartment, where her neighbors wouldn't have cared what happened to anyone in the middle of the night. Amrod's drunken near drowning the night before had been a nightmare, and the last thing Caroline wanted to do this morning was talk about it.

"Caroline," Ellie said, jiggling the younger woman's shoulder. "Did you hear me?"

Caroline stared at the cardboard box beside the table and groaned. When she'd arrived this morning, her store had looked as if a giant vacuum cleaner had sucked up half the merchandise. By now she should have unpacked the four dozen teddy bears in the box and displayed them out front, along with ten other cartons of merchandise.

Already customers were tapping on the front windows, even though her 1:00 p.m. to 6:00 p.m. Sunday hours were clearly posted on the door.

Ellie plunked a fresh cup of coffee in front of Caroline and eased herself into the chair across the table. She leaned forward on her elbows and wiggled her brows. "Must have been some night."

Caroline wrapped her fingers around the hot ceramic cup and let the aroma of French vanilla coffee tease her nostrils.

What she really needed was a few moments alone. Across from her, Ellie drummed her fingers on the table. Caroline could forget her privacy until Ellie got her explanation.

How could she admit to the older woman that Amrod had almost killed himself last night in a drunken stupor. She searched for words to make Amrod's nocturnal behavior sound justifiable, if not respectable, but all she could come up with was the truth. As usual.

"Amrod . . . well, he fell overboard while he was on the riverboat and almost drowned, but Luke dived in and saved him."

"Almost drowned?" Ellie's eyes grew as big as saucers behind her glasses. "Why didn't you come get me? Is he okay?"

Caroline nodded. "Luke and I were on the Queen, watching the fireworks, when Amrod fell off the back of the boat. We went with him to the hospital to make sure he was okay. Then we brought him home."

Ellie sat back in her chair. "That explains it then. When the dogs barked last night, I looked out my bedroom window and saw Luke carrying Amrod to the cottage. Earlier I heard the rescue squad siren, but I figured someone got hurt by the fireworks or got drunk. . . ."

Caroline stood up, avoiding Ellie's probing eyes, and thrust her arms elbow deep into the box of teddy bears.

Ellie reached over and touched her arm. "Is that what happened? Amrod got drunk and fell in the lake?"

Caroline hunched her shoulders and hugged two bears to her chest, finally bringing her gaze to meet Ellie's. "Oh, Ellie, it was awful."

The old woman sighed. "The poor man clearly has a problem. And it seems to be getting worse."

"What am I supposed to do about it? What would Momma have done?"

Ellie traced the rim of her coffee cup with one finger before fixing her gaze across the room. "I don't know. I'm not so sure what she would have done would have been the right thing anyhow."

"What do you mean?"

"Perhaps your mother should have gotten Amrod help a long time ago, instead of coddling him like a naughty child every time he went on a binge."

"You sound like Luke. He thinks I should get tough with Amrod."

Ellie pursed her lips and took a slow sip of her coffee. "I suppose Luke has a bit more experience at this kind of thing than we do."

"But do you agree with him? Should I be that harsh with Amrod? I'm all he has. If I don't show him some . . . love, he'll think nobody cares about him."

Ellie stared at Caroline for a long moment. There was something strange in Ellie's eyes—a mix of melancholy and pain and something else Caroline couldn't define. "Child, that would be wonderful. Might just make the difference in that poor man's life if you showed him you truly cared."

"You really think I could make a difference?"

"Yes, I do. But we've talked enough about Amrod this morning. I'm dying to hear about your date with Luke."

Caroline wondered what else Ellie had seen from her bedroom window last night. Had she seen her in Luke's arms, seen her look up into his eyes and quiver when he brushed his lips across her fingertips?

If she had, Caroline was in for a marathon grilling. That was one thing about Ellie. She let Caroline know what was going on in her life and wanted the favor returned.

"There's not much to tell," Caroline said, shrugging. "It was a disaster."

Ellie peered over her glasses. "You can be more specific than that."

Caroline lowered her gaze and tried to ignore the rush of blood to her face that the mere thought of last night generated. She scooped up several more bears and backed through the gingham curtains, the memory of Luke holding her in the moonlight flooding her senses.

When she was out of Ellie's sight, she closed her eyes and sighed. Her lips tingled as she thought about the way each of his fingers had felt at her waist, how he'd cupped her chin with his hands, how he'd—

"Caroline?" Ellie prodded, following her into the storefront. "If you think I'm going to let you get away with avoiding me, you've got another think coming."

Caroline spun around, knocking a hand-carved nativity manger from an antique rolltop desk. Ellie grabbed it before it hit the floor and handed it back to Caroline.

A warm, soft smile creased Ellie's face. "It's okay, child. Having feelings for a man sometimes makes a woman skittish, clumsy even."

Caroline lifted her chin. "It isn't like that at all."

"Oh, no? You should see your face."

Caroline pressed her palms to her cheeks and felt the warmth emanating from them. "What I feel doesn't matter. Luke and I are about as opposite as two people can be."

"Sometimes that makes it fun. Makes the sparks fly."

"If by 'sparks' you mean arguments, you're right. But I don't call that fun."

Ellie picked up a feather duster and attacked a shelf of ceramic miniatures with her usual vigor. "What did you two find to argue about this time?"

Caroline remembered her promise to Luke. Remembered it and regretted it. "We see things differently, that's all."

Ellie turned her back to Caroline and continued to dust, muttering something about young folks and ridiculous expectations.

"I'll say one thing for him, Ellie. He risked his life to save Amrod, like a real hero."

Ellie waited a moment before she answered, as if she were thinking out her answer. "That doesn't surprise me."

"It doesn't?"

"I guess there's something you don't know." Ellie stared at the ceramic Christmas tree in her hand for a moment before she returned her gaze to Caroline. "Luke's grandfather drowned in Lake Granbury."

"Oh, Ellie!" Caroline collapsed into a nearby rocker, visions of last night and Luke's determination to save Amrod flitting through her mind.

"I'm afraid there's more. George O'Connor was drunk, too, like Amrod. Luke found him on the shores of the lake. The man died in his grandson's arms."

A frown knitted Caroline's brow. "Poor Luke. No wonder he seemed driven to save Amrod last night." *And no wonder he was so insistent that I should help Amrod with his drinking problem.*

"That young man has a lot of character, Caroline. You'd best think twice about shutting the door in his face."

Caroline grimaced at Ellie's cliché. "Too late. I've already done that."

"Don't worry. I made my pies last night while I watched the game. You're free to cook a dinner for that nice young man this afternoon."

Caroline rolled her eyes. "I'd forgotten about that."

"I'm sure he hasn't. A man doesn't overlook the chance for a home-cooked meal, especially not from the likes of you."

"He won't be coming to dinner, Ellie."

"You mean I baked those pies last night for nothing?"

"No," Caroline said, flipping the sign on the front window from Closed to Open. "Now you have a free afternoon. Read a book, work in your garden. Say, wait a minute. Aren't the Rangers on TV this afternoon?"

Ellie chuckled. "I said I'd work this afternoon, so I'll work. You, child, are getting out of here, no later than four."

It was useless to argue with Ellie. Even though Caroline was the owner of Cain's Emporium, when Ellie got that look in her eyes, the older woman was the undisputed boss, and they both knew it.

True to her word, Ellie shooed Caroline out the front door at four o'clock. As soon as Caroline stepped out into the heat, she scanned the Square for Luke. Half disappointed at not seeing him, she took the shortest route to her house, which meant she had to walk directly in front of McNutt Brothers Hotel, where Luke was staying.

Okay, so she was darting glances over her shoulder, looking out for Luke, but only because she wanted to avoid another confrontation with the man. If she saw him, she'd quicken her pace so she wouldn't have to discuss Dino-Land with him again.

As she rounded the corner and crossed the street to the old jail house, she glanced up at the second floor of the hotel and wondered which room was Luke's. The silhouette of someone standing at a window caused her heart to skip a beat, and she jerked her gaze down at her red leather boots. Had it been Luke?

Slowly she looked up again, but whoever it was had disappeared from the window, leaving her with a strange sense of disappointment.

The walk was a short one. Amrod awaited her on the front steps to the veranda that wrapped around her house. He lifted his head from his hands and managed a thin smile. Caroline smiled back. He appeared scrubbed from head to toe. He'd shaved and had dressed in a crisp white shirt, with a blue Western tie secured at the collar with a turquoise-and-silver slide.

Standing, Amrod twisted his white straw hat by its brim. It looked like a Sunday hat. Maybe he'd been to church. Good. Perhaps the minister had instilled the fear of God in him.

"Afternoon, Miss Caroline," he said sheepishly.

"Afternoon, Amrod." She paused with one foot on the bottom step.

"I, uh, want to thank you, uh, for last night," he said, wrinkling his forehead into a frown.

"You were in pretty bad shape, Amrod. You know that, don't you?"

Staring at his polished boots, he nodded silently.

Caroline's heart melted. Seeing him standing there, contrite and all alone, she didn't have the heart to chastise him as if he were a naughty child. She held out her arms and gave him a big hug. "Oh, Amrod. I love you, you know that? I didn't realize how much you meant to me until last night. I don't know what I'd do without you."

He sniffled over her shoulder. "You—you love me? Even after last night?"

"Especially after last night."

"You forgive me, then?"

"Of course I do." She held him at arm's length and shook a finger in his face. "But don't do it again. You scared the daylights out of me. I was afraid I'd lost you."

"Jeez, I'm sorry, Miss Caroline. I won't do it again. I ran into some old buddies on the Square, and we got to talkin' over old times and shootin' the breeze, and we remembered the Fourth of July when we all went fishin' the last time on the river before they dammed it up. One of the men recalled we put away a few beers that day, so we decided to celebrate the Fourth the same way—without the fishin', of course."

He scratched his head. "Don't know what happened to the others. Last thing I remember, we ran out of beer and started on the flask Lloyd had in his boot."

Caroline couldn't help smiling. Even though Amrod was old enough to be her grandfather, he reminded her of a little boy rambling on to his mother so she wouldn't have a chance to scold him.

Amrod offered his elbow. She smiled and slipped her arm through his. At the front door she paused. "I've got an idea. What are your plans today?"

"Plans? Nothin'. Why? You need help? I could change my clothes and be back in a—"

"Amrod, I don't need your help. I want your company."

He puffed out his chest and straightened the slide on his tie. "I'd be pleased to oblige, Miss Caroline." He frowned. "But what're you doin' home this time of day? You must be busy as a cranberry merchant at Thanksgivin', this bein' the last day of the holiday weekend."

"Oh . . . Ellie's minding the store," she said vaguely as she let him open the door for her and motioned for him to follow her through the living room and dining room into the kitchen. She opened the refrigerator, removed a frosty pitcher of mint tea and filled two tall glasses. Why was she home, indeed! The thought of her aborted dinner plans gave her an idea. "Amrod, how'd you like to stay for dinner?"

"Dinner? Me? I'd be honored."

Caroline felt warm all over, knowing she was doing something to make Amrod feel better about himself. She would help him with his problem, without being blunt and rude and insensitive, as Luke had implied she should be. Amrod wouldn't wind up like Luke's grandfather. She'd see to it—but in her own way.

With the help of the old man, Caroline prepared a dinner of country-fried chicken, mashed potatoes, green beans and biscuits. They sat down to eat just as the grandfather clock chimed six times. Although it wasn't her kind of music, she let Amrod tune in the radio to his favorite station. They sat together at the lace-covered table in the dining room, licking their fingers and tapping their toes to country-and-western music while they ate.

As she was about to step into the kitchen to refill the mashed potato bowl, the doorbell rang.

"Must be Ellie," she reasoned out loud. With a chicken leg in one hand, she danced a jig across the living room, humming along to a lively blue grass number as she flung open the door.

Eyes of midnight blue and a voice as rich as velvet assailed her. "Looks like fun. Am I late?"

Caroline stood poised with her chicken leg in one hand, the brass doorknob in the other. Luke was

dressed much as she'd pictured him the day before—
khaki pants, a jade-green cotton sweater, the sleeves
pushed up his tanned arms and supple black leather
loafers on his feet.

One thing she hadn't pictured was the bouquet of
crape myrtle cuttings he held in his hand. "What are
you doing here?" she asked.

He opened the screen door, sniffed the pink blossoms and handed her the bouquet. His blue eyes sparkled as he touched the tip of her nose. "You asked me
to dinner—remember?"

She stuck the fist holding the bouquet on her hip and
waggled the chicken leg in his face. "I remember a lot
of things about last night."

He smothered a smile with his hand, but the mischief twinkled in his eyes. "So do I, Caroline.
So...do...I."

She felt a flush on her cheeks and heard Amrod's
chair scoot back from the table. When she turned
around, she saw him dabbing his mouth with his napkin.

"I'll be goin' now, Miss Caroline," he said, a nervous edge to his voice.

"No," she said, directing him back into his chair
with a flutter of her hand. "Sit down. Miss Ellie sent
the Williams boy over with a home-baked peach pie,
and you haven't had those seconds on mashed potatoes."

She looked back at Luke. "I never dreamed you'd
have the nerve to show up here this evening. Not after
the way you talked to me last night."

"I can be a nervy fellow when a pretty lady offers to
cook me dinner." He tipped a salute to Amrod with

one finger. "'Evening, Amrod. Good to see you up and around."

Amrod slipped his hands into his lap and lowered his gaze to his plate.

Caroline grabbed Luke's arm. "You're embarrassing him."

"Embarrassing him?" He bent to whisper in her ear. "If the man has something to get embarrassed about, he'll get embarrassed."

The swirl of Luke's warm breath in her ear prompted a line of goose bumps down Caroline's neck and across her shoulders. That sensation held her motionless while Luke strolled into the dining room and seated himself at the table across from her chair with his back to the double-hung windows. To his right sat Amrod, hunched over his plate.

"Glad you could join us, Amrod." Luke inclined his head at the chicken. "Is that as good as it looks?"

The old man passed the chicken platter, pushed back his chair and retrieved his hat from the sideboard. Twisting the brim in his hands, he glanced first at Caroline, then at Luke. "Time for me to . . . to watch Lawrence Welk."

Although Amrod's voice bore its normal gravelly tone from years of cigarettes and drink, Caroline detected a new, softer texture as he bid her farewell. "I'll be goin' now. You two'll be wantin' some privacy. Time for an old man to make himself scarce."

Caroline wrapped her arms around him and felt him hug her in return. "Please stay," she pleaded in a whisper. "I had no idea he'd come. We had . . . sort of an argument last night."

"On account of me?" Amrod whispered back.

"No," she said too loudly, narrowing her gaze at Luke, "It had nothing to do with you."

LUKE SUFFERED through long moments of embarrassing silence. Fingering the stem of his iced-tea glass, he watched Caroline flick another crumb off the lace tablecloth. She'd said all of two words since they'd sat down together, those two being "More chicken?"

He knew he'd taken a chance on showing up at her house tonight, as if they hadn't had cross words last night. But, dammit, the lady had haunted him in his dreams, as she had for years. Only now he knew how silky her skin felt above her jeans, how it felt to hold her in his arms. Argument or no argument, he had to see her.

That afternoon, just when he'd thought he'd shut out the vision of her firm little fanny from his mind, there she'd gone, sashaying it across the Square, turning every man's head in her path. The rest of the afternoon his thoughts had focused on the feel of her soft curls beneath his chin, on that damned gardenia scent of hers.

He hadn't been thinking too clearly when he'd decided to drop by. But, hell, he was here, and he wasn't a bit sorry.

Settling back in his chair, he smoothed his palm across his full stomach and nodded at the empty platter. "Best fried chicken I've ever eaten."

Caroline glared at him. "Save the compliment for Amrod. He cooked it. Now, aren't you ashamed for chasing him out of here?"

Luke leaned over and squeezed her elbow. "I didn't chase him away, sweet thing. He left on his own accord."

She jerked her elbow free of his fingers. "We were having a very nice time until you showed up."

"Did you talk to him—you know, about his problem?"

Caroline stood, picked up her plate and reached for Luke's. "We talked . . . some. I'll handle it, Luke. I'll do this my way." She turned to leave the room.

Luke scrambled to his feet, grabbed several dirty dishes and followed her into the kitchen. "Remember, you're all the family he has."

Caroline brushed past him on her way back to the dining room, her nose stuck in the air with a haughty tilt. Luke followed her.

"That's right. This is a family matter. A McAlester family matter. The McAlesters never interfered in your family business. We—that is, I—don't want you interfering in ours."

Luke gripped the back of his chair and clenched his teeth, resisting the urge to tell her a thing or two about her grandfather. "Look," he said, picking up the gravy boat and butter dish, "I'm not trying to interfere. I only want to help."

Caroline opened her mouth to speak, then clamped it shut. She glanced out the window, balancing the platter in one hand as if she wanted to throw it at him. When she looked at him again, the heat of anger had faded, and she spoke in a calmer voice. "I appreciate what you're trying to do. I know you want to help. But I think I can help Amrod without being . . . well, without being rude and pushy."

Luke followed Caroline into the kitchen again. As soon as her hands were empty, he cupped her elbow in his hand. "You've got to listen to me. If you don't, you'll be sorry."

She made no attempt to shake loose from his grasp. "Luke, did it ever occur to you there's more than one way to help Amrod? That maybe you don't know everything about his problem?"

Recognizing the signs of denial, Luke took her chin in his other hand and forced her to look at him. "I do have a little more experience with alcoholism than you do. Will you please listen to me?"

Her chin stiffened in his hand, and her eyes flashed a taunting dare. "It doesn't seem I have much choice, does it?"

He moistened his lips with his tongue and glanced from her lips to her eyes. She felt it, dammit. She felt it as much as he did. He watched her long brown lashes blink once, twice, then flutter. Each time she lifted her lashes, her eyes were a warmer, brighter blue. He let his gaze slide down her cheeks, over the freckles and the hint of sunburn, over her perky little nose that turned up cutelike at the end . . . and down to her moist lips.

How many times had he dreamed of kissing those lips? How many times had he dreamed of walking through the Square with her on his arm, of taking her to the Opera House, to Carmichael's Restaurant, to all the places his parents couldn't afford when he was a child, that he couldn't afford as a young man?

He closed his eyes and parted his lips, savoring the smell of peaches on her breath. God, he wanted to kiss her!

Caroline felt the cool ceramic tile of the kitchen counter press into her back as she tried to retreat from Luke. He lowered his gaze to her lips, then burned a path to her eyes, his fingers sliding down her chin to the tender skin on either side of her neck.

"What—what do you want from me?" she demanded, but her words rushed out in a whisper, revealing the urges building inside her. She swallowed hard, feeling her heart go wild in her chest.

Luke sucked in a deep breath. How he longed to tell her he wanted her—the lonely woman who denied her feelings for him. The woman he'd watched grow from a skinny child who delighted all the adults into a woman who could bring unmeasured ecstasy to a man if he were lucky enough to touch her. He wanted to be that man, but he wanted more than the physical pleasures she could bring him. If he could only find the words to make her listen to him.

The flash of her blue eyes sparked a realization. Words? He didn't need to tell her; he needed to show her.

As soft as a butterfly's wings, his lips touched hers, carrying the feelings he couldn't convey with words. The stiffness in her arm disappeared, and her lips lingered on his as he delicately stroked the curve of her jaw.

As he'd done a thousand times in his dreams, he gathered her into his arms and sifted his fingers through the soft mass of sunny curls at her nape. "Dear, Caroline," he said, voicing the words that had been in his heart for years, "I want you to give me a chance to get to know you. I can't help feeling that beneath our differences of opinion, despite our differences in background, there's the basis for a lasting friendship." *Dear God, please let it be more than friendship.*

Caroline pressed her palms against Luke's chest and pushed back, craning her neck so she could look up into his eyes. When he tightened his embrace, she narrowed her gaze and twisted out of his arms, retreating to the back door to gather her wits.

She grasped the doorknob firmly in her hands behind her to steady herself and willed her heart to slow its runaway beat. "You didn't come here tonight to try to persuade me to support your theme park?"

"No, I did not."

She bit her lip and regarded him for a moment. There was a sincere look in his eyes, but she had been fooled before by men whose eyes had hidden their selfish motives. "Okay. I believe you. But what about Amrod? Did you come here tonight to persuade me to get tough with him?"

Luke backed against the counter and planted his palms on the cool tile to his sides. "I was hoping we could forget about him tonight."

Caroline's mind considered his answers, while her heart considered the man. "Then why did you come here tonight?"

Oh, boy! If he told her why, she'd lash out at him with the fury of a west Texas tornado. How could he tell her he'd fantasized about her for years? That now that he'd felt her body next to him, he had to hold her again. "Because I enjoy your company. Is that hard to believe?"

"My company? That's it? No politics, no lectures?"

He shook his head. "All I wanted was to be with you and—" he grinned and inclined his head in the direction of the dining room "—eat that fine cooking."

The boyish smile on Luke's face melted what little reserve Caroline had left. Perhaps he was telling the truth. Maybe he had wanted to see her as much as she'd wanted to see him. Deep inside, she felt a pang of guilt for having invited him to dinner to have an opportunity to change his mind about the location of Dino-Land. But then she put aside all thoughts of the theme park. Tonight would be their night.

She released the doorknob and gestured toward the dining room, welcoming the sudden trust she had in him. "If you came here to eat, it would be inhospitable of me to send you away hungry. How about some more pie?"

Luke smiled. "What do you say we share a piece?" He took her hand and led her back into the dining room. While he sat down at the table, she took a clean dessert plate and two linen napkins from the sideboard.

Caroline felt him watching her every action. His eyes warmed her skin as she eased an ample serving of pie onto the plate, the ripe peaches sliding out from beneath the lightly browned crust sprinkled with crystals of sugar.

"You first," she insisted. "I'm really not hungry."

Their gazes locked as he lifted the first bite of pie to his waiting lips.

"Ellie bakes a great pie, doesn't she?"

He licked his lips and glanced at his plate, then back at her. "She sure does. Don't you want a bite? Just one?" Without waiting for her answer, he slipped his fork beneath a succulent peach slice and lifted it to her lips.

Luke had to work hard to keep his hand from shaking when her lips parted. Her eyes held his gaze as he slid the sweet, warm peach onto her tongue.

Caroline closed her eyes, savoring the taste. As she licked the syrup from her lips, she slowly lifted her lashes. His hand was poised before her, the fork between his fingers.

"Do you want more, Caroline?" He paused. "Do you want... another bite?"

She shook her head slowly and drew in a ragged breath. *I want you to kiss me. Kiss me now and hold me.*

CHAPTER FIVE

LUKE'S HAND SHOOK as he laid the fork on his plate with measured care, unprepared after all these years for the encouragement he found shimmering in Caroline's eyes.

Rosy circles highlighted her cheekbones—not the blush of an ingenue, but the flush of a woman imbued with vitality. It hinted at the vibrant quality that had always been uniquely hers. He remembered she'd had the same rosy cheeks when he was a boy and had snuck in to watch her dance at the Opera House.

Although she'd retained the rosy glow of her youth, she wasn't a little girl anymore, and he wasn't that adolescent boy obsessed only with her material possessions and her exalted social position. At the sight of her rosebud nipples straining against the thin, silky fabric of her blouse, he swallowed hard. She was a woman now, and tonight he wanted to possess all of her.

Unable to restrain himself, he circled her wrist with his hand. Beneath his fingers her pulse beat at the same quickened pace that brought the glow to her skin at the vee of her blouse.

Lifting her hand to his lips, he turned it over and kissed the tender skin on the inside of her wrist, pretending it was for him that she'd splashed the essence of gardenia there. She didn't withdraw from his touch but regarded him with a steady gaze, and moistened her lips with a telling sweep of her tongue. When he seared a kiss into the palm of her hand, he thought he detected a quick intake of breath and gained confidence that she, too, felt the blood racing through her veins.

The ache started in his loins—the ache that had been there since that sultry summer Caroline had blossomed into a woman. Home from college for a brief visit with his family, he'd mustered the nerve to call on her, but her mother had taken one look at him, stuck her haughty nose in the air and turned him away.

He might as well have asked for an audience with the queen, for Caroline was a high-and-mighty McAlester, and he, a working-class O'Connor. But the chasm between them hadn't lessened his obsession with her. His dreams of her had recurred through the years, dreams of resentment and envy—and in more recent years dreams of a grown man's desires.

He wanted to touch her. God help him, she seemed willing. In some dreams he'd fantasized about making love to her right there in her house, in the place denied him by his birth. Now that he was there, an inner voice told him that when he made love to Caroline, they would lie in each other's arms far away from anything tainted with Barron McAlester's power and influence.

Restraint knotted Luke's hand into a fist at his side, and he rose to his feet, expelling a ragged breath. "I could use some fresh air. How about you?"

Caroline read the heat in Luke's gaze. Fresh air wasn't what either of them wanted. She opened her mouth to speak, but Luke drew her up beside him, kissed her hand and led her through the living room and out into the warm night.

The air outside was heavy with the fragrance of English tea roses—roses planted by her great-grandmother when the house was built. The fragrance wrapped around them as they sat side by side, holding hands on the seat for two that hung from creaky chains on the veranda.

Caroline tried hard to ignore the yearning to be closer to Luke, but the feel of his hand about hers, the length of his arm pressing lightly against hers, prompted a tingling sensation that made her heart sing.

Luke's longer legs stretched out before them, swinging them in a slow, mesmerizing motion, stirring up the heady scents of roses, crape myrtle blossoms and the woodsy one that was distinctively his. Beside him she closed her eyes and didn't resist when his hand urged her cheek against his shoulder and lightly ruffled the curls on the side of her head.

"This is some house," Luke said. He smiled down at her, and when she returned the smile, he shifted her back against his chest, looped his arms loosely about her and rested his chin atop her head.

She welcomed Luke's arms around her, even though she sensed his attempts at restraint in the tensed muscles in his chest. "I never realized how much I'd missed it until I came back," she said. She paused, letting her gaze wander over the familiar gingerbread architecture of the house. "Now it's all that's left of my family—this house and the store."

"There's something more—the most important part—you," he said, giving her a gentle squeeze between his arms. "I expect someday you'll fill this house with children, and you'll tell them how your great-grandfather Cain built this place for his bride. You plan to have children, don't you?"

"Of course. Someday. If I don't, my family will cease to be when I die. I'm the last one on either side."

In the moment of silence that ensued, Luke's respectful comments about her great-grandfather echoed in her mind. Just yesterday Luke had talked about her family as if they were despicable, self-serving people. Why the sudden change in his attitude?

She narrowed her eyes as she let her gaze drift across the lawn. His respect had seemed to be for her great-grandfather Cain, while his animosity had been directed toward the McAlester side of her family, her father's side. Maybe that was a clue. The McAlester name had become a part of her family tree when Barron McAlester married Lydia Cain sometime during the depression. Their only child, Aaron, had been her father.

Aaron had died young, leaving her fatherless. Thank God for her grandfather. Barron McAlester had willingly assumed the role of her father. Even though Barron had been busy with his responsibilities as the town mayor and with his business interests, he had always found the time for her.

She frowned, unable to understand how her father or her Grandfather McAlester could have done anything to generate the kind of animosity she'd seen in Luke. She couldn't imagine that her father or grandfather had even been involved with the O'Connors. After all, the McAlesters hadn't mixed much with the lower classes. Could it be that there had been more to Barron's whispered conversations about George O'Connor, Luke's grandfather, than derogatory remarks about the man's drinking?

The feel of Luke's cheek against the side of her head drew her to the present, and she nestled her back against his chest. Tonight was their night—hers and Luke's.

"Next time you come over, I'll give you a grand tour of the house," she offered, beginning a mental walk-through of the old dwelling with its Victorian parlor and extravagant furnishings.

Her mental tour halted abruptly before her bed-room door, and she felt an awareness sing through her at the thought of inviting Luke into her bedroom. Her bedroom with the four-poster—the wedding-night bed for her mother and her grandmother and her great-grandmother before that.

"I'd like that," Luke said, smoothing her hair back from her face and kissing her temple.

She smiled to herself, wondering if Luke had read her thoughts.

"You seem happy here," he said. "What will you do if you don't stay?"

"My boss in Fort Worth is still holding my job for me."

"You must be a crackerjack accountant for him to be so accommodating."

"I don't mind working hard, and I've been at the firm since I graduated from college. CPAs with four years' experience in public accounting are pretty much in demand these days. My experience justifies his holding my job for me, but I'll have to make a decision soon. At the end of the summer, the firm's busy season starts again."

"You think you'll go back?"

"I don't know. I . . . like it here so much better than in Fort Worth, and I enjoy managing the Emporium. If I go back to my job, I'll have to hire a manager for the store, and that would wipe out my profits."

"I'd like it if we both stayed," he murmured into her ear.

His warm breath and his comment sent a line of goose bumps dancing down her arms. Then the impact of his words reached her brain. "The only way that'll happen is if you get approval to build your theme park here, right?"

"Right."

She started to comment on her feelings but remembered their conversation in the kitchen. "We weren't going to talk about that tonight, were we?"

"No," he said, picking up her hand and cradling it in his atop his thigh. "We weren't."

Feeling a muscle in his thigh flex, she closed her eyes and snuggled the back of her head into the curve of his neck, the pace of her heart quickening. It felt so good to be close to him. She'd been lonely during the past months, lonelier than she'd admitted to anyone, even Ellie.

She glanced about the moon-washed veranda, watching the shadows of the crape myrtle play across the weathered boards. A strange object propped against the wall on the far side of the veranda drew her attention. She frowned and lifted her head. "I wonder what that is," she said, pointing one finger at a long white cylinder. It didn't look like anything she remembered seeing there. What day was it? Sunday? Not a day for parcel deliveries.

Luke urged her head back beneath his chin. "It's nothing—just something I left on the porch when I came in."

"Something you left on the porch? Why didn't you bring it in with you?" She lifted her head again and sat up straight, turning to him for his explanation.

Luke's eyes darted across the porch and back to her. "It's . . . nothing, Caroline." He cupped her shoulders in his hands and kissed the tip of her nose. "Now come back here. I like the way you feel next to me."

She resisted the gentle pressure on her arms and tried to read the new expression in his eyes. "Is there something over there you don't want me to see? A secret, maybe?" She turned for another look at the cylindrical object.

No sooner had she turned her head than he caught her chin with his fingertips and eased it back around to him. "It isn't really a secret."

A growing suspicion brought her palms against his chest. "There is something over there you don't want me to see, isn't there?" She glanced at the white cylinder and back at him, sure that any minute he would explain the mystery.

Luke looked at her for a long moment before speaking. "Aw, Caroline, it's just something I grabbed when I walked out of my room. I thought we might talk about it. When I got here, I decided tonight wasn't the right time."

"Wasn't the right time for what?" Resolutely she stood up, walked to the opposite side of the porch and reached down to pick up the long white cardboard tube.

Immediately Luke moved behind her and reached over her shoulder for the tube. "Let me have that. I'll show it to you tomorrow."

Spurred on by the urgency in his voice, Caroline clutched the tube and twisted away from him. She drew it closer to the edge of the veranda and squinted. In the moonlight she could barely make out the label: "Sandifer, Morrow and Seligson Architects, Dallas, Texas."

Architects? She pursed her lips and felt her nostrils flare, confident that inside the tube were the plans for his theme park. And she'd believed this was their night!

The muscles in her shoulders tensed as she walked slowly back to him, swinging the tube vertically between two fingers. Disappointment and anger colored her words. "I thought you said you didn't come here to discuss your theme park. From the looks of things, that's exactly why you did come."

Luke took the tube from her and curved a hand around either end. "I wanted you to see these. I wanted to talk about them, but not like this."

"But you said you came here because you enjoy my company." She almost choked on the words.

"I do, but we have to talk about our differences of opinion. We can't pretend they don't exist."

Caroline turned her back to Luke and folded her arms across her chest. "Do you know what a curse it is coming from a prominent family, a family that swings a lot of weight in local politics? Every time you turn around someone tries to persuade you to support a cause, because more often than not your support will swing the community in behind a cause."

The tube tumbled to the porch as Luke reached for her arm. Her head bowed, she regarded his hand on her arm and pushed it away before she lifted her head to speak. "For a moment there I thought you cared for me—as a person, as a woman. You almost had me believing you and I—"

When her words caught in her throat, she turned her back on him again. Oh, God, she'd been such a fool. She hung her head and crossed her arms at her waist, clutching at the ache beneath her ribs.

Behind her Luke spoke, his voice no longer gentle but hard edged. "Do you realize you just accused me of trying to develop a relationship with you so you'd support my project before the city council?"

She turned and looked up at him. "Do you deny it?"

"If you think I'd do such a thing, you must have a low opinion of me...and a low one of yourself, as well."

Caroline stooped and picked up the plans. Grabbing one of Luke's hands, she pressed the cardboard tube to his palm. "I'm a fair woman. If you had told me you wanted me to consider these this evening, I'd have said fine, we'll do it after dinner. To be truthful, I wanted to talk to you about your project, too. But after dinner, you stood there in the kitchen and told me you didn't come here tonight to discuss your theme park. It's the deception that hurts. It's knowing you felt you had to hide these on the porch until you found a moment when I'd be amenable to discussing them."

"You're a fair woman? A reasonable woman? Tell me you were fair and reasonable when I told you about Dino-Land in your back room yesterday."

She felt her face burn with anger, but she was determined to show him she wasn't the hothead he thought she was. "I think you'd better leave. Have someone drop a set of your plans by my store, and I'll look them over before the city council meeting Tuesday night. But don't get your hopes up. Unless you have magic in those plans, I'll be in that city council meeting Tuesday, but I'll be there to fight you."

CAROLINE SAT in the city council chambers, waving an occasional greeting at others arriving for the meeting. Even though she tried to appear relaxed and confident, she tugged on the red silk tie at her neck and smoothed her navy skirt across her knees. She'd changed clothes a half-dozen times that morning, trying to decide what image suited her best. She wasn't sure she'd made the right choice showing up in her accountant's traditional blue. The folks around Granbury were accustomed to seeing her in much more casual attire.

She skimmed the agenda in her hands. Good. Old business would precede Luke's proposal. It had taken all her willpower, but she had kept her promise not to tell anyone about Dino-Land, not even Ellie. It had been tricky when a courier had dropped off a set of Luke's plans at the Emporium, but luckily Ellie had been in the bathroom at the time.

Caroline had poured over the plans the previous night and come to the same conclusion: Dino-Land didn't belong in Granbury. She was even more convinced of her opinion now, so convinced she'd made a decision. It was a decision likely to set Luke back on his heels.

She heard some commotion down the hall and shifted in her seat, which was near the center aisle halfway back in the chambers on the left side. Her heart fluttered when she saw Luke in the doorway. Dressed as professionally as a Philadelphia lawyer, he entered the chambers with a meticulously groomed, silver-haired man of about sixty.

Caroline couldn't help letting her gaze drift over Luke's tall, muscular frame. It would be easier to dislike him if he were bald or fat or smoked nasty cigars. There wasn't a thing about the man that didn't appeal to her—except his devotion to his dinosaur project.

Before she could avert her gaze, he turned around and caught her looking at him, returning her attention with a hard stare that chilled her. He inclined his head as if to acknowledge his adversary and looked away. Apparently he didn't have any trouble keeping his eyes off her.

Out of the corner of her eye, she watched him work his way through the crowd to the front of the room, shaking hands, greeting the councilmen as if they were lifelong friends. His light gray summer suit fitted him with the unmistakable touch of an expensive tailor.

So that's why the Western attire he'd worn on the Fourth of July hadn't seemed natural on him. So why had he worn it? To make people think he was still a small-town boy? To attract attention? He'd sure attracted her attention, with his tight jeans and custom-fitted shirt with those damn pearlized buttons that kept popping open.

Caroline clenched her jaw, admitting the man was a smooth operator. His decision to stay in the old McNutt Brothers Hotel on the Square had undoubtedly been calculated to give him frequent access to the town's opinion leaders, the ones who'd have the most influence when it came to the vote on his project.

She folded her hands in her lap and stared at her freshly painted nails. She'd begun to wonder if he'd planned their impromptu partnership in the Fourth of July bed race.

He flashed a smile at the woman who owned the store next to hers, that damn dimple creasing his chin. Caroline's eyes drifted lower to the burgundy silk tie secured in a perfect Windsor knot at his neck. If she could get her hands on him, she just might strangle him with it.

She focused on the back of Luke's head as he sat in the front row with that strange man, and she cursed the stirrings she felt deep inside.

Yesterday, while she'd polished the storefront windows, she'd caught sight of him walking into the courthouse, his long, muscular legs taking the limestone steps two at a time. She'd grabbed a handful of chocolate chip cookies and retreated to the back room, where she'd gobbled down all of them, one right after another.

Every time the bell on the door to the Square had tinkled, she'd glanced up, hoping it was Luke, hoping he'd say the words to persuade her she'd misjudged him Sunday evening, but he hadn't called, and he hadn't dropped by.

She lifted her chin proudly and stared at his back. Maybe it was for the best. If he had called, she might have told him her news. She sat up straighter in her chair and fingered the three-by-five note card in her hand. It was better, she told herself, that he learn about it this way.

The mayor called the meeting to order. In a few minutes it was time for the old-business portion of the agenda.

The mayor cleared his throat. "Not long ago," he began, "Granbury's young people were deserting the town in droves. We'd educate them, give them their values and lose them to the big cities, where they could get decent-paying jobs. Things are beginning to change. Some of our young people are returning to raise their families here, coming back to the wholesome small-town atmosphere they took for granted while they were growing up."

There was a murmur in the room. Caroline saw several people nodding at one another and smiling. The old gentleman next to her, whom she'd known since she was a child, winked at her and patted her hand.

"One of those young people is with us today," the mayor continued, smiling at her. "She came back under some trying circumstances, but she's decided to stay."

Caroline returned his smile and glanced about the room. Forgetting Luke for a brief moment, she let the warmth of her hometown surround her. Without these people, these friendly, caring people, she never would have been able to face her loneliness as well as she had after her mother's death. They were her family now.

"We're mighty anxious to keep her with us," the mayor continued. "Besides her youth and her beauty she has a quality Granbury needs—an interest in continuing her family's tradition of preserving our cultural heritage. That's why we're pleased she's agreed to accept an offer we made her a month ago. Folks, let's have a hand for Caroline McAlester, who today becomes Granbury's director of historical preservation."

He motioned for Caroline to stand, and she obliged, acknowledging the applause. Her eyes returned the warm smiles of the townsfolk in the room, but she held her breath when Luke turned around in his front row seat to stare at her. She searched his face to gauge his reaction to the news of her appointment. Unsmiling, he arched one brow.

She realized the mayor was talking about her again. "And I know your family," he was saying, "especially your mother and grandfather, would be proud to know you stand here today, ready to carry on another

McAlester tradition, that being a tradition of civic responsibility to Granbury. Caroline, come on up here, sweetheart.''

It was a long walk to the microphone at the front of the room. Every step of the way Caroline felt Luke's eyes burn into her. She couldn't resist the urge to look at him again. When she did, she was surprised to see a flicker of sadness in his eyes, and for the shortest moment she regretted what she was doing.

Standing before the microphone, she clutched her three-by-five card in one hand. Out of the corner of her eye she could see Luke to the left of her. She tried to ignore his penetrating gaze, but it invaded her consciousness as she spoke.

''I—I can't tell you how good it is to—to be back in Granbury,'' she stammered. She took a deep breath and willed herself to concentrate on the points she wished to make. ''I can assure you I'll do my best to carry on the McAlester tradition of preserving this beautiful town. When I was a small child, the Square was a bunch of run-down, boarded-up storefronts. Now it's our pride, the heart of our town.

''Before our ancestors came to this area, the Square was part of a wilderness of huge oak, pecan and cottonseed trees, a home for buffalo, deer, antelope and small game. The Comanche, Kiowa, Caddo, Lipan and several other Indian tribes used the Square itself as a camping site before being pushed westward. Then Granbury became a wide-open Western town, with a colorful history. Today the restored image of that Western town draws tourists to Granbury—and with them their dollars. That image, coupled with our magnificent lake, are the two jewels in the Granbury crown we need to polish.

"There are those," she continued, avoiding Luke's eyes, "who would use our fair town for interests inconsistent with these images. We must be ready to stand for what we believe, to make sure we control our own destiny. I look forward to serving you."

Everyone in the room applauded. Everyone except Luke and the silver-haired man beside him and another man she didn't recognize, who sat at the back of the room. Luke and his associate sat in the front row, conferring about something while Caroline returned to her seat. As she did, she had a better look at the burly man in the back row. Unsmiling, he glared at her as if he despised her. A dimple creased his chin.

Still feeling the icy gaze of the stranger on her back, she shook hands with several well-wishers sitting nearby, then turned, ostensibly to focus her attention on the mayor, who was attempting to discuss a previously tabled motion. But Caroline's gaze was drawn to Luke, to the black hair that curled over the collar of his pinpoint oxford cloth shirt. A vision of his magnificent chest in the white cowboy shirt sprang to mind, the mat of curly black hair tumbling through the opening above the pearlized buttons.

She felt sorry for him. She knew how these people thought, how they had agreed with her mother and her grandfather for years on what was best for Granbury. Her breast swelled with pride at the role her family had played in the renovation of Granbury, in the leadership the McAlesters and Cains had provided for generations. Luke didn't have that long tradition of Granbury civic responsibility to support him. But even if he had, she knew his Dino-Land proposal would fall flat on its face. The people of Granbury would never agree to it.

A half hour later the mayor introduced Luke in the new-business section of the agenda. Luke stepped behind the microphone and flashed a winning smile. After rambling on for a couple of minutes about how good it was to be back home, he said he had a proposal he wanted them to consider.

He nodded to someone in the back of the room, and the lights went off. A slide show was projected onto the screen at the front of the room as a deep, rich voice with a north central Texas accent explained the concept of Dino-Land to the hushed room.

Even in the semidarkness, Caroline could see Luke staring at her. He leaned against the wall on the side of the room, his arms folded at his waist. She tilted her chin upward and, pretending to ignore his gaze, focused her eyes on the screen.

When the presentation ended with an emotional swell of music and that deep, rich voice imploring the citizens of Granbury to approve the project for the good of their community, the councilmen joined in the general thunderous applause.

The lights went on, and Luke returned to the microphone, this time with his tie removed and the top button of his shirt undone. Nice touch, Caroline noted. Nice, earthy touch.

"Before we address your questions," Luke said, "I want to assure Caroline—" he gestured in her direction and executed a beautiful smile "—that Dino-Land would do nothing to threaten Granbury's fine reputation for historical preservation. On the contrary, I'm convinced Dino-Land would complement it and increase the tourist business on the Square and at the lake."

Caroline pasted her sweetest smile on her face and scrunched up her toes inside her navy pumps. He'd see. It wouldn't be too long now. He'd see she'd been right.

She complimented herself on her silence while Luke described the anticipated financial rewards to Granbury from his Dino-Land project. When he asked for questions, she decided to keep quiet. The people of Granbury would speak.

The first question dealt with what Dino-Land would cost Granbury in terms of streets, water lines, sewage treatment and police protection.

Luke thanked the man for his question and asked an assistant to flash a chart on the screen. It was an estimate for the new facilities he anticipated would be required through the first six months of the park's opening. He announced he and his backer were willing to pledge half that amount and assured the questioner that all parties would be more than compensated from the receipts and sales tax revenues generated by the park.

Caroline decided it was time for some tough questions. She stood and squared her shoulders. "Mr. O'Connor—"

"You can call me 'Luke,' Caroline," he interrupted. "After the bed race, I'm sure everyone here realizes we know each other on a first-name basis."

A light chuckle rippled through the room.

Caroline felt her cheeks grow warm. "This is business. That was monkey business." She waited while a second wave of chuckles swelled and subsided.

"I realize you're confident Dino-Land would produce the revenue to pay for these extensive civic improvements that would have to be made before the park could open. But this—" she waved her hand at a map of the theme park Luke's assistant had mounted on the wall "—would be a very expensive venture. Millions of dollars."

"That's right," Luke said. "Millions of dollars invested in Granbury."

She faced him squarely. "I do not mean to question your financial solvency, but I've heard about developers who've begun expensive amusement facilities and, coming on hard times, have stopped construction. Meanwhile the towns that poured tax dollars into streets and utilities had no way to recoup their losses. My question is, what guarantee do the citizens of Granbury have that you could follow through on this multimillion dollar venture once it's begun?"

Luke's eyes shone with the luster of deep blue star sapphires. He waited for Caroline to take her seat, then motioned for the silver-haired friend beside him to stand. "Caroline has a point, friends, but I'm sure her fears will be put to rest when I introduce the person who has agreed to provide the financial backing for Dino-Land. He is prepared to execute a bond to guarantee his investment. Ladies and gentlemen of Granbury, meet Conway Carriker of Fort Worth."

A hush fell over the room, but the name "Carriker" shot like a lightning bolt through Caroline's head. The Conway Carriker of Carriker Enterprises? Was Luke in business with the Carriker who controlled enough real estate ventures to fill an entire state?

Whenever Carriker got into something, he controlled it like a tyrant. Hooking up with the likes of that man had been a monumental mistake for Luke. Granbury would never agree to let an outside interest as powerful as Carriker take over the town.

The owner of a local restaurant asked for permission to speak. Caroline waited for him to voice his opposition to the Carriker influence, but what came out of the man's mouth made hers go dry. Instead of being opposed to Luke's project, he extolled its virtues, talking about the increased business for merchants and the national attention that would be focused on Granbury.

Caroline's hand shot up. "Dear friends," she began, "I think we're missing the point here." She smiled a sugary sweet smile at Luke and inclined her head. "Mr. O'Connor—Luke—has flattered us with his proposal. Any time someone of Mr. Carriker's prominence expresses interest in a town this size, it's a compliment.

"However," she continued, "I'm afraid Dino-Land is totally inconsistent with the character we've established for Granbury. If we permit such a theme park to be built here, it would consume us, obliterate the small-town Western image we've worked so hard to establish."

Thoughts of her life in one big city flashed across her mind, and she felt a chill dart over her shoulders. "We wouldn't be a small town anymore. And that stretch of land that gives us such a magnificent view of Comanche Peak would be filled with huge neon dinosaurs, noisy amusement rides and parking lots full of vehicles."

Luke addressed her in a brisk, businesslike manner. "Caroline, nobody wants to destroy what's already been accomplished here. We want to build on it. Besides, when it comes to historical preservation, how can you discriminate against dinosaurs?"

The sparkle in Luke's eyes fueled the fury that raced through her veins. She rolled her hands into balls and felt her fingernails dig into her palms. "Mr. O'Connor, there's a difference between preserving the actual footprints of those early-day inhabitants of our lands, as they've done near Glen Rose, and erecting fifty-foot neon replicas of the creatures that made them."

Luke glanced about the room and shrugged. "Why don't we let our citizens speak for themselves? Let them decide if they want Dino-Land here, where they can reap the benefits, or if they want to let some other town cash in on it."

"Fine," she snapped, scanning the room as Luke had. "Let's put it to a vote."

"I'd like to address myself to that issue," a city councilman interjected. "You two know exactly where you stand on this thing. I'm not sure the rest of us are ready to vote yet."

Caroline watched townsfolk nod in agreement, as she sank into her chair, a wave of doubt engulfing her. This was not the reaction she'd expected.

Luke relinquished the floor and turned the meeting over to the mayor. Back in his seat, Luke raised his hand, was recognized and stood. "My dear friends, our honored city councilman is right. This is an opportunity too important to be decided in an hour. I'd like to suggest we delay the vote on this project for thirty days. During that time Mr. Carriker and I and—" he gestured to Caroline with an open palm "—Miss McAlester will have ample opportunity to present our cases to the public. At the end of that time, the citizens of Granbury will make the decision by vote of this council."

Another councilman leaned toward his microphone. "Oh, no, you don't, O'Connor. This is too important for us—" his gaze swept the long table where the councilmen sat "—to make the decision on our own. I vote for an election, a referendum, if you will, in thirty days to decide if Dino-Land will be approved for Granbury, or not approved, as the case may be."

Luke flashed a victorious smile at her. "Any objections, Caroline?"

CHAPTER SIX

CAROLINE WILLED HERSELF to look more confident than she felt. "Absolutely no objections, Luke." Her gaze locked with his, as if their eyes were waging a battle. "Thirty days should give me all the time I need to let the citizens of Granbury know what they're in for if you build your project in our town."

Luke clenched his jaw as Caroline sat down in her chair. Whose town did she think it was, anyway, the McAlesters'? He watched her tilt her chin upward and stare down her nose at him. It was a look he remembered well from his childhood—the look those in positions of privilege and power used to intimidate those who weren't.

He sat down slowly. That kind of a look didn't intimidate him anymore. Caroline might be the granddaughter of the most powerful mayor in Granbury's history, but, by golly he, Luke O'Connor, was a force to be reckoned with, too. People might have gotten away with making jokes about his grandfather, but they'd show respect to this O'Connor. Not only would they listen to his ideas, they'd soon thank him for bringing a sterling opportunity for economic security to their hometown—his hometown.

He thought of his father, still living on a dirt road in the modest five-room house where Luke and his brother had been born. He wished his father would let him buy him a nicer, newer house. It wasn't that Luke was ashamed of his birthplace. He just wanted to make life easier for his father now that his health was bad and his twilight years had arrived. But every time the subject was brought up, his father refused to talk about it.

Luke let his gaze drift out the window. He couldn't blame his dad. Mack O'Connor wanted to stay where his poignant memories of Luke's mother made his loneliness a little easier to bear. Barbara O'Connor had been an accomplished homemaker, and evidence of her talents were scattered throughout the house like memories.

Luke shook himself from his reverie and glanced at his watch. In the thirty minutes since he'd finished his presentation, the councilmen had formalized his thirty-day, wait-then-vote suggestion on his theme park and whipped through the remainder of the meeting agenda. All that time, Luke had felt as though his back were sizzling from the fixed, searing stare Caroline had directed at him.

The next thirty days were going to be doozies. It wasn't so much the demand on his time that bothered him or the pressure of getting the job done. After all, his new park in northeastern Arkansas was running smoothly now, and Conway had whispered to him after the motion had passed that Luke should stay in Granbury until the referendum. Conway would find someone else to cover Luke's responsibilities at the management office in Fort Worth, so Luke could devote all his time to preparing for the big vote. Politicking, said Conway, would require Luke's total efforts if they were to ensure passage of the referendum.

Luke shifted in his chair and glanced over his shoulder at Caroline. What he didn't like was the prospect of spending an entire month sparring with the fiery little woman behind him. Damn, she was stubborn! If she ever opened her mind a crack, she might see how good Dino-Land would be for Granbury. But open-mindedness had never been a McAlester family trait, and she was definitely a McAlester. Good sense was apparently not one of Caroline's virtues, either. Even a fool could see she'd burdened herself with a load too heavy even for a superwoman.

Reluctantly Luke admitted he was worried about her. Even though she was one spunky lady, she'd tackled a triple load—store owner-manager, director of historical preservation and leader of the opposition to Dino-Land. Two of those jobs would keep a normal person busy. Three would keep Caroline so involved she wouldn't...what? Have time to see him? Was that what worried him most?

Even though he could still feel the sting of her words, he smiled. She was one spirited woman. He'd like to see how she channeled that enthusiasm and energy when...if...the two of them weren't at odds with each other.

It was strange she hadn't mentioned the preservation job. She'd told him she had to make a decision about her accountant's job in Fort Worth, but hadn't ever mentioned any directorship of historical preservation. Was it possible she'd decided to accept the job after their disagreement Sunday evening?

The thought was still on his mind as he stood up with Carriker and shook hands with the councilmen. His gaze darted several rows behind him to where Caroline's supporters formed a circle about her.

"I'll catch up with you at the hotel," he told Carriker. "I want to have a few words with Caroline."

"I should hope so," Carriker said, smiling at the man whose hand he was shaking. "She's already cost us thirty days." Carriker angled his head in her direction. "For a little bit of a thing she can sure make a lot of noise."

Luke glanced over his shoulder at her. "You forget she's a McAlester."

"Right. How could I?" Carriker said. "And she's every bit as opinioned as her grandfather ever thought about being." He narrowed his gaze. "You be careful there."

"I'll only be a few minutes."

"Tell you what, if you think you have things under control here, I'll get my driver to take me back to Fort Worth. I have a big meeting at the bank in the morning."

Luke frowned. "Anything wrong?"

"Nothing I can't handle. Seems they hired a new bank auditor who doesn't like the looks of some of the loans."

"You need me?"

Carriker clapped him lightly on the back and headed for the door. "When I do, my boy, I'll let you know."

While Caroline finished talking with the people who'd gathered around her at the end of the meeting, Luke helped his projectionist gather up the equipment.

His thoughts kept returning to her. She sure had the McAlester mystique. No sooner had she planted her feet in the middle of a cause than half the town's leaders appeared to agree with her.

Thank goodness he had a whole month to convince them to vote his way in the referendum. Without those thirty days, Caroline might have had the advantage, with her long-standing family tradition of shoving McAlester ideas down the throats of the townspeople before they had a chance to consider their alternatives. That's why he'd come up with the thirty-day waiting period idea, instead of urging an immediate vote.

Gradually the room emptied. As Luke stuck the last extension cord into a cardboard box, he looked around and found Caroline alone...finally. He shook hands with his assistant, grabbed his briefcase and headed down the center aisle.

Caroline sat in her chair, her back turned to the aisle as she snapped the locks shut on her navy leather briefcase, positioned on the chair beside her. Luke took one look at her shapely legs, following the curve of her slender calves to the delicate turn of her ankles, and tightened the grip on his own briefcase. Even in a business suit she had the ability to stir up his insides—just as she'd always done.

He lowered himself into the empty aisle seat beside her and reached out hesitantly. What he really wanted to do was sift his fingers through the sunny cloud that curled over the back of her suit collar. Instead he settled for tapping her lightly on the shoulder, but his hand twitched in protest as he touched her. "Caroline, still friends?"

She swung around in her seat and banged her knees against his. The hem of her snug straight skirt crept above her knees, drawing Luke's willing gaze as the warmth of her body blended with his.

"It's hard to be friends with an adversary."

"Why don't we try?" Luke saw a hint of a smile in her eyes and reached for her hand.

She snatched it away from him. "What do you think you're doing?"

"Have lunch with me, Caroline. I've missed you."

She stuck her chin in the air again and tugged the silk tie at her neck into a tighter bow. "Why should I?"

Without taking his eyes from hers, Luke ran one long finger along the creamy curve of her chin. "You haven't missed me...at all?"

"Not one bit." She glared at him, but Luke was quick to notice she didn't push away his finger.

"Liar."

She blinked and stared at him wide-eyed. "What did you call me?"

"Liar." He glanced down at their knees, still touching. "Your words say one thing. Your body tells me another."

Caroline shifted in her seat, swinging her knees away from him and banging them into the chair in front of her. "Ouch! That hurt." She rubbed her knees and grimaced.

Luke reached for her elbow to help her stand.

"I'm not an invalid, and I don't need your help." Her shoulder brushed against his chest as she stood, and her eyes registered the same jolt that shot through Luke's body.

"That may be, but I'm going to see you get it." Beneath his thumb he felt her quickening pulse at the bend of her arm. "You may not need me now, but someday...someday you just might."

Caroline's shoulders sagged. She appeared to be struggling more with herself than with him. "Oh, Luke, how in the world did you get mixed up with a guy like Carriker?"

The change in Caroline's demeanor gave Luke a kernel of hope for them. But she was wrong about Carriker. The man had been good to him, almost like a second father. "You can't judge a man by what you read in the newspapers. He's been my boss for years, and I've always found him to be honest and honorable."

"My grandfather got stung by that man when I was in high school. I remember what he was like then. If he hasn't changed, you could be in trouble."

"Conway told me about that business with your grandfather."

"He did?" Caroline's eyes registered a smattering of surprise. Bending, she picked up her briefcase. "Did he also tell you that whenever he's involved in something he controls it with an iron hand?"

Luke stood aside so Caroline could step into the aisle. "You sound like those newspaper stories again."

"I suppose I shouldn't feel this way—worried, that is, about what's going to happen to you. Maybe I shouldn't even be talking to you. But for some strange reason I don't want you to get mixed up with a man who's hurt a lot of people."

Caroline cared about him. She'd just said as much. Luke wanted to whisk her away to Tanzania or Iceland or Bora Bora or someplace where they could build on that center of caring. He swallowed hard, wanting to gather her into his arms, but he told himself to be satisfied for the present with one step forward and, for once, none backward.

Remembering all he owed to Conway, he continued. "There's a lot you don't know about the man."

"Like what?"

"If it weren't for him, I wouldn't be where I am today."

Caroline rolled her eyes. "You mean here in Granbury, fighting me over your theme park?"

"Of course not. I mean in business, and before that, college." He didn't feel like bragging about his successful business ventures, including his theme park in Arkansas, but he meant for her to know how special Conway had been to him since he was eighteen.

"What did Carriker have to do with you and college?"

"That's where I met him—at Tarleton State University over in Stephenville. I was going to school there, working for one of Carriker's subsidiaries as a handyman afternoons and evenings to pay for my tuition. One day he came to town to check on his business, and . . . well, the rest is history. He never had any children of his own, and I guess he got a lot of satisfaction from teaching me the business as he would have a son."

Caroline shook her head. "So, you're Conway Carriker's protégé. Great. Just great."

Luke narrowed his gaze. "I don't like the tone of your voice. Conway's a good man. If you'd give him a chance, you'd find that out for yourself."

"My grandfather told me enough about him to make me steer clear of him for a lifetime."

Luke wanted to tell Caroline she should have considered the source of that information, but he thought better of it. "Suit yourself. But you're wrong. Conway's a good friend, and we're going to be partners on Dino-Land. He wouldn't hurt me any more than he would hurt his own son."

Caroline paused beneath the clock over the door. "So there's something else we disagree about." There was a measure of sadness in her voice. "Look, it's getting late, and I've got a dozen things to do, and Ellie's going to be as mad as a wet hen if I don't get back to the store to help."

Her eyes softened as she placed a hand on the door. "I feel a compulsion to say something significant, such as 'may the best man win,' but instead I'm going to ask you to be careful, Luke. You and I may have our differences, but basically I think we're both good people. I'm not so sure about Carriker. I'd hate to see you hurt."

CAROLINE GLANCED UP from her battered desk in the modest office the city had provided her on the second floor of the restored jail house. The sound of the maid buffing the floors in the chamber of commerce offices downstairs made her long to do something mundane for a change.

In thirty minutes she had to speak to the Opera Guild ladies, and she hadn't organized her thoughts yet. Tomorrow night it would be the Lions Club, the school board the next and a garden club the next.

Her gaze fell to her appointment book, before her on her desk. With a groan she realized that every single night for the next three weeks she was booked to speak to another group, each one important in her campaign to reach the citizens of Granbury before they voted their consciences on Dino-Land.

So far, she and Luke had twice found themselves speaking at the same meeting. Both times Caroline had had trouble concentrating on what she was saying. Ordinarily she handled speaking engagements with panache, thanks to her experience on the stage, but the man had a way of unsettling her that was infuriating. To make matters worse, Luke spoke with a relaxed self-confidence that made her wish she had the nerve to pour a glass of ice water down his pants.

She admitted her schedule was killing her. Fatigue racked her body. The dark circles beneath her eyes were getting bigger by the day. Worry over Amrod had a lot to do with it. Her double duties as store owner-manager and historical preservationist left her precious little time to be with him, to help boost his self-confidence and feeling of self-worth.

Until tonight she hadn't had trouble persuading him to go with her when she spoke, although he'd tired of sitting quietly at the back of the room. Last night he'd fallen asleep while she'd spoken to a PTA group. She'd cleared her throat loudly to awaken him. And it worked, only he'd left the room for the remainder of her speech and she'd worried about what he might be doing.

Caroline picked up the current issue of the *Hood County News* and wrinkled her nose at Luke's picture on the front page. Dressed in a white dress shirt, his red paisley tie blowing over his shoulder, he was stepping onto a shovel at a ground-breaking ceremony. A local reporter had discovered that Luke and Carriker had already successfully launched a theme park in Arkansas. The local editor had gotten permission from the Arkansas newspaper to reprint the picture.

Caroline stared at the picture, letting her finger drift over the broad expanse of Luke's shoulders and slide down his long, muscular arms. A shiver of wanting snaked down her spine. It had been five days—five long days—since she'd sat in the cradle of his arms on

her veranda swing . . . five days since she'd discovered
how determined he was to get his project approved in
Granbury.

THE LAST CRIMSON RAYS of sunlight reflected off the
lake and through the windows of the posh private home
where the Opera Guild ladies were having their Sunday night meeting. Caroline's speech on maintaining
Granbury's preservation reputation had been well received by them. That hadn't surprised her. After all,
their favorite pastime was preserving the lovely Opera
House, built in 1886.

She took a sip of iced tea and selected a butter cookie
from the silver tray on the buffet table. Throughout her
speech she had felt uneasy about Amrod. He'd refused to spend the evening in the company of a room-
ful of ladies but had promised her he'd stay home and
watch television, without alcohol to fortify him. She
had no right to insist he join her, so she'd acquiesced
and worried all evening.

Concern for Amrod quickened her resolve to leave
the meeting early. She stuffed the rest of the cookie in
her mouth and gathered up her leftover handouts.

"Caroline?" a voice called from behind her.

The identity of the person came to her immediately.
"Miss Justine, what are you doing here? I didn't see
you when I was talking."

The tall, striking woman in her early forties had been
Caroline's jazz dance teacher in high school. She
hugged Caroline enthusiastically, then rested her slender hips against the back of a floral couch. Her brunette hair still had a healthy sheen. Secured at her nape
with a hammered brass clip, it fell midway down her
back. She closed her green eyes and sighed dramati-

cally, massaging the back of her neck with her palms. "I just drove over from Glen Rose. I got here at the end of your speech. I had to catch you before you left."

"Catch me for what?"

Justine twisted her mouth sideways, let her gaze drop to her feet, then slowly raised it to meet Caroline's inquiring eyes. "Before I tell you, let's get something straight. You're a woman now, so you can drop the title. Make it just plain 'Justine.'"

"Justine, then. What is it you need to see me about?"

Justine's eyes roamed over Caroline's frame. "You're still in pretty good shape, kid, just as they said."

Caroline laughed. "Remember the exercise room Granddaddy made for me?"

Justine nodded, smiling.

"I work out in it every day. Helps iron out the kinks. And heaven knows, I've got plenty these days."

"So I've heard," Justine said. "And I'm about to add another."

"Uh-oh."

"I don't know what I'll do if you say no."

"Say no to what? And who was it who said I was still in good shape?"

"I got a call this afternoon to sub as the director for the rest of the *Pal Joey* performances at the Opera House," Justine said. "Seems the director had a personal emergency and had to leave town for a couple of weeks."

"I heard a couple of the women say some relative of the director's was in a terrible accident, but I didn't get the details." Caroline smiled softly. "At least some good's come of it. I'll have a chance to see you again—

if I can find a few spare minutes in my crazy schedule."

"I'm afraid I'll need more than a few minutes."

Caroline didn't know what Justine wanted, but she could already feel herself saying no. "Justine—"

"Look, the director's brother was in the accident. Apparently the man's lucky to be alive, and she's his only living relative."

"I'm sorry. But what's that have to do with me?"

"Did you know two cast members were in the accident with the director's brother?"

"Oh, my God! Are they—?"

"They're alive, but they won't dance or sing anytime soon. I moved the two understudies into their roles. They're over at the Opera House right now, rehearsing. That leaves us two short in the dance ensemble." She squeezed Caroline's hand. "You could do it. We have a few days until the next performance. You always were a quick study."

Caroline groaned, her fatigue making her head spin. "Can't you just eliminate one couple?"

"Nope. Can't. Each person in the ensemble has several lines. We're already making enough changes as it is, and it's too late to rewrite the whole script. Now listen. I don't want to hear that nonsense about how long it's been since you danced. Once a dancer, always a dancer. And you can sing. Lots of dancers can't. When they called, they told me you were back in town, and I figured I could count on you to help. It should be easy enough to find a man who'd want to be your partner."

Caroline was so tired that she could hardly stand up. She couldn't say yes. She couldn't afford the time.

Justine grabbed Caroline's arms. "Will you do it? Please say yes. I need you."

Caroline sank into a cushioned chair and propped her elbows on the padded arms. "There's nothing I'd like better. I've missed dancing, but surely you know—"

"I know. You're busy running a store, preserving the cowboys and Indians and fighting dinosaurs, but I've already taken care of that."

"How?"

"Ellie's agreed to manage your store for two weeks."

"You're kidding! And give up her ball games and soap operas?"

A victorious look spread across Justine's face. "I told her she could bring her television set to the store. I hope you don't mind."

"But that still leaves—"

"Time during the day to slay your dinosaurs. We only have four performances. Thursday through Sunday—"

"And matinees Saturday and Sunday," Caroline added. She remembered her full schedule and shook her head. "It just isn't possible. I'm booked solid with speaking engagements for the next three weeks."

"If I can get them switched around to accommodate our performance schedule, will you do it?"

Caroline rubbed her forehead. "I don't know...."

Her old teacher grabbed one hand and pulled her from the chair. "I knew you'd say yes. Come on. We've got to get you fitted for costumes."

JUSTINE TOOK CAROLINE to the Opera House for a quick fitting session. After that she showed Caroline a video of the dance numbers and worked with her for a few minutes. Caroline picked up the steps easily. As for the script, she'd seen the musical twice already and had sat in on a couple of rehearsals while she ate her lunch. The two women sang "Bewitched" as Justine drove Caroline home.

The minute Caroline saw her house, lights on in every downstairs room, she knew something was wrong, and she instinctively knew it had something to do with Amrod. Panic lodged in her throat as she took the three steps to her door in a single leap.

Ellie met her at the door and pulled her through the entry hall into the living room, a grave expression etching wrinkles in her brow. She gestured to a couch. "You'd better sit down."

"What's going on?" Caroline demanded to know.

"It's Amrod."

Caroline grabbed Ellie's arm, guilt and fear and anger pumping triple doses of adrenaline into her bloodstream. "Is he okay?"

"If by okay, you mean alive, yes, he's okay. If by okay you mean sober, he's far from it."

"Oh, Ellie," Caroline cried. "Can't I leave him alone for one night?" Reason elbowed its way through her tangled emotions. "Something must have happened to him if you're here."

Ellie folded her hands in her lap and heaved a sigh. "The police found him staggering around the cemetery about an hour ago. They brought him back here. When you weren't home, they knew enough to try my house. It took all three of us to get him into bed. He was a mess—crying, blubbering about what a failure he's been all his life." Her gaze fell to her age-spotted hands. "He—he kept saying he's hurt so many people."

Caroline arose from the couch. "I'll go see him."

Ellie grabbed her arm, pulling her back down on the couch beside her. "No, you won't, child. You'll sit right here and listen to me. He won't know you're there. It'll be noon before his liver gets rid of the fifth of whiskey he drank tonight."

"A whole fifth?"

"That's the way it looked, judging from the near-empty bottle he had in his hands and the smell of his breath."

Caroline's words formed around a lump in her throat. "What am I going to do, Ellie?"

With her fingertips Ellie brushed an errant curl from Caroline's face. "I'm not sure you can take much more, child. Perhaps it's time to get some help."

Caroline felt the blood pound in her head like a bass drum. It wasn't fair that this fell on her shoulders. She wasn't Amrod's family. She shouldn't have to be responsible for him and his disgusting binges.

Glancing across the room, she saw an old picture of her grandfather, his back straight as a board, his dark hair slicked into a middle part. Staring straight at her, he seemed to be telling her she was responsible for Amrod, like it or not.

THE NEXT MORNING Caroline dragged herself from bed at eight. After her shower she checked on Amrod and found him snoring away his stupor. She drew back her shoulders and sighed. Let him sleep. She wasn't any more ready to confront him than he was able to talk.

With forced efficiency she tackled her list of things to do, to which she reluctantly added a new item: tell Justine to find someone else. Amrod needed her.

Her first stop was the store. There were bills to pay, and this morning the ladies would be in to pick up their checks for the handcrafted items Caroline had sold the past two weeks.

When Ellie arrived at ten, Caroline grabbed a cup of coffee and a chocolate chip cookie and headed out the front door for the Opera House. She wanted to tell Justine in person she couldn't help her. After that, she'd stop by her new office to organize her preservation plan. Then she meant to confront Amrod about his behavior the night before. Finally she planned to spend an hour or two looking through her attic. Her mother had once mentioned something about family memorabilia she might find interesting. If she was lucky, maybe she could find something useful for her new job.

She didn't mind stopping at the Opera House. Every time she stepped inside the narrow lobby that ran the width of the pristine limestone building on the Square, she felt a flutter in her chest. Polished brass coach lamps gleamed against walls painted a cheerful peach. To the left, steep stairs angled to the balcony entrance. The place smelled of wood and Oriental rugs tempered by time.

Today she could hear Justine's familiar voice through doors that opened up into the quaint performing center that seated just over three hundred. "That's wonderful. You'll do just fine! Let's try it again. Remember to count. Step-two-three-lift!"

Caroline felt a pang of regret at what she had to tell the dear woman. Apparently Justine had found her a dance partner, and he was already learning the lifts. If only she had the time.... Caroline stopped that line of thinking before it got her into trouble.

She grabbed the doorknob, opened the door, stepped into the room and gasped.

CHAPTER SEVEN

"HE'S THE PARTNER you got for me?" Caroline asked in disbelief as she stalked down the center aisle to the stage, where Justine and Luke were practicing. "Do you have any idea who that man is?"

Justine smiled up at Luke and rolled her shoulder seductively. "Quite a looker, isn't he? Did I do okay, or did I do okay?"

"Justine!" Caroline jabbed a finger up at Luke as she reached the foot of the stage. "I can't dance with him. He's the one I told you about. The one I'm fighting!"

The dance instructor pinched her lips with her forefinger and thumb and glanced sideways at Luke. "Well, I'll be!"

Caroline bounded up the stairs on the left of the stage and headed for Luke. Although she'd intended to berate him, when he looked at her with a sheepish grin, she felt her anger ebb and admitted she was disappointed she wouldn't be the one to dance in his arms. Still, she skewered him with a suspicious look. "How did you manage to arrange this?"

Justine stepped in front of Luke protectively, only partially obscuring his large frame from Caroline's penetrating gaze. "Wait just a minute. Luke's only trying to help."

Luke rubbed the back of his neck with his hand and smiled innocently. "At breakfast the waitress told me Justine here was desperate for a man who could dance, so I volunteered. I don't have much experience, but I don't have a jealous wife like most of the men she says she's called."

"Probably 'cause nobody'd have you," Caroline muttered.

"What did you say?" Luke asked.

"Nothing." She turned to Justine. "Look, it doesn't matter, anyway. I came over to tell you I can't do it. I know I told you I would, but, well . . . something came up last night, and—" she looked down at her tennis shoes "—I have other responsibilities that have to come first." She felt the corners of her mouth droop, realizing how much she had looked forward to performing again.

Luke quickly closed the distance between them and cradled her elbow in his hand. "Could you use some help?"

For the life of her, Caroline couldn't understand why she wanted to pull Luke's comforting arms about her and lay her head on his chest. He was the reason she had to work night and day. He was the one who was threatening to make Granbury grow into a big, impersonal city. He was the one who kept throwing barbs at her family—at people who weren't alive to defend themselves.

She lowered her lashes and stared at his fingers stroking her fair skin. If she swallowed her pride and asked, he also might be the one who could help her with Amrod. "I—I think I can handle it."

"Sure she can. The kid's as tough as nails," Justine said. But from the corner of her eye, Caroline saw the woman arch one brow, as if she were seeking Caroline's reassurance.

Caroline focused for a moment on Luke's midnight blue eyes, which held her gaze with a warmth that felt strongly protective. Yet at the same time his gaze prompted—no, demanded—a response from her. She smiled softly, an appreciative smile, and saw a flicker of understanding register in his eyes.

"She may be tough, but she's human," Luke said to Justine, his eyes still holding Caroline's gaze. "If she says she can't dance, she can't." He slipped an arm around Caroline's shoulders. "Better find someone else."

Astonishment was too mild a word for the feeling that settled over Caroline. Luke somehow knew she'd reached the bottom of her reservoir of strength. She slipped an arm around his waist and felt renewed by the feel of his body next to hers.

"Why don't you call the college and see if one of the drama students can fill in?" he suggested. "Better find two." He winked at Caroline. "Surely there's some guy over there who can dance better than me."

"Wrong," Justine replied tartly. "I've already tried there and the high school. If you two don't do it, I don't know who will."

Caroline looked up at Luke and remembered the day of the bed race, when he told her how he'd always wanted to perform at the Opera House. She wanted him to have that chance. She wanted to be the one to dance with him, to feel his hands on her body as they responded to the music.

The voice of reason burst her dreamy bubble. *What will you do about Amrod?* Desperately she searched for an answer that would allow her to be Luke's partner.

Amrod seemed to go on his binges at night, after he'd completed his gardening chores and whatever odd jobs he had around town. She could bring him to the rehearsals with her, couldn't she? And to the performances? Couldn't she count on his cooperation for two measly weeks?

"Well," she said, breaking the silence, "I might be able to arrange it."

Luke's face lit up like a kid at the circus. He bent and thanked her with a quick kiss. "Are you sure? You look awfully tired. *Drained* is a better word. You aren't sick, are you?"

She wasn't sick; she was dizzy after the teasing touch of his lips. "I'll tell you about it later," she whispered to him, certain his concern for her had been prompted by the fatigue in her face from worrying most of the night about Amrod.

"Well, if we're going to put this show back together by Thursday night, we're going to have to work our little bunnies off," Justine said. "Are you two ready to work?"

"I need to warm up if we're going to dance," Caroline said, glancing down at her loose-fitting red cotton pants. "I think I can do it in these." She bent at the waist and touched her palms to the floor, stretching the hamstring muscles on the backs of her legs.

She saw Luke watching her, and asked, "You can dance, can't you?"

"He sure can, honey. He's got some great moves on him," Justine said, walking behind Luke and rolling her eyes. She squeezed his biceps, peeked around his torso and winked at Caroline.

For the next hour and a half Caroline and Luke worked side by side on the stage, executing the steps over and over until Justine smiled as they danced. "Okay, you two. Let's see how you look together."

Caroline's heart, already pounding, thumped wildly as Luke came to stand behind her. He spread his legs behind hers and wrapped his arms loosely around her waist, nestling his chin on top her head as they swayed side to side. She was surprised how easily he'd picked up the steps and how naturally they danced as a team.

"Are you sure you haven't done this before?" she asked him halfway through a turn.

"Ever see the Women's League show in Fort Worth?"

"No, when I lived in Fort Worth I worked so many hours I didn't have much time for entertainment." She remembered going home alone to her darkened apartment. To her loving dog, Jessie, until...

"Ouch!" Luke muttered as she crunched his instep.

"I'm sorry," Caroline apologized. "My mind was someplace else."

"What's wrong?" he asked in a concerned voice.

"Nothing." Now that she was back in Granbury, she felt safe again. "What were you saying?"

"I said I danced in the Women's League fund-raiser."

He was a natural for that production. The Women's League recruited attractive, eligible bachelors to form a co-ed chorus line.

Caroline and Luke swayed face-to-face. "Had the time of my life." He lowered his voice to a husky whisper and squeezed her waist, lifting her above his head and turning a full circle before he slowly let her slide down his hardened torso. "That is, the time of my life until I got you into my bed."

Caroline groaned and rolled her eyes. He winked at her as he sat down on a chair and led her by one hand to sit on the flexed muscles of one thigh.

"You know the routine well enough to work on it by yourselves," Justine announced. "I've got some errands to run. You can use the place for another hour. Then I have to work with the cast members who took the place of the kids who got hurt."

She rewound the tape player. "Have fun. We'll work together every night until show time." As she descended the stage stairs, she spun around and added, "Caroline, why don't you two work out in your exercise room tonight? Take the tape with you when you leave." She smiled. "Remember, the more you practice, the better you'll be."

The hundred-year-old Opera House echoed with Justine's retreating steps. Caroline wiped her palms on her polished cotton pants and heard a door in the lobby slam shut.

Luke's tennis shoes made light, padded sounds as he walked a wide circle around her. His legs glistened with perspiration below the snug yellow shorts that stretched across his hips. "Seems strange, doesn't it?"

She reached for a towel that hung across a chair, wiped her forehead and offered it to Luke. "How's that?

"You and me." He accepted the proffered towel and wiped his own forehead, then tossed the towel back on the chair. Then, wrapping his fingers around Caroline's firm upper arms, he looked at her with an expression that did little to cool her rising temperature. "Whenever we do things together, we're good."

She felt him draw her closer and saw his gaze slide to her lips. With one finger she traced the single button on his yellow-and-white striped shirt. "I—I wish we didn't see things so differently."

"We don't have to, you know."

She laid her hand flat over his heart and felt it pound beneath her fingers. "Yes, we do. It comes from here with you and me. We follow our hearts."

"Caroline—"

She silenced him with her finger, which he kissed. When he opened his mouth to speak, she pleaded, "Let's not talk. I've enjoyed today too much to ruin it with more angry words."

The sound of someone clearing his throat echoed from the back of the Opera House. It took Caroline a moment to find the man who'd interrupted them. He had bushy salt-and-pepper hair and was seated on one of the chairs in the auditorium. She squinted and felt a lurch in her chest. He was the same burly man who'd sat on the back row of the city council meeting and glared at her after she'd spoken.

"Dad!" Luke pressed his palm to Caroline's back and urged her toward the stairs on the right side of the stage. "He said he might drop by to watch me rehearse. I'd like you to meet him."

Luke's father? Why hadn't she guessed? She forced a smile and prayed the man had overcome his hostility.

As they approached him, he struggled from his seat, a flicker of pain crossing his face.

Caroline extended her hand. "Mr. O'Connor, I'm glad to meet you. It's nice of you to drop by to watch Luke."

The older man shook her hand with obvious reluctance and little enthusiasm. "'Afternoon, Miss Mc-Alester."

"Oh, please," she said, "call me 'Caroline.'"

Unsmiling, he took a toothpick from his shirt pocket and peeled off the cellophane wrapper. "Caroline, then."

Caroline looked to Luke for guidance, her brow worried into a frown. His eyes were focused on his father, and he wasn't smiling, either.

"Your son's a good dancer," Caroline said, trying to be courteous and cheerful but finding the task a difficult one.

"Guess so," the man answered, pulling the toothpick from his teeth. "Never put much stock in dancing and singing, though. This young man's made his way by hard work. Honest hard work."

That Luke's father was a man of simple means was obvious. That he disapproved of her was even clearer. Although she'd never been one who had to have the approval of those around her, this was one man she knew she wanted to please. She knew it wouldn't be easy.

"Why don't we all go to my store for a glass of mint tea?" she suggested. "I made a fresh pitcher this morning, and there's a little table in the back where we could sit and talk."

A cloud of gloom descended over Luke's father's face. "No," he said abruptly. "I don't want to go to your store."

"Dad—"

"I'm going home," Mack O'Connor announced, interrupting his son. "Are you coming?"

Things were not going as Caroline had hoped. Luke's father obviously didn't care about making friends with her, and Luke seemed to understand, although he didn't appear to like it. Caroline searched for something to say that would melt the invisible barrier the older man had erected between them. "Luke told me you make beautiful nutcrackers. I'd like to see them sometime."

The ice in Mack O'Connor's eyes melted around the edges. He looked at Luke and shrugged. "Bring her over sometime. She can look at them if she wants."

Thank God she'd remembered his hobby! "I've had people ask for nutcrackers in the store. I'd be honored if you'd let me sell your work."

"In Cain's Emporium? My nutcrackers?" The man snorted and ground out his reply. "No way in hell!"

"Now, Dad—" Luke began, but Mack had already turned on his heel and was headed for the door of the Opera House in a slow, arthritic gait.

When Caroline started to go after him, Luke gripped her arm. "You'd best leave him alone."

She stared after the man. "What did I do to make him so mad?"

"You're a McAlester. That's enough for my dad."

"I'm a McAlester." She repeated the words out loud, as if measuring their meaning. When the lobby door slammed shut, she turned to Luke, disbelief converting to anger. "What did someone in my family do to make your father feel such animosity toward me? I've never even met the man before!"

Luke puffed out his cheeks and blew out a deep breath. "Something happened—a long time ago. Something my father will never forget."

Caroline's heart pounded like a thundering race horse. "What was it? If you know, tell me. I have to know what somebody in my family did that hurt your father so much."

Luke gathered her into his arms and stroked her back. "Sshh now. It isn't important. What's important is you and me—our new beginning today."

Caroline stared up into Luke's eyes, wondering if his father was always so volatile or if his angry outbursts were reserved for people he hated...like the Mc-Alesters. "Your father wouldn't even set foot in my store," she said with disbelief. "It's obvious the man hates me."

"He doesn't hate you, Caroline. He just doesn't trust you, that's all."

"And what about you? Do you trust me? Or do you blame me for something someone in my family did a long time ago?"

A muscle in Luke's jaw flexed. When he spoke, his voice was laced with emotion. "I trust you, Caroline. You and I haven't gotten off to a very good start, but you haven't given me any reason to believe you're anything like...like how my father remembers your family.

"I'm sorry for the way he treated you. You didn't deserve that. I'll talk with him when I get home and try to make him understand that you're a dear, sweet—" his eyes lit up, and he bent to kiss her "—and very kissable woman."

Caroline smiled. "Thanks for the vote of confidence."

"You're welcome." He placed a lingering kiss on her parted lips. "Just don't ask me to vote your way in the referendum."

Caroline boxed him in the chest. "Why did you have to ruin things by reminding me about that?"

"You would've brought it up if I hadn't."

"It'll all be over in a couple of weeks. Then one of us will have to get used to a new way of thinking. I hope it won't be me."

"And I hope it won't be me," Luke said seriously.

Deciding she better not pursue this topic, Caroline returned to the stage for the music cassette.

"You didn't look like you felt so hot when you got here," Luke said from the foot of the stage. "You look a lot better now."

She fidgeted with the cassette in her hand, wondering if she had the nerve to tell him about Amrod's recent binge. "I—I had a bad night, that's all."

"You did, or Amrod?"

Her shoulders sagged. "How did you know?"

"You forget. I've been there."

She nodded, her head aching again from worry about Amrod as she descended the stage stairs.

"What are you going to do about it?"

"I thought I had things under control." She gripped the cassette tightly in her hand and walked with Luke to the door of the Opera House. "I left him alone one night—just one night—and poof! There he went, back into his bottle."

"So what's next?"

Caroline noticed Luke wasn't telling her what to do this time, just asking her questions. This approach was easier to take. "For the next two weeks, I'm going to make him come with me to practice and to the performances."

"Won't work. You still can't monitor what goes in the man's mouth. He has to learn to do that himself."

"But how?"

"The place to start is Alcoholics Anonymous. They'll match him with a man who'll help him. Amrod will have to admit he has a problem. He'll have to decide he'd rather be sober than drunk. But the A.A. way has worked in more than a hundred countries and with a lot of men—hopefully, it will work for him."

"You know a lot about A.A. Did your grandfather go?"

Luke sighed. "Yes. Finally. I just wish he hadn't waited so long to admit he had a problem."

"He meant a lot to you, didn't he?"

Luke glanced over her head as if he expected to see his grandfather there. "Yes, he did. He still does."

When he looked back at her, pain was etched in his eyes. "Someday I'll prove what a wonderful man he was. He opened his heart to everyone, trusted without question. Unfortunately that made him an easy mark."

Caroline puzzled over Luke's words. "Were my grandfather and yours ever friends?"

Luke's eyes flashed surprise at her question. "Yes, Caroline. They were—at one time."

"Did they have a fight? A serious disagreement? Is that why your father doesn't trust anyone with the McAlester name?"

Luke stared at her, as if weighing his answer, then brought her fingers to his lips and kissed them. "I'd say we have enough problems without dwelling on the past."

"But I want to understand," she said, pleading with her eyes as well as her words.

"Understand this, sweet thing. When I look at you I don't think about your grandfather. I don't think about mine. I don't even think about Dino-Land. I think about how much I want to do this."

He cupped her chin in his hands, lowered his head and paused for an agonizingly long moment while he let his gaze roam over her face. Caroline curved her hands over his. "Luke, I . . ."

With his thumb he stroked her lower lip, while he drew her close to his body. His bare legs were so warm the heat penetrated her thin cotton slacks.

"I've waited a lifetime to do this," he whispered, and with gentle pressure on her chin, he parted her lips and settled his mouth on hers.

At their moment of touching, Caroline reached for him, sliding her hands up around his neck and tangling her fingers in his coal-black hair.

When at last they broke the kiss, Caroline splayed her trembling fingers across his chest and tried to catch her breath.

"My God, you feel it, too," he said. Gathering her to his chest, he murmured, "I can't wait to see you tonight."

CHAPTER EIGHT

LUNCHTIME HAD COME and gone by the time Caroline walked into Cain's Emporium, and all she had eaten that day was the morning's chocolate chip cookie. Her hunger, however, wasn't the kind that could be sated by food. Nevertheless, when Caroline found Ellie attacking a huge salad in the back room, she discovered that one kind of hunger didn't necessarily drive out another.

Ellie took one look at her and smiled with twinkling eyes but said nothing. She speared a cherry tomato with her fork, then nodded in the direction of the refrigerator. "I brought enough for you, too."

Caroline gratefully retrieved the extra portion of salad from the refrigerator. Sitting down across from Ellie, she dug into the spinach and lettuce leaves. She wondered if she looked as radiant as she felt. Finding her voice, she commented in a nonchalant manner, "You'll never guess who my dance partner is."

Ellie poured a wide swath of blue cheese dressing across her half-eaten salad. "Bet I can."

"You knew?"

A nod told Caroline Ellie did. "Why didn't you tell me before I went over there?"

"I was afraid if I did, you wouldn't go."

"But how did you know?"

"Word gets around in a town this size," Ellie explained. "You should know that by now."

Caroline turned the fork over in her mouth and licked off the dressing. "He's really good."

Ellie chuckled. "At what?"

"Ellie! Dancing, of course." But Caroline smiled, not really minding that Ellie could read the glow on her face. "It's too bad he didn't have lessons when he was a kid."

"Seems to me he's done all right for himself without dance lessons."

"I don't mean that. It's just that he seems to enjoy dancing so much."

"Maybe what he really enjoys is dancing with you. Did that occur to you, child?"

Caroline let her thoughts drift to the way she'd felt when Luke had held her, when they'd moved together to the music, when he'd filled her soul with his kiss. Her body hummed in anticipation of their practice session that evening. "It's a flattering thought."

"Um-hmm."

"I met his father."

Ellie braced her wrists on the edge of the table. "You met Mack O'Connor?"

Caroline nodded, standing to clear the table. "He came over to watch Luke practice. Not the nicest man I've ever met, and he sure has a vendetta against my family."

"He was rude to you?"

"Rude? He was downright uncivilized!"

Ellie pressed her lips into a thin line. "When will it end?"

Caroline wheeled around. "What do you know about all this? What are you keeping from me, Ellie?"

Ellie pressed her palms to the table, stood and ambled to the back door. Caroline waited while the old woman stared out the window, seeming to focus not on anything in particular, except her thoughts and perhaps another time.

After a long moment of silence, she turned to Caroline. "There was a . . . a problem, I guess you'd say, between your grandfather and Luke's."

"Must have been some problem!" Caroline said, but she kept the rest of her thoughts to herself and waited for Ellie to elaborate on the mysterious problem. But Ellie wasn't talking. She stared out that window, as if she hoped divine intervention would supply her with the explanation Caroline wanted.

Caroline crossed the room and joined Ellie at the window. "What problem was so big it's lasted all these years? Whatever it is, Luke's father seems to hate me because of it—because I'm a McAlester."

Ellie's gaze slipped to her feet. "That's entirely possible, child."

"Look at me, Ellie. If you know something about this, you've got to tell me. Luke won't."

The expression on Luke's father's face at the city council meeting and again in the Opera House flashed in Caroline's mind. Those looks of unconcealed contempt were conjured up just by the sight of her. She deserved to know why Mack O'Connor had judged her before he knew what kind of a person she was.

"All I'm going to tell you is that Barron treated George O'Connor in an unconscionable manner. I suppose your grandfather told you George was a no-good drunk. Well, George may have been an alcoholic, but he was a good man. I knew him from the time I was a child. George O'Connor was a kind, loving man.''

"Then why did Granddaddy treat him so poorly?'' Caroline asked.

"It's best left alone, child.''

"But why can't you tell me?''

Ellie's flashing eyes and tight-lipped gaze told Caroline she'd brook no further questions. When Caroline dropped her own gaze, the older woman took her youthful hand and squeezed it affectionately, a soft smile returning to her face. "Perhaps you and Luke can put an end to this nonsense between the McAlesters and the O'Connors.''

"How can I put an end to the nonsense if I don't even know what it is?''

Ellie gave Caroline's shoulders a gentle shake. "That isn't important. What's important is for you and that young man to forget all this nonsense and live your own lives.''

Later, while Caroline cut across the courthouse lawn on her way to her preservation office, she played Ellie's advice over in her mind. If only it were as simple as Ellie had suggested.

Even if Caroline and Luke could disregard any problems that had plagued their grandparents, there were no guarantees Mack O'Connor could be persuaded to do the same. If that man didn't change his opinion of her, he could cause trouble for her and Luke. Besides, she didn't like the idea of being responsible for bad feelings between a man and his father.

She plucked a crape myrtle sprig from a nearby tree and brought the delicate pink blossoms to her nose. Inhaling the heady scent, she closed her eyes and savored the memory of Luke's arms about her and the breathless feeling she'd felt when he had poured himself into his kiss.

She opened her eyes and glanced around the quiet Square, sure Luke's kiss had rendered her brain incapable of functioning. It would never work for them. She and Luke might have grown up in the same hometown, but their orientations to life were as different as their upbringings.

The town had a special place in her heart. After her stay in Fort Worth, she'd come to appreciate Granbury for all the wonderful things it was—a small town where people cared about one another, where a child could skip around the Square without the fear of being abducted, where the scent of new-mown hay lingered in the summer air. It was a place a person could feel free . . . safe.

She quickened her pace as she felt the frustration rise within her. Luke didn't seem to care about these things, but she supposed his growing-up years hadn't engendered the memories that would endear Granbury to him. On the contrary, he seemed filled with unhappy memories of his childhood. He acted as if he wanted to exact revenge on his hometown.

Caroline was back for good—regardless of what happened with the referendum. Her phone call last week to her boss in Fort Worth had settled that once and for all. Now a growing part of her hoped Luke would stay on in Granbury, too. But would he stay if he lost the referendum? And even if he won, would he stay after Dino-Land was finished, or move on to another town to develop yet another theme park?

Caroline girded herself for the truth. Of course he'd leave. He seemed to have come back for one reason and one reason only—business, pure and simple. If the referendum failed, he'd have no reason to stay. If it passed, he'd stay as long as he was needed. Or, she thought, remembering the slick, silver-haired man who had accompanied him to the city council meeting, until Conway Carriker decided to send his protégé someplace else.

The thought of Luke's leaving saddened her. These days, each time she stepped outside, her heart fluttered in anticipation of a chance encounter with him. Would the streets of Granbury lose their magic if Luke were not in town? Even now her heart beat faster knowing she'd be in his arms tonight, if only to dance.

For a brief moment she closed her eyes, conjuring up the woodsy scent that lingered in his hair, in his clothes and on his glorious chest.

That vision stayed with her as she climbed the metal stairs to her office and sat at her desk. She plucked a pink slip of paper from the tail of her brass mouse paperweight and saw that it was a note from Justine. As promised, she had rescheduled Caroline's evening speaking engagements, at least through Sunday.

Caroline made the changes on her calendar and said a silent prayer of thanks. Glancing at her clock, she saw it was two in the afternoon. She could probably accomplish all the tasks on her list, practice with Luke and still get to bed by midnight.

First she had to get serious about this preservation business—develop a plan. She took a pad of yellow lined paper from her desk. Her mother and grandfa-

ther had spoken of Granbury's preservation potential
for so many years that the plan practically poured from
her pen.

The number one priority was to complete a list of all
the pre-1900 buildings in Granbury. The second, another list of those built between 1900 and the end of
World War I. Although the local residents had done a
commendable job of renovating the Square and a few
older homes, she was sure there were other structures
worth saving. She'd need to know the names and
whereabouts of the property owners and their inten-
tions for the buildings.

For number three she made a note to assemble a
book with past and present pictures of each structure,
along with the legal description of the location.

The next item made Caroline smile as she jotted it
down: document oral accounts of Granbury's history.
Each time Granbury lost an older citizen, it lost a
wealth of stories passed on by early settlers. She wished
she'd written down her grandfather's stories; now she'd
do it for other people's elders.

As a final item, she made a note to appraise the me-
mentos stored in trunks in her attic. Hopefully her
mother had been right when she'd said Caroline might
learn more about the beauty of early Granbury by examining the possessions her grandmother and great-
grandmother had saved for posterity.

She reviewed her plan and developed a comprehen-
sive time table, the third generation of McAlesters to
do something constructive about a fierce pride in the
community. Until Luke had revealed his theme-park
plans, she'd never realized she had the spark burning
within her. But she knew now she'd been raised for this

role—to save the town from financial exploitation, while she worked to preserve its rich heritage.

In a way it was a curse. Her breeding and her family traditions had pitted her against the one man who made her want to forget everything, the past included, and savor the moment. But she couldn't help feeling the way she did about Granbury. It was a part of who she was.

That thought weighed heavily on her during her calls to the county courthouse records section and to the National Trust for Historical Preservation in Washington, D.C. Then, resigned to an unpleasant task, she dialed the number for Alcoholics Anonymous that Luke had written on one of his business cards for her before they'd parted at the Opera House.

At the end of a lengthy conversation with an A.A. counselor, she left for home, feeling better equipped to confront Amrod.

She found him in his cottage, cleaning out his hamster's cage, an old fish aquarium.

"'Afternoon, Miss Caroline."

"'Afternoon, Amrod."

"Miss Caroline," she repeated to herself as she sat down at the green Formica table in Amrod's kitchen. "Please, Amrod, call me 'Caroline,' will you? Why is it everyone here seems to think I expect to be addressed formallike."

Amrod looked up quickly from his task as he knelt on the kitchen floor. "Guess 'cause your granddaddy insisted on it from the day you were old enough to meet people, Miss—sorry—Caroline."

Of course—her protective grandfather. But she hadn't come here to discuss her relatives. "Amrod, we have to talk about last night."

The aquarium slipped from his grasp and landed on his knee. He grimaced and rubbed his joint, managing to avoid her gaze. After a long moment of silence, he turned to her, his face flushed a cherry red. "I'm sorry. I let you down again, didn't I?"

Caroline rose from her chair, knelt on the floor beside him and squeezed his hand. "No, you didn't. The important thing, at least, is you let yourself down. You know that, don't you?"

He looked at her hand, tears forming at the corners of his eyes. When he nodded his assent, the tears trickled down his time-weathered cheeks.

Please give me the strength to do this. Caroline smoothed away his tears, feeling him tremble when she touched his skin. "Why do you do it, Amrod? Why do you keep doing this to yourself?"

He rubbed his knuckles against his eyes, and sniffled. "Sometimes a man drinks to forget the past. To forget mistakes he made."

"Do you want to talk about your mistakes? They say confession is good for the soul. Besides, nothing you could have done is as bad as what you're doing to yourself."

More tears sprang to Amrod's eyes. "A long time ago, when I was a young fella, I...I hurt some people." He paused, as if to gather the loose ends of his emotions. "Did you know I used to be the postmaster?"

Unable to follow Amrod's line of thinking, Caroline nodded. "I think I recall Momma saying something about it."

He regarded her with a worried look. "What did she say? What did she tell you?"

"Not much. What's there to tell?"

He stared at his knees but said nothing.

"Amrod, are you okay?" She ran her hand lovingly over the curve of his shoulder and felt the tension in his knotted-up muscles.

He nodded but still refused to meet her gaze. "If only I could do things over. Maybe then I'd be able to look at myself in the mirror."

"There's another way to get back the good feelings about yourself you deserve to have," she assured him.

They had told her it wouldn't be easy, but the pain in Amrod's face tore at her heart. He was looking to her for answers but would surely resent what she was about to tell him.

"I have a few things to say to you." Her voice broke as she forced the words. "First I want you to know I...I love you, Amrod. I didn't realize it until these past few weeks, but I do. I'm afraid I took you for granted all those years while I was growing up and you were gardening for us. As I recall, you and I had some pretty good talks. You're my...my family now—the only family I have left."

She pinched the bridge of her nose between her thumb and forefinger and shut her eyes as a sob escaped her throat. When she opened her eyes, Amrod's head was bowed. One fist pressed against his chest, and his shoulders shook. Oh, God, it was going to be harder than she'd thought.

Needing to touch him, she curled her fingers around his arm and squeezed it. "I—we can't go on like this. We—that is, you—have to get help for your drinking problem."

Amrod drew her hand to his dry lips and kissed it. "I won't do it no more. Promise."

"No," she said, emphatically, pulling her hand away. "It's too late for promises. You have to get help, before it's too late. Before you wind up like Luke's grandfather."

Amrod's body stiffened at the mention of George O'Connor. "What do you mean?"

"I mean," she said, "you're going to kill yourself if you don't stop drinking. George O'Connor did it. I won't stand by and see you do it to yourself."

Amrod's hand fell to his lap, and his gaze darted to the window. The rays of afternoon sun deepened the grooves the years had etched in his face. He squeezed his eyes shut and hung his head.

"Amrod—"

He snapped his head up and rose to his knees. "Hand me that goldfish bowl over there, will you?" He nodded at the glass container where his hamster was temporarily housed.

They had warned her he would try to ignore her. "Amrod, I won't leave until I get my answer. Will you or will you not get help—go to Alcoholics Anonymous or to therapy or to dry out somewhere?" She handed him the bowl. "And I don't want to hear you can't afford it. I'll pay whatever it costs."

As if he hadn't heard her, Amrod scooped the frisky hamster into his hand and drew it to his chest. He cooed and stroked the animal's snowy fur, then bent over and placed the creature in its clean quarters. After watching the animal scurry about and sniff its clean surroundings, Amrod lifted his gaze to Caroline's. "And if I don't?"

She sighed and shook her head. "If you don't, Amrod, I—I want you to move out."

DISCOURAGED BY AMROD'S REFUSAL to answer her, Caroline trudged up the stairs to her attic and wished she could talk to Luke, but she knew he didn't have a telephone in that old hotel room. Besides, he had said something vague about business appointments in Fort Worth that afternoon, so she'd have to wait until that evening for his advice and concentrate as best she could on the next task before her.

As she slipped the key into the attic door, she puzzled over the family habit of securing memories behind a lock, while they had left the front door to the grand old house unlocked night and day. The family idiosyncrasy reinforced the relief she felt at being back home, where she could choose whether or not to lock or bolt a door. It was so unlike her life in Fort Worth.

Memories of her childhood washed over her as she stepped through the doorway and looked around the small, rectangular-shaped room. Now, as then, daylight streamed through the gable window that overlooked the back lawn.

Four trunks lined the wall opposite the window. Scattered about the attic were cardboard boxes, an antique dress form, an old rocker, a chandelier that had hung in the dining room and Victorian antiques her mother hadn't been able to discard. There, too, were the toys Caroline had persuaded her mother to save for the next generation of McAlesters.

Caroline spotted her Mickey Mouse record player in one corner and grinned. Were her records still there? Yes, there in a box on the floor. She pulled an Elton John record from its jacket, plugged in Mickey and began to move her feet to a scratchy rendition of "Crocodile Rock."

Humming the once-popular tune, she let her fingers trail over the curved lid of a scarred wooden trunk. Although it had been off-limits to her as a child, occasionally she had peeked inside at the elegant dresses and dreamed of wearing them as she danced in the arms of a handsome man.

At that moment she pictured herself dancing in Luke's arms—she in a bustled ball gown of palest pink silk taffeta, he in a satin-lapelled black tuxedo.

Smiling at the fairy-tale vision, Caroline knelt on a faded rag rug before a trunk and lifted the heavy lid. The scent of the trunk's cedar lining filled her nostrils.

She smiled at her mother's work. Each garment had been neatly folded and zipped into a clear plastic bag with a label as to its owner. Some tags documented when the dresses had been worn, by whom and for what occasions.

One by one she lifted the antique garments from the trunk, until she found a vision of white satin, lace and illusion. A tag was attached: "Wedding gown of Lydia Cain McAlester, June 14, 1930, created by a seamstress in Glen Rose after the Paris-inspired fashions popular at the turn of the century."

Wondering why her grandmother had chosen to wear a gown designed for another generation, Caroline unzipped the bag and removed the garment. No wonder her grandmother had loved it; the gown was exquisite.

Awed by its beauty, Caroline stood and draped the gown across her body, one hand pressing the Victorian neckline to the pulse point at the base of her neck, the other clasping the garment to her waist. The pearl-encrusted lace that edged the hem came to within an inch of the floor. Her mother had always told her she had inherited her small stature from her Grandma Lydia—and her stubbornness and quick temper from her Granddaddy McAlester.

She wondered how her grandmother had felt on the day of her wedding, marrying the ambitious, debonair Barron McAlester. What a handsome couple they must have made, dancing at their reception.

Closing her eyes, she dared to picture how her grandmother had looked on her wedding night, and a vision of her own self and Luke popped into her mind. He was standing at the foot of her four-poster bed in the Western attire he had worn the Fourth of July. With trembling hands he was slowly unbuttoning the row of satin-covered buttons that fastened the front of a wedding night negligee.

The tiny buttons made the task of undressing her deliciously slow. Each time he slipped the loop over a button, he bent and kissed the newly exposed skin that blazed beneath his lips.

She opened her eyes and felt the pulse in her neck pound beneath her fingertips, the thought of sharing wedding night intimacy with Luke overpowering her senses.

Drawn to the trunk again, she found another bag with a second satin gown, this dress the color of golden ivory and most assuredly that of another bride, although it bore no label.

Caroline unzipped the bag, removed the dress and felt her heart flutter. Similar to the first, the gown was about the same turn-of-the-century vintage, but romantically different. Regarding the two creations, she decided her favorite was the second gown, the one with lots of lace, trimmed in tiny satin rosebuds with trailing ribbon streamers knotted at the ends. It, too, had been worn by a petite woman. Perhaps Ellie knew whose dress it had been.

As she repacked the lovely dresses, she promised herself she'd devote a full day to them after the referendum. Today she had work to do.

Inside another trunk she found only papers, and judging from the typeface and staples, they certainly weren't antiques.

Typed in the center of the first paper was a title: "Wallace H. Winthrop, born 1896, Granbury, Texas, age 88." What followed appeared to be the transcript of an interview her mother had done with Wallace Winthrop in 1984.

Caroline sat in the rocker and skimmed through the transcript, which contained marvelous stories Wallace's father had told him about the days when he'd first crossed the Brazos to settle in what was now Granbury.

The second transcript contained more stories of the past, told by another Granbury elder. The trunk was full of similar transcripts, along with several rejection letters from publishers to whom Meredith McAlester had obviously submitted the true stories.

So this was what her mother had meant when she had told her to check the attic. Now she had exactly what she wanted—a documented oral history of the area for her preservation plan.

That her mother had attempted to sell the stories surprised Caroline. The daughter of one of Granbury's wealthiest families, Meredith McAlester had been concerned with the spending of money, not the earning of it. Perhaps she had attempted to raise money for a favorite charity.

At least Caroline had found what she'd wanted, with time to spare before she changed clothes for her practice session with Luke.

WHEN THE DOORBELL RANG, Caroline was upstairs in her bedroom tugging on the high leg of her red French-cut leotard and fretting over her appearance. Maybe she should have worn something less revealing, something that would hide the extra pounds she attributed to chocolate chip cookies.

Shrugging off her indulgence, she tightened her stomach muscles and bounded down the hand-carved cypress stairs, her heart all aflutter when she saw Luke's head through the fan window at the top of her door.

"Hi," she greeted him. "Come on in, and we'll get to work."

"Work?" he said, stepping inside. "Who said anything about work? I came to dance."

A mischievous grin played across her lips as she leaned back against the door to close it. "So, you think dancing's easy?"

Luke winked at her. "Digging ditches is work. Dancing's fun."

"We'll see what you think after tonight," she cautioned him, thinking of the warm-up routine she'd designed especially for him.

While his gaze wandered about the entry hall and into the living room, she regarded him with an appreciative eye. He cut a fine, muscular figure in a soft blue T-shirt the color of a summer sky. Stretched taut across the firm swells of his chest, the T-shirt disappeared into the elastic waistband of a pair of snug blue athletic shorts. Lower still a smattering of dark fuzz softened the hard contours of his thighs. Long, vertical muscles told Caroline he didn't spend all his time in a business suit.

When she heard him clear his throat, she reversed her gaze from its downward appraisal and focused on Luke's face.

Luke met Caroline's gaze, having enjoyed every second of her thorough assessment. While she had been so distracted, he had done some serious looking of his own.

When she'd opened the door in that brief red thing, she could have knocked him over with a feather. Once he'd let his eyes drift below the seductive dip of her vee bodice, he'd almost lost his footing. Below her waist a little red triangle no bigger than his hand was flanked by smooth, high-reaching stretches of skin. Okay, so her flanks were covered by something thin and shiny that only looked like skin. His imagination still kicked into fantasy mode and made his pulse race.

Determined not to let his hormones wreck the evening now that he'd finally had the opportunity to call on Caroline in her mansion of a home, he cleared his throat and tried to think of something to say.

Caroline broke the awkward silence. "I, uh, talked to Amrod. You know, the way you wanted me to—about his drinking."

Luke stepped forward, resisting the urge to pull her into his arms. "That couldn't have been easy."

"What wasn't easy was leaving him without his promising he'd get help."

"Don't feel bad if you don't succeed your first try."

"I backed him into a corner," she said. "I told him if he didn't get help, he'd have to move out. I hope he doesn't make me keep my word."

"Give him some time, Caroline. If you need help, I'll be there. God knows I've been through those confrontations enough to tell when someone's trying to con me."

"Did your grandfather do that?"

"Con me? You bet, until I got tired of being suckered by his sob stories and elaborate excuses."

"What makes a person drink like Amrod does?"

"It's hard to tell. Some people who grow up with alcoholic parents get the impression drinking's the way to cope with problems. Some say there's a hereditary link."

"Was that how it was with your grandfather?"

Luke looked away. "No. Neither of his parents drank."

Caroline frowned. "Then why?"

Luke stared at her so long Caroline began to feel uncomfortable, and she remembered what Ellie had said that afternoon. "Ellie told me my grandfather didn't treat your grandfather very well. Is it possible that had something to do with your grandfather's drinking?"

Luke's eyes brimmed with emotion. What he didn't say tore at her heart. "Someday we'll talk. Tonight I want to dance. What do you say we get started?"

Welcoming the chance to end the discouraging discussion about Amrod, Caroline turned to ascend the stairs. When she realized Luke wasn't following her, she turned around and saw him at the base of the stairs, his hands on the banisters. "Aren't you coming?" she asked him.

He motioned past her shoulder with a slight lift of his chin. "We're going upstairs?"

"Of course. That's where my practice room is."

The moodiness that had silenced him a moment ago gave way to his usual teasing demeanor. His eyes sparkled with mischief as a grin brightened his face. "So are the bedrooms, sweet thing."

Caroline grinned back, then spun around on the ball of one foot. "Don't get your hopes up, buster. By the time I get through with you, you won't have the energy to think about bedrooms."

CHAPTER NINE

SEATED OPPOSITE CAROLINE on her practice room's polished hardwood floor, Luke tried to match the easy way she bent herself in two like a taco shell. "Oooh boy!" he complained. "This exercise is killing me."

"You need to stretch until it burns, until it hurts a little," she said, a smug look on her face.

He grinned, already feeling the tightness in his hamstring muscles. "That's easy. It hurts just watching you do it."

"If you don't stretch out, you could pull a muscle. Then you might not be able to dance Thursday night."

"If I do what you just did, I'll be lucky to walk by Thursday." He winked at her. "What do you say we move on to the fun part."

She nodded at the long wall to the left, the one covered in floor-to-ceiling mirrors. "If you're sure you're ready, we'll run through the two routines in front of the mirror and see what we have."

Luke struggled into a standing position. She'd certainly proved her point. Unlike the simple routine he'd done with the Women's League in Fort Worth, this dancing business of Caroline's was work—hard work. Good thing he was in reasonably good shape from racquetball and jogging.

He watched her walk to the carpeted recreation area at the far end of the room and click the *Pal Joey* cassette into a wall stereo unit. Old man McAlester hadn't spared the bucks when he had indulged his granddaughter with her very own practice room. Besides an expensive-looking sound system, there was a refrigerator, television set and pastel floral couch at the end of the room.

Luke wondered if Caroline had any idea how it felt to want something...or someone...she couldn't have. He doubted it, but before long he expected she would experience the pain of disappointment, and he couldn't help worrying how she'd cope with it.

As the speakers boomed the introduction to the song, Caroline darted across the room and struck up the beginning pose in front of him. That began an hour of concentrated rehearsing, punctuated by occasional laughter when one of them stepped on the other's foot. After they'd gone over and over their two routines until they could do them without making a major mistake, they took a break with tall, frosty glasses of lemonade.

Seated beside Caroline on the couch, Luke tipped his head back and took a long drink, watching her over the rim of his glass. In the past few minutes she had slipped into a blue mood of sorts. He wasn't accustomed to seeing her like that. One elbow propped on the curved arm of the couch, she was staring down into her glass, poking an ice cube with her forefinger, watching it bob in the lemonade.

He drained his glass and set it on the coffee table, determined to relieve her of the thoughts that had knitted her smooth brow into worry lines. Because he was confident Amrod was the reason for her pensive mood, he wanted to comfort her, as he had needed comforting at a much younger age. Shifting sideways on the cushion, he draped his elbow across the back of the upholstered couch and considered taking her in his arms and nestling her head beneath his chin.

So far, by concentrating on the mechanics of the dance routines, he had been able to resist letting his hands wander over her lovely body, but the mere thought of her cuddling next to him energized his libido. He clenched his fist until his knuckles ached and resolved to keep his hands to himself. If he touched her now, he wouldn't stop at consoling her.

He could tell how much she needed to be held, to be loved the way he knew he could love her. He drew in a deep breath and wondered how much longer he could wait to make love to her as he had in his dreams for years.

Suddenly she turned to him, as if his movement had shaken her from her thoughts. "How long did your grandfather and mine know each other?"

Luke expelled a ragged breath and raked his hair with his fingers. Why couldn't she bury the business about their grandfathers? Nothing either of them could say or do could change the past, and talking about it could only build a higher barrier between them. But he could tell by the determined look in Caroline's eyes that she wouldn't relent until he'd answered her question.

"They were friends as kids. Two Huckleberry Finns on the same street in a small town in northeastern Oklahoma. According to my grandfather, both families were dirt poor. My grandfather's family moved here during World War I, when he was still a kid. I gather Barron moved here somewhat later, by himself, when he was a young man out of school."

Caroline's eyes widened in disbelief. "My grandfather's family was poor?"

"Hard to believe, isn't it?"

"I wonder why he never told me that."

"Probably because he didn't want you to know."

She frowned. "But why not? There's nothing disgraceful about coming from a poor family."

"Oh, no? Do you have any idea how cruel people can be?"

She reached for his hand. "Luke, I'm sorry. I—I guess you had it rough as a kid."

Luke matched the fingers of his hand with hers and couldn't help noticing her perfectly manicured fingernails. His mother had never had a manicure or a store-bought dress, but she had never complained. On the contrary, she had spoken of the riches of her family, of the love she and Mack O'Connor had for each other and their children.

"We were rich in many ways, Caroline. Someday I'll tell you about it."

"I'd like to hear about your family."

The warmth of her smile encouraged him, but the look of determination that followed warned him she wasn't through asking questions.

"I'd like to hear how our grandfathers' friendship dissolved into downright hatred."

Luke shook his head. "You won't give up, will you?"

"Do you blame me?"

"No, not really, but you have to understand I don't know all the details." He paused, trying to pack what he knew into a concise statement that would exorcise the subject once and for all. "It had something to do with a—a woman."

Caroline pressed her fingers to her lips. "What woman? My grandmother? My Grandma Lydia?"

Luke gripped her upper arms gently, but firmly. "Now, Caroline. I told you, I don't know all the details, but surely you can understand how a love triangle could tear a friendship apart."

Caroline stood and paced the carpeted area in front of the couch. "A love triangle. Your grandfather and mine in love with the same woman. How awful, how absolutely awful for all of them." She paused and cast him a suspicious look. "But why is your father still so angry—angry with my grandfather, who's dead, angry even with me?"

Luke went to her, sorry he'd told her as much as he had. "I can't account for my father's attitude, but I can account for mine. I don't want to think about the past. I want to think about now. About you and about me. About us."

Caroline fingered the button on his shirt, and after a long pause looked up at him. "That's something that's been bothering me. What do you think people will say when they see us together on that stage?"

"What do you mean?"

"We're supposed to be adversaries, right?"

He pinched her nose playfully. "Do we look like adversaries right now?"

"Come on, Luke, admit it. It's bound to be confusing to folks around here. They've seen us battling each other over this project of yours. Then there we'll be, up there on that stage, dancing together as if...as if..."

"As if we were lovers?" he provided.

She dropped her gaze to his button again. "Something like that."

Luke slipped a curved finger beneath her chin and tilted her head until she looked into his eyes. "What's the matter, Caroline? Don't you want anyone to know we . . . well, we care about each other?''

"Care about each other?'' She said the words softly, as if she were considering their meaning.

"We do, you know. It's written all over our faces. I can see the caring in yours, and I'll bet you can tell how I feel about you when you look in my eyes. If we can see it, it's a sure bet others can, too.''

No longer able to resist the urge to touch her, he rested his hands on the graceful curves of her shoulders and let his thumbs stray over to her warm, bare skin. "I like the idea myself—you and me together.''

As he had for years, he wondered how it would feel to lie beside her, to claim her as his own, she, the mayor's granddaughter; he, the painter's son.

His gaze drifted lower, detecting the telltale flush of desire on her upper chest, and lower still to her leotard-covered nipples that even now invited his touch. God, how he wanted to touch her!

Blue eyes, wide and trusting, stared up at him, the dark, luminous pupils telling him she wanted him, too. He threaded his fingers through the soft, blond curls at her nape, feeling her shiver as his thumb slid over the curve of her jaw to the dainty narrow tip of her chin.

When she tilted her chin upward, the blood hammered in his ears, and he ran his thumb down the silky expanse of her neck. There in the hollow, beneath his thumb, he felt an erratic pulse that matched his own. Whether she admitted it or not, she cared.

But she backed away from his touch, leaving his hand suspended in midair. "Luke, I can't.''

When at last she met his gaze, the wide-eyed trust had vanished. He reached for her, unwilling to let go of the goodness that had begun to grow between them. "Can't what, Caroline? What is it you can't do?"

"I can't let my feelings get in the way of what I have to do. No matter what I feel for you, it won't change my position on your project and how it affects Granbury."

Who said anything about Granbury? He gripped her shoulders again, wanting to shake her because of her comment, yet at the same time wanting to hold her. "Is that what you think this is all about? You think I'm trying to get close to you so I can change your mind about Dino-Land?"

"No, of course not."

"Then why?"

"Because it bothers me!" she blurted out. "Can't you see that?" She brought up her hands between his arms and pushed them away from her shoulders. "Because when I'm with you sometimes I...I forget what's important to me."

Again Luke fought the urge to take her in his arms, to kiss her as he'd done in his dreams and show her what was really important.

A question formed in his mind, a question he had to ask her. "What is important to you, Caroline? Do you really know?"

Her gaze drifted to the window at the end of the recreation area and back to him. "I'll tell you what's important to me. This town—this little town, with these dear, sweet people who care about each other, about me."

Her eyes skimmed the room in a visual caress. "And this house. My family's house. It's all I have left of them really."

Luke narrowed his gaze and cupped her shoulders again. "You've left out something important."

She pushed his hands off her shoulders once more and diverted her gaze across the room. "I'm afraid I don't know what you're—"

"Yes, you do, dammit!" He grabbed her arm and pointed at his chest. "Look at me. Look in my eyes and tell me you don't know what I'm talking about. Us! You're forgetting us!"

She glanced at the hand that gripped her arm like a vise, then sighed and shook her head. "Until the referendum is over, there can't be any us. I can't cope with the mixed-up feelings. Besides, I'm beginning to wonder if the bad feelings that existed—maybe they still exist—between our families will make it impossible for us ever to become more than friends."

Luke drew his lips into a thin line. "We could be more than friends—a lot more—if you'd give us half a chance."

"But we don't think the same," she said, anguish wrapping her words in soft-spoken despair.

"Hell, Caroline! Who cares what we think? It's what we feel here—" he slapped his palm against the center of his chest "—that counts."

She stared at him for what seemed like an eternity, her sky-blue eyes softening as they studied the contours of his face. Her gaze lingered on his lips, then slid to the narrow indentation in his chin, down his freshly shaven throat and over the hard muscles of his chest.

He waited for her to come to him, to step into his arms and lay her head on his chest and admit she ached for him as much as he ached for her.

"Uh, we...really should practice the lyrics," she half whispered. "Justine said—"

"I don't give a damn what Justine said!" he bellowed. His restraint drowned in a wash of long-denied desire, he stepped forward and framed her face in his hands. "You can try to ignore it, but I know what you feel." Before she could speak, he lowered his lips to hers and summoned a kiss from her soul.

Frightened by the intensity of her response, Caroline struggled, pressing her palms against Luke's chest, then tried to peel away the steellike fingers that imprisoned her face. But he only deepened the kiss, stroking her back as he stoked the embers in her heart.

Caroline whimpered into the moist recesses of Luke's mouth, feeling the last ounce of her resistance slip away. Slowly she relaxed, not fighting, but giving, taking and giving again, until her body hungered for him.

Luke tore his lips away and held her at arm's length. "Now tell me you didn't feel that. Tell me, if you can."

Caroline's fingers trembled as she pressed them to her swollen lips. "Oh, Luke, I do care about you."

Her words filled him with joy. He gathered her into his arms and shuddered as she slipped her slender arms around his waist. "I knew it," he groaned. "I just knew it."

When she nestled her head against his chest, he squeezed his eyes shut and felt a tear roll down his cheek. "If you only knew how long I've wanted to hold you like this."

"You—you make me feel so good, so wanted."

"Then I'll show you what's important," he said. Determined that she blot all negative thoughts of them from her mind, he parted his lips and kissed her as he had kissed no other woman.

Caroline felt a flame fan down her neck, race through her aching breasts and begin to burn furiously deep inside her. When their lips parted, she pressed her cheek against his chest and felt a thundering beat beneath the soft blue of his T-shirt.

She pressed her lips to the muffled sound of his heart, while her hands moved up the hard, flexed muscles of his chest to curl around his neck.

Luke's hands slid down her back, lower, lower, until his hands cupped her hips. She gasped as he lifted her from the floor and pressed her against him. A summer-hot heat uncoiled within her and raged through her body.

Then suddenly, when the world was spinning around her, he gentled her down until her feet touched the floor. Why, why was he stopping?

Unable to hide the wanting, she looked up into his eyes and felt the kiss of his gaze.

"Caroline?" he murmured, his breathing as ragged as her own.

"Yes?"

He kissed her hand, drew it to his chest and pressed it to his thundering heart. "Feel that?"

She felt the erratic cadence and nodded. Her hand still over his heart, she quivered inside as he slowly trailed one finger of his other hand down the vee neck of her leotard and paused over her pounding heart.

He lifted the fingers of her other hand and pressed them on the inward curve of her breast. "And that? Do you feel that?"

She nodded, feeling her heart race even faster.

"*That's* what's important, sweet thing. What I feel for you. What you feel for me. More important than anything else in the world."

THE FEEL OF THEIR HEARTS pounding in their chests, that special moment of touching, haunted Caroline for days. By Thursday she felt like Dr. Jekyll and Mr. Hyde. In the early mornings, before her business day began, she rehearsed with Luke in her practice room, looking forward more every day to the sound of his distinctive knock on her door, to dancing in his arms, to the joyful laughter that echoed through the second floor of her house when he was there.

Each night after the full-cast rehearsal, when, spent from exertion, she slipped between her cool sheets, she fantasized they'd have a few private moments together the next day, moments to satisfy her longing to touch and be touched again. But one day Ellie stopped by to watch them practice, and the next Amrod kept interrupting them for instructions on a repair job Caroline had asked him to do. This morning Justine was the intruder, there to make sure they had smoothed out the rough spots in the routine.

After each morning practice, Caroline showered and scurried off to her office, then to that day's luncheon or civic club meeting or other campaign appearance. Through it all, she somehow managed to voice her opposition to Dino-Land, but in her heart she longed to be in the arms of the very man she was supposed to be fighting.

It became more and more difficult to paint him as an unprincipled scoundrel who cared nothing for Granbury and easier to admit he was just a man whose opinions differed from hers—a man for whom her affection grew daily.

To make matters worse, she began to feel she was slipping in her unofficial poll of the voters.

On Thursday after morning practice, she stopped by the store to discuss her concern about the election with Ellie and to see if Amrod had told his old friend that Caroline had confronted him about his drinking. Perched on a step ladder, the old woman was giving the top shelf of a display case a brisk application with a feather duster.

"What do you think, Ellie? How are we doing?"

"I suppose you're referring to the election."

Caroline nodded, needing to hear what she knew would be Ellie's honest appraisal, yet dreading her answer.

"I'm afraid the news isn't good."

Caroline slumped into the rocker, not caring that she had rumpled the freshly ironed Raggedy Ann pinafores on the cushion beneath her. "Have I been wrong all along?" she asked, looking up at the woman. "Am I alone in my opposition to Dino-Land?"

"Of course not. I'm afraid, though, it isn't as simple as you see it, child."

"What do you mean by that?"

Ellie paused in her dusting chores. "Let me put it this way. Do you depend on the money you make here in the store to put food on your table?"

Caroline shook her head.

"To pay your electric bill? Your house payment?"

Caroline lifted one shoulder and sighed.

"Do you have kids to put through college? Relatives who need extra cash? A sick child?"

Caroline leaned back in the rocker and stared about her store. "What you're saying is that I've been selfish, that I haven't considered how other people might benefit from Dino-Land."

"I didn't mean to imply you've been selfish. I'm talking priorities. Most folks in this town would probably do just fine if things never changed, but some could use the extra cash Dino-Land would bring. What I'm trying to say is, I guess folks have to decide what's important to them."

Luke's tender words filled Caroline's ears. *"I'll show you what's important."* She closed her eyes, remembering the touch of his hand over her heart, then opened her eyes and sighed. "You think I should give up?"

Ellie regarded her for a moment. "You believe in what you're doing—really believe?"

Caroline nodded. "I think we'd all be so sorry if we let go of what we have here. I've lived in a big city. I know how rare this friendly, caring atmosphere is. I don't want to see us lose that, and I think we will if Luke's allowed to build Dino-Land here."

Ellie poked her glasses to the bridge of her nose. "There's your answer. Follow your heart, and you won't go wrong. Then, no matter how the election turns out, you'll be able to live with yourself."

Caroline stood and made a halfhearted attempt to straighten a display of handpicked pecans. "Luke told me something the other night—about Barron and George. He told me they were childhood friends, but their friendship dissolved over the love of a woman. Was that woman Grandma Lydia?"

Ellie climbed down the ladder and shook a finger in Caroline's face. "I told you I was through talking that nonsense. Leave it alone, child. Leave it alone, or it'll destroy what you and that young man have."

Caroline watched Ellie bustle around the store as if she'd been offended and decided that if she was to unravel the mystery of the McAlester and O'Connor feud, she'd have to question somebody else. Caroline pursued another topic.

"You should've seen the kids at one of the elementary schools the other day when Luke and I both spoke. I didn't know he was speaking before me until I got there. I walked into the classroom as he finished up."

She paused, remembering how his face had lit up and how her own breath had caught in her throat at the sight of him.

"You two didn't argue again, did you?"

"We didn't," Caroline said softly. "He had two kids on his lap, one on each knee. He'd taught the younger ones a lesson on dinosaurs and passed out coloring books."

"Some people might object to his trying to get to the voters through their kids."

"They were neat books, and the teachers appreciated the reinforcement of their classroom lessons. That's one thing Luke pledges to do—give back to the town some of what his theme park brings him."

Ellie peered over the rim of her glasses. "Sounds like you're changing your mind about this Dino-Land business."

"No, I'm not. I'm against it as much as ever. But you're right. I can see why some people think I'm crazy to oppose it. It has its good points, as well as its bad."

"Before long we'll have an answer, and it'll be settled once and for all," Ellie remarked as she walked behind the counter to put the feather duster away in a box beneath the cash register. "Are you and Luke ready for tonight?"

Caroline recognized Ellie's attempt to change the subject. Still, the older woman's words stirred up the butterflies in Caroline's stomach. She couldn't remember how many times she'd danced on that stage when she was younger, but even then she'd always had an opening night case of the jitters. She pressed both hands over her abdomen. "I hope I'm ready."

"Nervous?"

Caroline nodded, but Ellie's spontaneous smile settled the covey of butterflies in her stomach. "Are you going?"

Ellie pointed beneath the cash drawer in the register. "Got my ticket right here. Front row balcony. Got a ticket for Amrod, too." She fingered the tickets and smiled softly. "He's picking me up at seven."

If Caroline had been Ellie, she would have pressured the older woman for the feelings that prompted the glow on her face. Delighted to know Ellie and Amrod would have each other's company for the evening, Caroline decided to be discreet about her observation. "Has he said anything to you about our talk?"

"Some, but he won't admit he has a problem."

"I had hoped that by now he'd have come to grips with the ultimatum I gave him. I couldn't bear to see him move out. I'd worry that someday someone might knock on my door and tell me something horrible had happened to him . . . like drowning in the lake."

Ellie snapped the drawer shut and toyed with one of the keys. "Amrod and I—we go back a long way— been friends a long time. It would mean a lot to me to see him get his life straightened away."

"It won't be easy for him, shaking a terrible, self-destructive habit like that. He could use your friendship, Ellie."

"Just you have faith in him, child. With your help, I think he can make it."

Ellie smoothed her apron with her hands and glanced at the clock. "Enough talk about Amrod. Go have yourself a bubble bath. Does wonders for the jitters."

"Thanks. I just might do that—after I check on a couple of things over at the office. Can you close up?"

"Not only can, I plan to. My gift to you on your opening night."

"Ellie, you're such a dear," Caroline told her, wrapping her arms around the woman's shoulders. "By the way, sometime when we both have a few minutes, I'd like to ask you about some things I found in the attic."

Caroline was halfway to the front door, when Ellie called to her. "Oh, by the way, you had a phone call this morning. From Wilson over at the bank."

Caroline frowned. "Do I have to call back today? He does go on so."

Ellie shrugged. "Didn't say. I suppose it could wait. From what he said I gather it has something to do with your mother's estate."

CHAPTER TEN

"TWO SINGLE DIPS in sugar cones and two Texas tea cakes."

The high school girl behind the counter at the Nutt Shell Eatery tilted her head flirtatiously and smiled. "What flavor, Mr. O'Connor?"

Luke looked down at the seven ice cream tubs in the display case and ran his tongue slowly over his lips as if he were savoring each flavor. A mischievous grin on his face, he turned to Caroline and bent to whisper in her ear. "I'm having peach. How about you?"

Luke's warm breath and his reference to the succulent peach pie they had shared generated welcome visions of intimacy in Caroline's mind. When she lifted her lashes and nodded, she couldn't help smiling at the man who had inspired those visions.

While she waited with him for their cones, she glanced around the eatery, where the cast had chosen to unwind after the Thursday evening performance. With its high ceilings, old wooden booths and vintage ice-cream parlor fixtures, the narrow strip of a shop on the corner of the Square near the Opera House looked as if it belonged in an old-time movie.

Right now its oak floors were crowded with customers, in a gay mood after an evening of lively entertainment. Thanks in part to Luke's and Caroline's premier performance, the evening had been laced with a good measure of laughter.

Caroline's face was still flushed with excitement. Although she and Luke hadn't danced in perfect unison with the ensemble, the crowd had been forgiving. They had applauded their efforts good-naturedly and given them a cheering round of support during a special curtain call.

Caroline looked around in time to see Justine walk through the front door with the woman who played the piano during the sing-along before the show.

Next came the mayor and the editor of the *Hood County News*, followed by a somewhat subdued Ellie on Amrod's arm. How much longer could the seventy-six-year-old woman keep up with the demands of running the store? It hadn't been quite a week and already Caroline regretted her decision to take advantage of the woman's good nature.

While she worried over Ellie, Caroline picked up the giant sugar cookies called Texas tea cakes and followed Luke to the back of the parlor. There they took seats opposite each other at a table commandeered by cast members.

Bob Brown, an outspoken member of the group, tipped his chair back onto two legs and stroked his chin as he glanced first at Caroline, then at Luke. "You know, you two aren't half-bad."

"I've been trying to tell her we're good together," Luke said, and giving his peach ice cream a lingering lick, winked at her.

The wink found its mark. So did Luke's stockinged foot as it slid up and down her calf beneath the table.

A few minutes later the editor of the local newspaper approached their table. After some small talk, the editor patted Caroline on the back and in a more masculine gesture clamped his other hand on Luke's shoulder. "You two are the talk of the town. How about an interview?"

Luke wiped his mouth with a white paper napkin and looked into Caroline's eyes with a devilish glint in his own. "What is it you want to know?"

"What makes you two tick. It isn't every day we see a couple of homegrown young folks like yourselves who care enough to wage war on a local issue. The fact that you're able to forget all that to help us out at the Opera House makes us all curious how you manage it."

Caroline squirmed in her chair and wondered what story the editor was after. Was it possible he'd guessed at the attraction between her and Luke? If the journalist planned to exploit the feelings that made her heart sing at the sight of Luke, he could forget it. She'd refuse to give him the ammunition to take shots at them.

"What do you say we all get together tomorrow morning for an interview?" the editor suggested. "It'd make a grand story for the Sunday edition."

Luke looked first at Caroline, then at the table, as he fiddled with a toothpick. She glanced about the table, painfully aware of the silence that had settled over the amiable group.

Luke answered the man's question for both of them. "Perhaps it's best you interview us individually. What do you think, Caroline?"

The sudden, cool expression on Luke's face reminded her of the way he had looked at her when he'd walked into the city council chambers. Gone was the sparkle that had made his eyes dance a few moments earlier, and so was the light-hearted banter she loved.

Instead she sensed the familiar competitiveness in the tilt of his chin, in the pursing of his full, sensuous lips into a thin slash.

When amusement sparkled in the editor's eyes, anger simmered within her. Tensing her leg muscles beneath the table, she fought to control her tongue; she didn't want to lose her temper in front of all these people.

Gratefully she thought of the press release in her purse as a way to hide her resentment at the invasion of their privacy.

From her shoulder bag she pulled the legal-size envelope containing the story she'd written in the early hours of the morning. "You might want to use this for Sunday," she suggested, handing the envelope to the editor.

The journalist's curious nature was evident as he slipped his thumb under the envelope flap. "What's this?"

"Just preservation business," Caroline said, hoping the editor would have the good manners to wait until later to read what she'd given him.

"Oh, well, then I'll look at it when I get to the office tomorrow. Stop by and see me about nine in the morning, will you, Caroline?" He turned to Luke. "Is ten convenient for you?"

Luke nodded and looked at his watch. "Ready to go, Caroline? It's getting late."

"Ready," Caroline answered quickly.

After a round of farewells, she and Luke stepped outside, where a light breeze carried the fragrance of crape myrtle blossoms about the Square. In full bloom, the trees shimmered like pink clouds. Spotlights on the courthouse lawn cast eerie shadows on the white lime-stone walls.

Lively strains of blue grass music drifted across the Square from Rinky-Tink's, tempting Caroline to ask Luke if he'd like to drop in for a few minutes. The banjo picking would begin soon, and she'd heard that one of the old-timers had agreed to play the spoons.

The faraway look in Luke's eyes warned her he was no longer in the mood for festivities. "Want to go for a walk?" he said.

"Sure." As they rounded the corner from the Nutt Shell Eatery and headed in the direction of the lake, she wondered what thoughts were running through his mind, fairly certain his solemn mood had been precipitated by the editor's query.

A rare chill in the night air sent goose bumps skittering over her shoulders and down her bare arms. She wished she'd brought the jacket to her blue linen jumpsuit. She stole a glance at Luke and wished, instead, he'd warm her with his arms.

Once the Square was behind them, he paused and raked the fingers of one hand through his dark hair. His white polo shirt with the navy collar emphasized his dark features, the swells of his chest, but even in the moonlight she could detect tension in the way he held his lips.

"What are you going to tell him? What are you going to say is the reason you're dead set against Dino-Land?" he asked her.

"I thought we agreed not to talk politics tonight." She turned away, wishing that for one night they could pretend their differences didn't exist, but Luke grabbed her arm and looked at her with a questioning gaze.

"You know how I feel about your project," she said, looking up at him. She didn't want to talk about Dino-Land. She wanted to hear Luke tell her again how much it meant to him to hold her in his arms.

"Admit it, Caroline. There's more behind your opposition to my project than your insistence on historical preservation. You know as well as I do that could be worked out—compromised. What is it? I want to understand."

Explaining her feelings meant reliving memories, memories she'd worked hard to suppress. She took a deep breath and thought about his question for a moment. Maybe she could explain her feelings with broad strokes of the brush. "You live in Fort Worth, don't you?"

"When I'm not traveling."

"And you've probably been in a lot of big cities on business."

"Yes, I have."

She shivered, more from where her thoughts were leading than from the chill in the night air. "Don't you miss Granbury when you're there? Don't you feel like a tiny fish in an ocean?"

"You're cold." He drew her close to him and ran his hands over her back. Smiling down at her, he asked, "There, is that better?"

She nodded, wishing he'd forget the next day's interviews and kiss her. Instead he answered her question.

"Do I miss Granbury? Of course. It's my home. But I like Fort Worth, Dallas, Washington, Boston—all those big cities. Sure they have their problems, but there's an air of excitement, a dynamic quality in big cities, that I miss here." He drew back and looked down into her eyes. "Couldn't you feel that excitement when you lived in Fort Worth?"

At the second mention of Fort Worth in a minute, she closed her eyes and snuggled closer to his chest, willing away the memory of the four years she'd lived there, especially those last six months before she'd moved back to help her mother. "I felt a lot of things, and I don't miss one of them."

Cupping her chin in his hand, Luke lowered his head and teased her lips to a kiss. "Tell me about your feelings. Tell me why just the thought of them made you shiver just now."

She thought for a moment before answering. "People...don't...care about each other there as they do here." Would that be enough to satisfy his curiosity?

"I've found they do if you give them a chance."

"You think I didn't?" His insult burning in her ears, she slid from his embrace, turned away and with long, purposeful strides headed for the lake. Had she been mistaken, or had he just accused her of being a snob?

Luke stepped in front of her and grasped her arm. "Hey, wait a minute. I didn't mean to insult you." He paused, as if waiting for her forgiveness. When she didn't voice it, he said, "What I meant was, have you ever met people who won't give a new place a chance? Who go on and on about how wonderful it was where they lived before and talk about how terrible things are in the place you love?"

That explanation only fueled her fury. With a shrug she was free of his grasp again and on her way to the lake. If he didn't do a better job of apologizing, she'd leave him and walk home alone.

Immediately he was beside her. "Please, don't be mad."

"For your information, it wasn't like that. Besides, most of my neighbors weren't Fort Worth natives, either. I tried every way I could to make friends with them. I baked cakes for their birthdays, invited them to parties, offered them rides, took care of their pets while they were away—pets that sometimes urinated on my carpet. Whenever anybody needed a friend, there I was—good old Caroline."

She stopped suddenly and wheeled around, the blood pounding in her head so forcefully she felt dizzy. "But where were they when I needed them?"

Luke narrowed his gaze. "What do you mean, when you needed them?"

She turned away, feeling her throat constrict from the memory. "I—I was in my apartment one night with my dog Jessie."

Luke reached for her, but she stepped back, knowing the warmth of his arms would destroy her fragile control.

"It was last July—July 31. After a week of hundred-degree days, we were blessed with a cool summer night. I lived in a ground-floor garden apartment, a place where they'd let me keep Jessie. That wasn't easy to find. Jessie was a big dog—half shepherd, half chow. I loved her so much.

"When I went to bed, I left the patio door open a couple of inches—"

"Caroline, you didn't."

"I love fresh air." She inhaled deeply and closed her eyes. "I was tired of air-conditioning. About three in the morning Jessie woke me up with a low growl. She always slept on the floor by the side on my bed. When her growl grew more menacing, I reached for my robe. Jessie bolted for the living room, as if she were a mad dog. I wasn't sure what I should do. I'd never seen her like that.

"When I caught up with her, she was throwing herself against the patio door so hard I thought she'd break through the thick glass. Then, by clawing at the opening, she managed to slide the door back enough to squeeze through."

Caroline's vision of the moonlit lake in the distance became only a blur. Turning to Luke, she leaned into his chest. "Oh, Luke, I don't know why this still gets me so upset. It could have been so much worse. After all, I wasn't even really harmed."

"Sshh, it's okay. You don't have to tell me the rest."

But Caroline didn't want to stop. She felt driven to tell the rest of the story, as if finishing it would make the memory go away. "As I grabbed a butcher knife, I heard a shot and a voice—a man's voice."

Luke's hold on her tightened.

"He laughed and yelled, 'Hey, lady. How do you like your dog now?' He stuck his head through the open door, looked at me and wolf-whistled."

"The son of a—"

"He killed my Jessie." The picture of Jessie's adoring eyes as the life drained from her body silenced Caroline's sobs. "She...she died in my arms."

Luke's hands stilled on her back for a moment, and he cleared his throat. "He didn't hurt you, baby?"

"N-no. He left. I think he was afraid the gunshot would bring the neighbors, and he'd get caught. I sat there beside Jessie for hours, waiting for him to come back—afraid to move, afraid not to. When he ran off I screamed and screamed, but nobody came. Not one of my neighbors even called.'' Caroline took a deep, shuddering breath.

''Sshh, it's okay now. I'm here.''

For a few moments she let herself be soothed as Luke rocked her in his arms. Somehow his closeness lessened her pain. ''So I called the police. They said they'd get there when they could. It had been a bad night. It was an hour, but it seemed like a year.''

''I'm so sorry. If I'd been there, I would've—''

''I know,'' she said, lifting her tear-stained face to look into his eyes. ''You're from Granbury. You're different. You care.''

''More than you know, sweet thing.''

''There were . . . other incidents,'' she continued.

''Did that man come back?''

''I don't know. I moved the next day, but I had a new problem. There were so many car thefts in the area, I got a burglar alarm for my car. To show you how bad it was, within three months the alarm went off twice—once outside a bank I was auditing, another time in front of a grocery store in broad daylight. And they weren't false alarms.

''Then someone started vandalizing the mailboxes at the new complex I'd moved to, so I had to get a post office box. Things just kept getting worse.''

Luke swore under his breath. ''I hear crime's getting bad in some big cities. Guess I've been lucky so far.''

He took her hands in his and kissed the tips of her fingers. ''If you're ever in trouble, I want you to call me. I don't care where I am or what time it is, I'll come to you. Will you remember that?''

She nodded, luxuriating for a moment in the feeling, so rare for her lately, of being protected. "I'll remember."

"And never, ever leave your doors open at night—promise?"

"But don't you see? I can do that here. I can walk away with my door unlocked and not worry that some deranged person might try to get inside. I can leave my windows open. I feel safe in my home here in Granbury, where only a few thousand people live. But if you build Dino-Land here, this little town will grow until we have the same problems the big cities have. I can't let that happen."

Now that her feelings were out in the open, she wondered if they would give Luke a different perspective on his project. He looked out over the lake but said nothing to indicate he'd changed his thinking.

"Maybe you ought to take me home," she told him.

His gaze flicked back to her with a thin smile. "Okay."

But the way he hung his head and stuffed his hands in his pockets told Caroline he hadn't taken care of a need of his own, the need that apparently made him want to take the walk in the first place. As he turned toward the Square and slipped an arm around her waist, she stopped him. "You still want to go for that walk, don't you?"

He shrugged. "I didn't think you were up to it."

"Of course I am."

His smile widened. "You're sure?"

She nodded. "I feel better now, thanks to you."

It was a short walk. In five minutes they were on the shore of the lake, standing beneath the canopy of two oak trees as old as the town. Overhead, branches embraced and rustled with lush summer greenery.

Almost absentmindedly, Luke released her hand, crouched and picked up a twig that lay beneath the closest tree. His gaze drifted across the water that lapped at the nearby shore. The lights of a few night fishermen in small boats reflected like shimmering gold ribbons on the water. The occasional mournful howl of a dog and the hoot of an owl mingled with the symphony of crickets and frogs.

Luke seemed to forget she was there. Caroline watched him as he ran his fingers across the stick's dry bark. Then suddenly he gripped it tightly in his hand.

Caroline stood quietly beside him, sensing his need for solace but not knowing whether to speak or touch or walk away. Had it not been for the tension she saw knotted in Luke's jaw and the knuckles of his fingers, showing white in the moonlight as he gripped the twig, she would have enjoyed the serenity of the rare, peaceful moment—and the place. But she sensed that tonight wasn't the time for peaceful reflection.

Luke's eyes were fixed on some distant point across the lake. Anxious to help ease his pain, she knelt beside him and draped her arm across his back, but his muscles tensed at her touch.

Taken aback, she removed her arm, wondering what would cause him to recoil at a touch she had meant to be comforting. "What's wrong? What is it? Have I done something? Said something to upset you?"

Luke looked at the moist ground before him and shook his head, still not speaking. Scraping aside the decaying tree leaves, he traced triangles in the dirt with the twig, then turned to her. "I'm sorry."

Except for the sadness in Luke's eyes, she wished she could have had a picture of him there, the wash of moonlight highlighting the smooth, strong features of his face—the slightly square jaw, the full, moist lips, the dimple in his chin, his dark hair as it tumbled onto his unblemished forehead. The man with eyes of midnight blue in a night as dark as his eyes. "What do you have to be sorry about?"

"My mood. I know I'm not much fun tonight."

"Nonsense. Why don't you tell me what's bothering you? You're not the only good listener around here."

Luke made a futile attempt to smile, but the corners of his mouth dipped even lower. "I don't want to talk to that editor tomorrow."

She nodded. "Same here. I have a feeling he's after more than he told us."

"And if we don't cooperate, he could murder us in print."

"There's more to it than that, though, isn't there? There's something else on your mind."

His lashes sent feathered shadows across his cheeks. "You're a perceptive woman, but in a way it's all connected to that interview." He paused. "Do you know what next Saturday is?"

"The day before our last performance?"

"It's that, but it's more. Fifteen years ago next Saturday I...I found my grandfather right over there." He lifted one finger and pointed to a gnarled tree root that extended into the water. "It was a dark night, a night as dark as—"

"Midnight blue," Caroline finished for him. She curled her fingers around his forearm and pressed her cheek against the sleeve of his shirt. "Ellie told me about it the day after you fished Amrod out of the lake."

Luke hung his head and shook it, his words tumbling out in a rush of grief and guilt. "I tried so hard to make him live, but I was too late. If only I'd gone to look for him a minute earlier. If only I'd found him sooner..."

"Luke, don't. You're beginning to sound like me when I tried to take responsibility for Amrod's drinking. You couldn't help what happened to your grandfather. From what I hear—"

He snapped his head around. "What did you hear? That old George O'Connor boozed it up one time too many? That he met his buddies at the tavern and didn't know when to stop?"

A helpless feeling swept over Caroline as she saw Luke's face twisted in anger and pain. "I only heard he'd been drinking and—"

"Well, you heard wrong!" he said, his booming voice silencing the night creatures. "My grandfather had quit drinking three weeks before that night. I ought to know. I was the one who finally convinced him to go to Alcoholics Anonymous."

"But, Luke, three weeks isn't that long when you've been drinking as long as he had."

"You don't understand, do you? There was something unexplainable about that night."

"Luke! Are you telling me you suspect foul play in your grandfather's death?"

"Do you know what I smelled when I found him, when I pulled him out of the water and tried to revive him? Gin—lots of it."

"But he could have had a weak moment and—"

"No! My grandfather never drank gin. He was allergic to it or to something in it. He knew that if he had one ounce of the stuff, within thirty minutes his throat would swell shut and he wouldn't be able to breathe. That night he'd had a lot more than an ounce. You can't imagine the smell."

Caroline's nostrils flared with the remembrance of Amrod's breath the night Luke had saved him from drowning. She slipped her arm around Luke's waist and hugged him close, sensing his anger, feeling his pain at the awful reality his grandfather had committed suicide.

"I know what you're thinking," he said, turning to her with dark eyes that flashed in the night. "You're thinking my grandfather killed himself."

Caroline said nothing. Her honest streak wouldn't permit her to contradict him.

The twig snapped in his fingers, and the anger was apparent in the whip of his arm as he stood and threw the two pieces in the lake. "Well, you're wrong. He never would've done that. He was a deeply religious man. To him, suicide was the same as murder. He knew a man once who killed himself with rat poison, and he told me he was sure the guy'd burn in hell."

Caroline rose to stand before him. "Are you saying you think your grandfather was . . . murdered?"

"I have my suspicions, but I've never been able to prove anything."

"But why would anyone have wanted to kill your grandfather?"

Luke paused before answering her. "I don't know. Everyone who knew him loved him—almost everybody, anyway."

"Did you tell the police? About the gin, I mean?"

"Of course I told them. I told them he never drank gin. I told them he drank only bourbon, and you know what? They laughed at me. They said, 'No disrespect intended, son, but your old grandfather would drink anything that didn't drink him first.' They wouldn't investigate, wouldn't even discuss it with me. The coroner ruled death by asphyxiation brought on by an allergic reaction."

"Oh, Luke, I'm so sorry. You and your family must have been devastated."

"You can't imagine what it was like to have people act as if my grandfather didn't matter. As far as they were concerned, there was one less drunk to litter the streets, to occupy a jail cell while he was drying out."

"I wish I'd been there for you."

With the hint of a smile he squeezed her hand. "I appreciate that. I know it would've helped, even though you were only—what? Eleven? Even then I knew you were special."

He paused, as if trying to decide whether or not to continue. "I used to watch you and wonder what it would be like to be a McAlester, to live in that big house of yours. I wanted to despise you for...for what you stood for, but I couldn't. Every time I saw you I knew...someday I'd feel this way about you."

"And how do you feel, Luke? How do you really feel about me now?"

He stepped closer and cupped her head in his hands, letting his gaze drift over her face before he spoke. "Don't you know by now?" He smiled softly and traced her cheekbones with his thumbs. "I love you, Caroline. I guess I've always loved you."

"Oh, Luke. I—I feel so—so honored."

A muscle twitched in his jaw. "I want you to feel more than honored. I want you to love me, too. I want you to lie awake at night and wonder what it would be like to make love to me."

She opened her mouth to speak, but he stopped her with words of his own. "No, don't say anything. You know how I feel. That's enough for now. Someday—soon, I hope—you will love me. The feeling is growing within you. I can see it in your eyes." Reverently he kissed each one, then rocked her in the cradle of his arms.

As the wind sifted through her hair, she shut her eyes and listened to her heart repeat the words he'd so reverently spoken.

"God, it feels good to finally tell you, lady of my dreams."

She smiled up at him. "I—I've dreamed of you, too."

"Good dreams, I hope."

She nodded and, standing on tiptoes, twined her arms around his neck. "Stop talking and kiss me."

Luke's lips closed over hers in a smile. Caroline felt her feet leave the ground as he lifted her in his arms and pressed her willing body full length to his. What a magnificent, giving body it was! As his hard muscles flexed, they seemed to gather her closer to him and the desire that burned within him.

When at last he lowered her to the ground, her body sang with the need for him. "I—I wish we didn't have to—have to stop," she said.

"When I make love to you, sweet thing, it won't be on the shore of a lake where someone might happen by and ruin what we're sharing." His gaze drifted over her head, and a haze clouded his eyes. "Especially this lake."

His hold on her relaxed, and she stepped back, knowing there was unfinished business in his heart for that night and that place.

The sound of laughter echoed across the water from one of the fishing boats, and Caroline watched the anger gradually repossess Luke's body.

"I'll tell you what," he said, the passion for her in his voice replaced by the passion of anger. "If I ever find out someone was responsible for my grandfather's death, I'll crucify him. I don't care who he is. I'll see he rots in jail for the rest of his days."

The vindictiveness in Luke's voice sent a shudder across Caroline's shoulders. In almost the same breath, he'd talked about his love for her and revenge for the possible murderer of his grandfather.

She tried to think of some way she could help him let go of his long-held hatred and anger. "Did your grandfather say anything before he died? Did he tell you why he'd been drinking gin—or why he smelled as if he had been?"

"He said only one word."

"What was it? Maybe there's a slim chance I can help. Perhaps you overlooked something—a connection somewhere."

"It's late. I've got to get you home."

"But what was the word?"

"I really don't want to talk about it anymore. I just want to go back to my room and go to bed."

She gripped his forearms securely in her hands and forced him to look down at her. "Weren't you the one who lectured me about trust?"

"It has nothing to do with trust. It's, well, something personal, something private."

"But how can I help if you won't tell me?"

"It's too late. It can't save my grandfather now."

"But I don't want you to kill yourself over this unfinished business!"

He frowned. "What do you mean by that?"

"It's because of the way your grandfather died that you acted so crazy the night Amrod fell into the lake. In your mind that was your grandfather, and you jumped in to save Amrod just as you would've saved your grandfather if you'd had the chance."

Luke clenched his jaw, his eyes ablaze in the moonlight. "I saved Amrod because it was the decent thing to do. A person doesn't just stand by and watch another person die. If he does, he might as well strangle him with his own hands."

"But you took such a big chance diving into the lake at night. I didn't mean to imply—"

"I know." He picked up a rock and sent it skipping across the water. "I just wish I could make people understand what a good person my grandfather was. I wish I could redeem him somehow in the eyes of all the people in town he considered his friends."

Realization dawned on Caroline with the force of a sledgehammer. "That's why you want to build Dino-Land here, isn't it?" She remembered something she'd seen on his plans, something she hadn't thought much about at the time. The full name of Luke's planned theme park was "George O'Connor's Dino-Land."

"You want to build your theme park here as a tribute to your grandfather, don't you?"

Luke turned around slowly, his body rigid, his hands clenched at his sides. "And what if I do?"

CHAPTER ELEVEN

SLEEP DIDN'T COME EASILY for Caroline that night. Every time she closed her eyes she saw Luke kneeling on the shore of the lake, cradling a man's lifeless body in his arms, tears of agony streaming down his young face, while his impassioned cries for help went unanswered.

Awake enough to feel the pangs of conscience eating at her, she tried to picture the old man's face in her mind, aware, even in her drowsy state, that she'd never known George O'Connor because she'd never tried to be his friend. All those years in Granbury she'd never tried to befriend any of the O'Connors. She'd regarded them and people like them as outside her social circle, as she'd been raised to think. Guilt nagged at her like an ulcer.

Shortly before dawn Friday she abandoned attempts to sleep, slipped into pink shorts and T-shirt and sat on the front porch in the moonlight, twisting a fragrant sprig of crape myrtle between her thumb and forefinger.

The rustle of bushes near the corner of the house startled her. "Who's there?"

"That you, Missy?"

It was Amrod. Since she'd insisted he quit calling her "Miss Caroline," he'd dubbed her "Missy." She liked the way he said it, softlike, as if she were a cherished child.

"It's me," she answered. "What are you doing up this early?"

"Thinkin' mostly." He shuffled to the front porch in baggy work pants, a white T-shirt and house shoes with fluorescent rims around the soles. Bracing his hands on his knees, he lowered himself to the step just below her. "Is that what you're doin'?"

She could tell from his breath and his steady movements he hadn't been drinking. Thank God for that. She plucked another sprig from the tree, and admitted, "I couldn't sleep."

"Somethin' botherin' you?"

There sure was. She didn't like the kind of person she'd been while growing up in Granbury. Because of her snootiness, she'd missed knowing the gentle person who had been Luke's salvation when he was a child.

She found herself wanting to know everything about Luke—the little things that made him happy, his favorite foods, what his home looked like, what he wanted in a woman, but now especially she wished she knew what she could do to ease the ache in his heart. "I was thinking about Luke."

Caroline could swear Amrod's eyes twinkled at her words.

"You two been seein' a lot of each other, have you?"

She didn't try to hide the grin that came with the thought of them as a couple. The fact that Amrod could read her feelings so easily didn't bother her. He was amazingly easy to be around—when he was sober. "Strange, isn't it?"

"Not so strange. He's a fine-lookin' young man. You're a pretty little miss. Good match, I'd say."

Caroline narrowed her gaze. "Sounds like you've been talking to Ellie."

"Maybe. Maybe not."

"Why you devil! You two are trying to get Luke and me together, aren't you?"

Amrod planted his palms on his thighs, winked at her and shrugged sheepishly. "Beats gettin' lit, wouldn't you say?"

"Oh, Amrod, you're a dear." When she wrapped her arms around his neck, his bear hug filled her with a sense of belonging she'd missed. "I'm lucky to have you, and I've been so proud of you lately." She scooted down onto the step where he sat and laced her fingers through his.

"So, thinkin' about Luke, you say? Would it be nosy for an old man to ask exactly what you were thinkin'?"

Why hadn't she thought to ask him? Amrod might be able to tell her what the scuttlebutt was when Luke's grandfather had died. He might help her unravel the mystery of his death. "How well did you know George O'Connor?"

Amrod's callused hand stilled in hers. He cleared his throat and looked away. "What makes you ask?"

"Oh, nothing really." Then, after a moment's thought, she added, "No, that isn't true. Luke and I went for a walk down by the lake Friday night after the show, and he told me how his grandfather died."

Amrod sat silently beside her and stared down at his house shoes, his forearms propped on his knees.

"It's been fifteen years, and Luke's insides are still eating away at him," she said. "I think he blames himself for not finding his grandfather in time. I'd like to help him prove there was nothing he could've done to save him.''

After a long pause, Amrod said, ''It wasn't Luke's fault.''

The old man's somber expression prompted Caroline's query. ''You know something about George O'Connor's death?''

Amrod's furtive sideways glance told her he might, but he stood, shoved his hands into his trouser pockets and diverted his gaze to the coral-pink glow on the eastern horizon. ''That young man's got to forget the past, Missy. Put it behind him. You'd best do the same. Take it from an old man who's just beginnin' to learn.

''Guilt, blamin' yourself for things that happened a long time ago—things you did, things you didn't do— can eat away at you till you don't want to live, till you drink so you can live with the pain. A man—or a woman—has got to find happiness in the present, in the everyday things, like that sunrise over there, like the look you young folks get when you look at each other, like the sparkle in your pretty blue eyes. Not in the past, Missy, not in the troubles of your granddaddies. Because of you, I'm beginnin' to learn that. I want you to learn it, too.''

''But—''

He bent to kiss her forehead. ''Remember what I said now. Promise?''

Caroline quietly thought over his words. ''You're doing it, aren't you, Amrod? You're getting help somewhere.''

While he stood there staring at his house shoes, she prayed his answer would be yes. She didn't want to have to make good on her ultimatum and kick him out of the only home he'd known for fifty years.

But if she thought he'd cooperate with her so easily, she was mistaken. He reached over and squeezed her shoulder lightly. "I expect my hamster's gettin' hungry."

Caroline bit her lip and said nothing, then watched him disappear around the corner of the house.

She had wanted to tell him more, how in the early morning hours, with the shadows of the tree dancing across her sheets, she'd finally come to realize Luke had captured a place in her heart—a place he'd hold forever. There had been men in her life, two in particular with whom she'd fantasized about a future together, but she'd never felt the dull ache, the longing for completion that she experienced when she wasn't with Luke.

It was a wild, out-of-control feeling, as if she'd just skied off a cliff and were whooshing through the air with nothing firm beneath her. The thought of Luke's lips pressing against hers with bruising force made her heart jumble around in her chest. God help her, she loved him.

She smiled as she whispered the word to the morning: "Love." A warm word, a word that created a melody in her heart, a word meant only for Luke.

Aware of movement in the street, she glanced up and saw Luke's silver Porsche roll to a stop in front of her house. Anxious to see him, she hurried down the path.

He hooked an arm around her neck and kissed her uplifted face. "You're up. Good. I was afraid to call. Thought you might be asleep."

"I—I couldn't sleep."

His eyes danced with amusement. "Does that mean what I think it means?"

Not answering his question, she slipped an arm around his waist and nestled her head against his chest, which smelled of fresh soap and cedar.

"Hmm. Something tells me your insomnia worked in my favor."

"Depends on what you have in mind."

"First this." He drew her into his arms and kissed her, filling her with a happy, singing feeling. When at last he broke the kiss, he looped his arms loosely around her waist, and said, "I also came to apologize. I was insufferable last night."

She ran her fingertips over his lips. When he stilled her hands and kissed her fingers, she smiled. "That word did cross my mind."

"I'm sorry. Sometimes I get carried away when I think about the way my grandfather died."

"You have every reason to be upset."

"Look, I promised myself I'd put my dreary mood behind me. I came here to ask if you could spare the morning. Dad's leaving to visit my brother and his family in Maryland, and I promised I'd give him a lift to the airport, then take care of a few things at the house. Conway's sending his private plane to fly him to Maryland directly. It's the only way Dad can go. If he flies commercial, he'll have to change planes and sit around airports too long. Too hard on his hips. I was wondering if you'd like to go with me to pick him up."

She was glad Carriker was good for something. "Oh, Luke, I don't know. Your dad doesn't like me much."

"He will when he gets to know you better. That's why I'd like you to go. Besides, last night you said you'd like to know more about my family."

Caroline hesitated, remembering Mack O'Connor's steely gaze the day at the Opera House. She also remembered how, only a few moments ago, she'd agonized over the way she had shut the O'Connors from her life. "I'll have to change," she said, glancing down at her shorts. "Do you have a few minutes?"

He looked at his watch. "Sure. I'll wait here." He bent and kissed her again. "That is, unless you need help."

The truth was, she would like Luke's help...only then, they'd never make it to the airport. As she rummaged through her closet, looking for something appropriate to wear, she couldn't help smiling at Luke's teasing remark.

Should she wear jeans and cowboy boots? Too casual, but a dress was definitely overdoing it. Realizing they probably had little time to spare, she grabbed red slacks and a matching sleeveless blouse that buttoned demurely to her neck, hoping the outfit didn't look expensive or pretentious.

HOLDING HANDS, she and Luke drove west of town until he turned onto a dirt road in a sparsely wooded area. Over a rise to the left Caroline saw a small red-brick home nestled beneath tall pecan trees, twenty feet back from the road. Behind the modest ranch-style house stood a detached garage with an old blue pickup truck parked in the gravel driveway.

"This is where I grew up," Luke said. "Dad refuses to move, although he did let me remodel the old place. We used the dream plans Mom drew up a year or so before she died. I just wish she could see how it turned out."

"Your mother must have been a creative woman."

"She had what I guess you'd call a flair. You can see for yourself inside. Her touch is everywhere."

Caroline felt a glow, a strong sense of family, the minute she stepped inside the house. Country furnishings in dusty rose and blue created a casual, relaxed atmosphere. A hand-stenciled Danish design decorated the borders of the living room's wide plank floors and the kitchen's natural oak cabinets.

"What a lovely home," she said. She stood in the middle of the small living room and slowly turned around to take in the many handmade treasures that bore Luke's mother's initials. "It's friendly, warm, personal."

"Just like Mom."

"I wish I'd known her," Caroline said, running her fingers over a quilted wall hanging edged in ecru lace.

"She would've liked you." He tapped the tip of her nose and winked at her. "She had your same spirit, the same fire in her eyes. Just like you, she attacked everything she did with the energy of three people."

Heavy footsteps resounded on the plank floors of a hallway that led off the living room. Mack O'Connor's burly frame loomed in the doorway, his gaze fixed on Caroline with a strong measure of disdain. "What are you doing, Miss Caroline? Slumming?"

Luke knotted his hands into fists and stepped forward. "Dad, I won't let you talk to Caroline that way."

Caroline grabbed Luke's arm and stepped up beside him. "No, Luke. It's okay. He has a right to say what he did. I—I'm the one who should apologize."

She looked to Luke's father and prayed she'd find the words to make him understand what was in her heart. "You have a lovely home, Mr. O'Connor. I'm sorry I never met your wife to tell her so myself. If I'd been friendlier, well . . . who knows?"

She fumbled with the white scarf tied at her waist and continued. "I've recently learned my grandfather treated your father rather poorly, Mr. O'Connor. No one will tell me how or why, only that your father suffered because of Barron McAlester and that there was a woman involved, a woman I gather both men loved. My grandfather's dead. He can't apologize for what he did to your family, but I can apologize for him. I—I'm sorry, sir."

Blue eyes, almost as dark as Luke's, softened, reflecting a gentler side of Mack O'Connor—a side Caroline had hoped existed. He stared at her a long moment before speaking. "I accept your apology, Miss Caroline."

She closed her eyes and let out a deep breath. "Then please, will you drop the 'Miss' and call me just plain 'Caroline'? If anyone should be addressed with a title here, it's you."

Mack stepped forward and laid a heavy hand on her shoulder. "I don't cotton much to titles...Caroline. Now, I expect we'd better get a move on if we're going to make that plane on time."

In Luke's car Caroline sat in the back seat so Luke's father wouldn't have to suffer the pain of maneuvering his arthritic hips there himself, but Luke held Caroline's hand while he drove, glancing over his shoulder and in his rearview mirror to smile at her every minute or so.

The drive was a short one. Luke extended his hand to help his father up the stairs to Conway's private plane. One foot on the stairs Mack paused, then gestured for Caroline to join him. Willingly she stepped forward and felt the older man's callused hand enclose hers.

"I've been wrong about you, Caroline. Luke's been telling me what a fine lady you are. It appears he's right. You'd be a fine match for my son." He squeezed her hand and bent to kiss her cheek. "My friends call me 'Mack.'"

"YOU SURE WON Dad over," Luke said, grinning as he drove back to his father's house.

"He's not so tough, once you get to know him."

"Something tells me you could wrap him around your finger, and he'd love it. He always wanted a daughter."

That comment made her wonder where Luke's thoughts were leading, but she was afraid to think for a moment that someday Mack O'Connor could have a daughter—her. And maybe some grandchildren? She decided to change the subject. "I don't understand why you stay in the hotel when you could be with him."

"We talked about it. Dad usually goes to bed shortly after dinner. I'm a night owl. If I were only here for a weekend, I'd stay with him. I wanted to be on the Square for a couple of reasons. You were—or you became—one of them. I thought I'd have a better chance of seeing you there. I was right, wasn't I?"

She ran her hand over his forearm, enjoying the fuzzy feel of the dark hair on her palm. "I'll bet that's not what you thought that first day, after I ripped into you in my back room. What was your other reason for staying at the hotel?"

He trained his gaze on the road. "I think you know the answer to that question. Business."

"Oh." The omnipresent barrier between them loomed clear in her sights, a barrier she'd been pretending didn't exist.

Caroline was still thinking about their differences after they arrived back at Luke's father's house. Luke repaired a torn window screen while she busied herself making lemonade. Then she tidied up the kitchen, watching Luke through the window over the sink as he changed the fan belt in his father's pickup. The bunched-up muscles on his back and arms glistened with a sheen of perspiration as he toiled in the morning sun.

Enjoying the domestic atmosphere, she felt a pang of remorse as she heard his booming voice singing "Bewitched" from *Pal Joey*. If only life could be as simple as the morning they were sharing.

By way of distancing herself from him, she did as he had suggested earlier and checked out the other rooms of the house so she could see the work he and his father had recently completed.

When she opened the door to the second bedroom, a warm swirl of mint and ivory and peach beckoned her into its interior. Covered in mint-green lattice, the ceiling rose to a peak at the far end of the room. There coach lamps on either side of a fireplace mantel illuminated another one of Luke's mother's needlepoint creations. Midmorning light streamed through French windows, warming the brass bed's peach-and-mint coverlet to a welcoming glow.

"You like it?"

Startled by Luke's voice, she turned around and found him shirtless, leaning against the door frame, his tight faded blue jeans slung low on hips. He handed her a glass of lemonade and took a long, slow drink from his. Caroline watched his Adam's apple bob up and down as he drained his glass. Still holding her gaze, he set the glass on a table by the door and wiped the perspiration from his forehead with his arm.

She let her gaze drop to his magnificent chest and felt a lump form in her throat. "I—I didn't hear you come in." To gather her wits, she turned her back to him, feeling her heart flutter at the thought of being alone with him in the house. In the bedroom. "This room is lovely."

"So are you, sweet thing." He reached over her shoulder for her glass and grazed her back with his chest, then came to stand behind her. In a warm breath that whispered through her hair, he said her name, the husky tenor of his voice a clarion of wanting. "Caroline, you love me, don't you?"

With the gentle pressure of his hands on her shoulders, she turned to him, her gaze moving to his full sensuous lips, to his glazed and glowing eyes. She let her fingers drift over the contours of his face, still moist from his labor in the sun. It was the face of the man she loved. "Yes, Luke. I do love you."

Her heart fluttered as his lips descended toward hers, and she closed her eyes in anticipation. But from some deep, hidden place worries of problems, of differences, nagged at her, forcing two words from her throat. "But I—"

"No buts, Caroline. For too long we've let unimportant things get in the way of how we feel about each other. I love you. I've loved you for years, though not like I love you now, and now you love me, too. You just told me, and I've seen it in your eyes for days." He tilted her chin and teased her lips to a kiss.

Caroline splayed her fingers across his chest, a strange, twisted fear standing between her and her love for him. "But don't you think—?"

He ran his thumb over her lower lip, feeling desire course through his loins. "I'm tired of thinking, and I'm tired of talking." He ignored the fingers lightly pressing against his chest and lowered his lips to hers. No matter what she said, he knew she wanted him as much as he wanted her, and now that he knew she loved him, the waiting was over at last. Her mumbled protest faded beneath the pressure of his lips.

Her instant response fueled his desire to fill her with the love he carried in his heart. She would relax that ridiculous McAlester facade, and he'd teach her how beautiful love could be. Any problems they had would pale in comparison to what they shared.

With a whimper, her lips parted, providing his tongue access to the silky tenderness inside, so he could give her a hint of what it would be like if she parted her thighs and let him stroke her, love her there.

Her groping hands slid up and kneaded his nape. Her petite body molded insistently against his large one, needing him, wanting him, at last destroying the barriers between them.

Breaking the kiss, he sifted his hand beneath the sunny curls at her nape and watched her eyes open slowly, the sky-blue pupils luminous with wanting. "I'm going to love you," he murmured, "and you, I know, are going to love me, too."

Luke's hands trembled as they settled on the curve of her shoulders. While she fixed her gaze on his eyes, he took her hand and pressed her fingertips to that special place on his chest where his heart thundered its wanting.

Feeling the flush of desire on her face, Caroline drew Luke's fingers to her heart, which pounded beneath the raw silk of her blouse.

"You remembered," he said in a husky voice. His fingers lingered on the beat, while his thumb strayed out to circle her breast.

"How could I forget how I felt when you touched me?"

"Sweet thing," he moaned, "I'm going to do more than touch you." With one finger he traced a figure eight around her breasts, then lifted his finger to her flushed cheek. "I'm going to love you until you glow."

Her thick lashes fluttered, obscuring her aquamarine eyes. She moaned at his touch. Her lips parted in invitation. Restraint and a determination to go slowly dissolved as he crushed her to his chest, taking her sweet lips with his own, tasting the juices she willingly offered. Her tongue was hot, teasing him to an unbearable arousal. My God, she was going to be a beautiful lover.

Aching as he withdrew from her lips, Luke smiled softly at the flicker of pain that crossed her face at the parting. "Come here, love. Share my bed with me at last."

They seemed to glide then to the bed, pausing hesitantly like innocent lovers beside it in the wash of the rising sun, their trembling hands lingering on each other's shoulders. Luke's gaze followed his fingers to the first tiny pearl button at the neck of her blouse. After what seemed like an eternity he freed the button from the tight loop around it. Anxious to taste her, he lowered his head and kissed the freshly exposed inch of skin at the hollow of her neck.

"I dreamed of you doing this," she murmured, raking her nails through his hair and arching against him each time another button was freed, another inch of flesh was exposed for his touch.

For a brief moment he lifted his head, his raven hair disheveled from her wandering hands. "Sometime I'll tell you about my dreams, but now—now I'm going to live them."

Caroline trembled as he slid the blouse over the curves of her shoulders. The wisp of a lace bra supporting her ample breasts strained at the front closure. His hands slid up to cup her breasts, his eyes watching hers and seeing, she knew, her pleasure reflected there.

His eager gaze followed her fingers to the bra closure. No modesty hindered her movements, the flick of her fingers to unsnap the bra, the release of her swollen breasts to his touch.

It was his undoing. Pulling her down beside him on the bed, he devoured her breasts with his eyes. Her rosy nipples hardened to tight red peaks as he pleasured them with his fingers.

The heat spread to the deepest parts of her. Her breasts strained toward him as his tongue, hot, wet, swirled around each nipple, his teeth nipping at each titillated peak. Then, cupping her hips in his hands, he pressed her hard against the full length of his body, while his mouth, warm and forceful, demanded and received the response of her lips.

In another moment red slacks joined blue jeans on the floor by her blouse, and only a scanty strip of virgin-white lace and his low-rise bikini briefs separated their bodies.

Luke reeled with the intense need that throbbed beneath the strip of sky blue. His thumbs dipped beneath the delicate lace, hers beneath the sky blue, each tugging off the last thin barrier to loving.

For a long, delicious moment he let his gaze wander over her body. "You're even lovelier than I dreamed."

While his adoring words filled her with joy, his mouth hungrily claimed her swollen lips. He slid his hand between her legs, stroking the silkiness there, sliding up, up, until his fingers found the heart of her wanting. With a moan that filled the room, she dug her fingernails into his back, and his fingers drove her to a pulsing need.

"Ah, yes, love, go with it," he said, then kissed a path from her navel to the hollow of her throat.

It was her turn to pleasure him. Tentatively she curled her fingers around his silken rod and stroked him. She felt his body tense, saw his eyelids drift shut over eyes glazed with the agony of restraint.

"Oh, God, Caroline! I wanted to go slowly, but when you touch me like that I...I..." His body went rigid, and his arms shook with need.

"Come to me," she cried out. "Love me. Love me now!"

Without speaking, Luke rolled her shoulders to the sheet and slid one knee between her glistening thighs. Cupping her head in his hands, he stroked the damp curls from her face with his thumbs, and told her in a ragged breath, "I'll try not to hurt you, but you're so...small."

"Nothing you do could ever hurt me," she whispered.

His eyes worshiping the woman before him, he knelt between her thighs, his trembling body towering over her.

She felt him there, gently probing at first, and watched a veil of passion descend over his eyes. Winding her legs around him, she arched her back and thrust her hips upward, a combined joy of pain and pleasure shooting through her as she felt him, all of him, inside her. Visions, sounds, scents all blurred into a surrealistic whirl that caught her, caught them, in its vortex until she felt his final fevered thrusting. Her body, his body—both dissolved in a sated mass of quivers.

How long they lay there, entwined in each other's arms, he a part of her, she a part of him, Caroline didn't know. When next she opened her eyes, she felt his tongue swirl along the sensitive spot beneath her ear, and she squeezed that special part of him and guided his lips to her breasts.

"Hmm, you like that, huh?"

Arms around his neck, she hugged him to her breasts. "I like it all."

His low chuckle brought a grin to her face.

"Now I know why you like to wear red. It suits your bedtime personality—hot!"

Playfully she batted his head and scooted down until her eyes were level with his. His head cradled in her hands, she traced the smooth contours of his face, and her tongue dipped to the shadowed cleft in his chin. "Dear Luke, I love you."

He hugged her fiercely. "And I love you, sweet thing." He settled her into the curve of his arm and stroked the smooth skin on her cheek, while they both stared at the latticed ceiling. "You know, when I was a young boy, I thought you were cute. A bit on the stuck-up side, but cute."

"But you didn't even know me."

"Oh, didn't I? I used to get on my bicycle and ride into town whenever I didn't have chores to do, and I'd ride around your house in hopes I'd get a chance to see you.

"Then, one day," he continued, "you weren't a cute little girl anymore. You were a woman—a woman I couldn't get out of my mind. Since that day I've wanted to—to possess you, I guess. Not in the sense of owning you, but in the way a man aches to have the woman he loves. Only then I didn't really understand what love was—not like I've come to understand it since I've actually come to know you…because you're a million times more wonderful than I'd ever imagined anyone could be.''

"Well, you've got me now. Warts and all.''

He turned to look at her, slinging one leg possessively over her lower torso, the dark hair on his thigh coarse against her softer texture. "You don't have any warts. Just a mole—'' he stroked the underside of her left breast "—right there.''

His touch sent a shiver across her chest and a lazy smile to her lips. "Do that again.''

"This?'' His eyes twinkling, he propped his head on his fist and watched the effect of his caress on her nipples.

"Uh-huh. I'll give you a couple of hours to stop. How long did you say your dad would be gone?''

He chuckled. "Long enough for a lot more loving.''

Caroline arched against him as he gathered her into his arms. She would make love to him until his arms fell off.

CHAPTER TWELVE

FORTUNATELY FOR CAROLINE, his arms stayed right where they were, on the man who loved her as she'd never been loved—tenderly, yet with an explosive passion that left her spent and delightfully sated.

Early in the afternoon they reluctantly discussed business appointments that couldn't be ignored—speaking engagements at the same ladies' garden club at four o'clock. Teasing each other about what the ladies' garden club members would think if they could see them together at that moment, they dressed hurriedly, destined for separate showers before the meeting.

"I—I feel like we've been in a time warp, where nothing matters but you and me," she said as Luke pulled up in front of her house and turned off the ignition.

Luke leaned over and tucked an errant strand of hair behind her ear. "We have to put each other first. Everything else has to come second."

"Everything?" she asked with a look meant to test him. "You think because we love each other, we're going to change our minds about this big obstacle between us?"

The sparkle faded from his eyes, and he glanced away.

Because she knew the park was more a shrine to his grandfather than a business opportunity or investment, Caroline wished she didn't feel the way she did, but she couldn't change her convictions. "I thought not."

"Can't we find some common ground? Some way to compromise?"

"I'd like to think we could, but it's the basic concept itself of a big theme park that I object to more than anything else. Luke, you have to believe I honestly think Dino-Land is wrong for Granbury."

She glanced down at her hands, which lay open and motionless in her lap. "I'm still going to fight you on it."

BY SUNDAY MORNING Caroline's emotions were so jumbled that she once again abandoned efforts to sleep and arose at the first light of day. In her bare feet she made tracks in the dew across the lawn and scooped up the Sunday paper. There, on page one, was the picture of her and Luke, taken in the gazebo on the Square that morning after their interviews.

A smile stole across her face. Amrod was right. They shared a special glow when they looked at each other.

For the most part the editor had been fair and impartial in his story about them. Her feelings of anxiety—and Luke's—had apparently been unfounded. Thank goodness the man hadn't been privy to their conversation at the lake Thursday night. She couldn't bear the thought of seeing Luke's private pain exploited for the sake of a story. If his personal motivation for building Dino-Land in Granbury were made public, Luke would have to be the one to do it. She wouldn't.

On the way back to house, she flipped the newspaper over and saw the story about her mother's manuscript. Caroline couldn't help feeling excited about donating it to the town for a book she'd decided to call *Granbury on the Brazos*.

If the printer she'd contacted had given her accurate figures, she estimated Granbury could raise almost fifty thousand dollars within a year of publication. With four to six thousand tourists visiting the Square each weekend, the book would probably sell as quickly as souvenirs, and she felt certain Texas libraries would order it, as well.

Her printer friend had told her she was crazy to donate the manuscript and do all the work for the book without some compensation. But she had enough to live on, with the profits from the store and her historical preservation job, and, of course, she had the house.

Her gaze traced the familiar lines of the Queen Anne dwelling with its turrets, gables, balconies and intricate trim. How she loved the big old place, dressed now in its summer garden finery.

Ellie ambled across the lawn in a splashy floral housedress, her newspaper tucked beneath her arm. "'Morning, Caroline." She nodded at the paper in Caroline's hands. "I came to see how you're doing after reading that."

"I guess I got all worked up over nothing about the interview."

Ellie arched one brow and looked at Caroline over her glasses. "Nothing? Apparently you didn't see this." She thrust her folded newspaper into Caroline's hands and pointed at an editorial.

Disbelief rooted Caroline to the lawn as she read the editorial "Good for Granbury," which called on the voters to support Luke's theme park as financial common sense. The editor called Caroline's opposition to Dino-Land irrational, based on incidents in her life that had rendered her incapable of looking at the proposed theme park objectively.

Caroline gasped. She'd said a few words to the editor about the problems of big cities, but she hadn't gotten emotional. Yet here he'd practically slandered her, made out she was some sort of nutcase! How could he? Unless... Caroline glanced in the direction of the McNutt Brothers Hotel. Had Luke told the editor about her apartment robbery and her resultant fears? She prayed he hadn't betrayed her confidence.

Forcing herself to read on, she found that the editor had projected Granbury to be a bustling, prosperous city of at least one hundred thousand within five years if the voters endorsed Dino-Land in the upcoming referendum. He foresaw plenty of jobs and the ability to keep Granbury's young people from moving away if the citizens voted yes in the referendum in two weeks.

"Oh, God, Ellie." The five zeros in the population figure swam before Caroline's eyes and made a knot swell in her stomach. It had never occurred to her that the editor wouldn't support her.

"This isn't going to help you win that referendum, that's for sure."

Caroline barely heard what Ellie had said. "I told Luke some things Thursday night in confidence. I was sure I could trust him. But reading this, I—I don't know."

Ellie shook her head and sighed. "When I first read that editorial, I was madder than a hornet. I figured

Luke must've done some fast talking to persuade the editor to write that. But I can't help feeling Luke's a man a woman can trust. That's something you'll have to decide for yourself, child, but in the meantime, you've got a job to do if you expect to win that referendum. You've got to get your message to the voters. You'd best get busy, though heaven knows there aren't enough hours in the day to do what you need to do. I wish you'd never taken that preservation job.

"Oh, that reminds me," Ellie said, deftly changing the subject. "Did you want to look at those things in the attic this morning? I have an hour before it's time to get spruced up for church."

Still numb from shock, Caroline sent Ellie into the parlor and started up the stairs, but the phone halted her progress. It was Luke.

"I didn't do it" was the first thing he said.

There was no sense in pretending she didn't know what he meant. She waited for him to continue.

"I didn't tell that editor what you told me at the lake Thursday night—about the robbery in your apartment, about Jessie and the rest of it. I knew that's what you'd think when you read that editorial."

She pinched the bridge of her nose between her thumb and forefinger. "The thought crossed my mind."

"You've got to trust me. I told the man nothing about that night."

She wanted to believe him. Maybe if she let him come over, take her in his arms and tell her how much he loved her, he'd chase away the niggling doubts that lingered in her mind.

"I appreciate the call," she said. Damn that editor! Making out as if she had a real problem. Still, she was glad it was just the editor who was a creep, not Luke. "But Ellie's here right now," Caroline said. "We're going to go through some things in the attic before church."

"Then I'll see you this afternoon. Tell Ellie hello for me."

Since Ellie didn't ask any questions about the phone call, Caroline didn't volunteer an explanation, choosing instead to think over Luke's words in private.

The cheerful parlor with its hand-blocked Victorian rose wallpaper and intricate rococo furniture improved her spirits somewhat. The morning sunlight flooded the high-ceilinged room Caroline's mother had redecorated lavishly in rose and subtle shades of green.

Ellie's eyes gleamed as she watched Caroline drape the vintage dresses across two Louis XV chairs. Ellie had a story for each dress, and Caroline recorded them all for her book.

"I've saved the best for the last," Caroline said half an hour later. "Close your eyes now."

Once she'd spread the two wedding gowns across the adjacent chairs, she stepped back. "Da-da! Open your eyes, Ellie!"

When the older woman looked first at one gown, then the other, her expectant smile faded. Caroline had the distinct impression the woman had seen a ghost.

"Ellie, are you all right?" Caroline scooted across the room and dropped to her knees beside her, thinking how insensitive she'd been to suddenly conjure up so many poignant memories in Ellie's mind.

The old woman pursed her lips and dug a handkerchief from her pocket. A faraway look in her eyes, she muttered, "Poor Lydia."

Caroline stroked the woman's fleshy arm, recalling that Ellie was one of the witnesses whose signatures appeared on the wedding certificate for the 1930 ceremony joining Lydia Cain to Barron McAlester. "We don't have to do this now," Caroline said. "I can see it's painful for you."

Ellie dabbed at her eyes with her handkerchief, then looked up with a measure of determination. "What was it you wanted to know about the dresses, child?"

Caroline looked at Ellie carefully and decided she was composed enough to go on. "I was hoping you could help me identify these dresses. The label on that one over there—" she pointed to the first dress she'd found in the trunk "—says it was Grandma Lydia's wedding gown."

She gestured to the one with the rosebuds of delicate pink satin. "That's my favorite, but whose was it? It's also Victorian, but apparently Momma forgot to label it."

Ellie pushed herself from the sofa and ambled over to the wall adjoining the fireplace. Summer sunlight streamed through the long, vertical windows in the French-style doors. When Ellie opened one of the panels, the delicate lace sheers billowed and the scent of English tea roses drifted into the double parlor.

With a sigh she turned and pointed at Caroline's favorite gown. "Lydia's mother—your Great-grandmother Cain—got married in that gown. Lydia had always planned to wear it when she married, but...she changed her mind." Ellie pointed a disdainful finger at the other dress. "That's the gown she wore."

"What made her change her mind?"

"She had her reasons. Barron was one of them."

That caught Caroline's attention. "Tell me the story, Ellie. I'd really like to hear it."

Ellie sighed. "Someday I'll tell you all about it, child. But . . . not today."

Amrod's distinctive knock echoed down the hallway that led from the back porch to the parlor. Puzzled by Ellie's half answer, Caroline stuck her head through the parlor doorway and motioned for Amrod to join them.

With a tip of his hat and a warm smile for Ellie, he handed Caroline a vase full of yellow roses.

"Oh, Amrod, how thoughtful of you!" Caroline drew his whiskered cheek next to hers for a kiss. "I've missed having fresh flowers around the house."

Turning to place the vase on the piano against the wall, she thought of the bouquet of fragrant crape myrtle cuttings Luke had brought her. She couldn't help savoring that moment with him, and remembering how her heart had hammered when they'd shared a piece of peach pie.

Amrod's voice interrupted her daydream. "So, what are you ladies doin'?"

"I brought these old dresses down from the attic so Ellie could tell me about them," Caroline said. "Look." She drew Amrod deeper into the parlor. "This one was Grandma Lydia's wedding gown, and that one, her mother's. Aren't they beautiful?"

Amrod's hat slipped from his fingers. "Lydia's . . . weddin' dress?"

His wide-eyed gaze darted suddenly to Ellie, who stepped around Caroline and the dresses to stand beside Amrod and hook her arm through his. When Caroline stooped to pick up the old man's hat, Ellie's frown warned her not to ask questions.

Caroline followed Amrod's fixed gaze to her grand-mother's wedding dress and back. What was it about that gown that had upset both Ellie and Amrod?

"You'll have to excuse us, child," Ellie said, nudging her stunned charge in the direction of the hall. "It's getting late, and Amrod promised to take me to church this morning, didn't you?" Ellie gave Amrod's arm a sharp little jerk and glared at him.

"Uh, yes, ma'am. Church. That's what I was goin' to do. Take you to church. Better go change."

"And shave," Ellie added.

"Wait a minute," Caroline said. "Will someone please tell me why you two are acting like you've seen a ghost?"

Ellie shot her another warning glance. "We'll talk about it later, child."

WHEN CAROLINE arrived home from church, she found Royce Wilson, the banker, waiting for her in his car in front of her house. She pulled her late-model red Subaru close to the curb and tooted her horn.

The balding banker with the pasty-white face squeezed from behind the steering wheel and tugged his vest over his paunch.

"Good grief, Mr. Wilson, aren't you frying out here in this heat? Why didn't you wait for me on the porch, where it's cooler?"

"I was afraid I'd startle you, Miss Caroline." He mopped his brow with his handkerchief.

"Please call me 'Caroline,' won't you?" she asked, wondering if predictable Mr. Wilson could surprise anyone about anything.

When they were seated comfortably opposite one another on two Queen Anne chairs in the parlor, she asked, "What brings you here on a Sunday, Mr. Wilson?"

The banker perched on the edge of the chair. "Because you haven't returned my phone calls."

Caroline sighed. "I'm sorry. I've been so busy with the play and my new job and this referendum business that I've let a few things go. What was it you wanted to talk about?"

The portly man craned his neck and ran a pudgy finger around the inside of his collar. "It's most definitely not a pleasure to do this."

Caroline didn't have to be a student of human behavior to figure out that what Mr. Wilson had to tell her wouldn't be pleasant—probably a hitch in settling her mother's estate. So far it had gone rather smoothly. Meredith McAlester had been in trouble financially, letting money trickle through her fingers like water, with several donations to her favorite charities. But Mr. Wilson had repeatedly assured Caroline that with careful financial management she could survive her mother's excesses.

"I'm afraid there's trouble regarding your house."

Caroline felt her heart lurch. Her house? "What kind of trouble? I thought everything went smoothly on the title transfer."

"Indeed it did, but this pertains to a different matter. You remember I told you your mother overextended herself on this house?" His gaze briefly roamed the room for which, Caroline knew, her mother had squandered twenty-five thousand dollars on hand-blocked wallpaper to match the room's original pattern.

"I remember. You said she mortgaged this house to the hilt, but she had the loan set up so she only had to make an annual interest payment, with a balloon payment due this year and every five years after that.''

"That's right, and that first large payment was to be due September 1.''

Caroline settled back into her chair. "There's no problem, Mr. Wilson. I can make the payment.''

The man shook his head. "I'm afraid there's a more serious problem.''

If Mr. Wilson wanted to play twenty questions, he'd picked the wrong time. She was due at the Opera House in an hour. As a hint, she looked at her watch.

Mr. Wilson removed a piece of paper from the breast pocket of his suit. "One of the provisions of that loan was an option on the part of the bank that made the loan. Each year they may review the loan and decide whether or not to renew it. In essence, that made it a one-year loan, renewable each year.''

"Whether or not to renew it?" The phrase reverberated in Caroline's head. "But they've always—''

"Not this time.''

A silence hung over the room like a pallor. The grandfather clock on the second-floor landing chimed once, the sound echoing down the stairs, along the hallway and into the parlor.

"Why? Wasn't Mother always on time with the annual interest payments? Isn't my reputation—the family reputation—enough to guarantee the loan?''

Mr. Wilson shook his head. "The McAlester reputation has nothing to do with it. A new auditor at the bank in Fort Worth took it upon himself to do some digging. He brought it to the attention of the board of directors that your loan is risky at best. On today's market, the house wouldn't sell for the amount of the loan. The board voted not to renew it.''

"How much?" Caroline asked, trying to maintain her composure. "How much do they need and how soon?"

"All of it—the entire quarter of a million dollars in thirty days, or they'll take possession of your house."

"That's preposterous! They can't do that to me!"

Mr. Wilson handed her the bank's letter. "I'm afraid they can."

Caroline sank back into her chair and in a daze read the demand letter from the Fort Worth bank. The words blurred before her eyes, and she glanced around the room, her gaze settling on the pictures on the table by the window of four generations of Cains and McAlesters. Her grandfather's steely look filled her with determination. Nobody was going to take away her home!

With a proud tilt of her chin, she turned to Mr. Wilson. "First thing Monday morning I'll be in your office to complete the paperwork for a loan. I assume you'll be able to handle it for me. You always took care of Mother."

Mr. Wilson shook his head again. "It's natural for you to expect we'd be able to accommodate you, but the truth is, your mother borrowed far more on this house than it's worth. The reason she approached the Fort Worth bank for the loan was that we turned her down. I've already consulted our board of directors. With your projected income and the rather sizeable amount you need to borrow—" he pulled at the knot in his tie and looked down at his feet "—I'm afraid we'll have to refuse you. If only you hadn't donated your mother's manuscript to the city...."

"What does that manuscript have to do with this?"

"If you'd retained ownership of the book, that might have been enough to convince the bank to loan you—say, one hundred thousand dollars, assuming, of course, you would agree to mortgage the Emporium."

Numbers swam before Caroline's eyes. "I still would've needed a hundred and fifty thousand dollars."

"Yes, but it would have shown you had the potential for earning a tidy sum on reprints, and that might have kept the wolves from your door."

"The wolves from your door." Was that why her mother had tried to market her manuscript? Because she'd been tipped off the bank would force repayment of the loan?

"I wish I could help," Mr. Wilson said. "I hate to think of you losing your home."

Gathering her pride, Caroline stood and fought to control the tears. "I'll call when I decide what to do."

When the door closed behind Mr. Wilson, the click echoed across the entry hall's cypress floor. Caroline leaned back against the door, her body shaking from the effort to hold back the tears.

It would be next to impossible to raise a quarter of a million dollars in thirty days. She looked up the richly carpeted staircase, a flood of sweet, poignant memories of childhood and family and friends smothering her, as if each were anxious for a special, lingering farewell.

Through misty eyes she saw the portrait of her and her grandfather in a gold-leaf frame at the top of the stairs. Her mother had commissioned an artist from Dallas to paint the portrait to commemorate her coming-out party, the pompous affair for all the uppity-ups Meredith McAlester and Granddaddy had known.

Looking at the portrait, she could almost feel Grandfather McAlester's arms about her, see the proud way he'd displayed her as they'd glided around the dance floor he'd had installed on the back lawn for the occasion.

She dragged her feet up the staircase and down the hall to her bedroom. Any minute now she'd wake up and discover today was a bad dream, the dues she had to pay for eating a dozen ice cream bon bons and six chocolate chip cookies at two in the morning when she couldn't sleep.

Sleep—where would she sleep if she lost the house? In a rented room? On a rollaway in the back room of her store? And what of Amrod? Dear, sweet Amrod, who was trying to come to grips with his own problems. She was sure he was. Now he would have to cope with her problems, as well. The cottage was part of her property. Amrod would lose his home when she lost hers.

She couldn't let that happen to him. Tomorrow she'd drive to Fort Worth, see the bank president, request a review of the bank's decision—or at least request more time to find the money. Bile rose in her throat at the thought of driving to Fort Worth, away from Granbury—away from her beloved house.

First she had to get through the matinee without dissolving into tears. It wouldn't be easy, dancing with Luke. He had a way of knowing when something was bothering her, but she couldn't talk about it yet, not if she intended to maintain her composure.

An ache knotted her stomach as she felt the need for his arms around her, his soothing support, his constant encouragement. Doubts about the editorial nibbled at her confidence in him. *Oh, Luke, I can trust you, can't I?*

"AREN'T YOU FEELING WELL?" Justine asked Caroline at intermission. "You look a little peaked."

Backstage, crew and cast members were scurrying about, making last-minute adjustments to the scenery and costumes for the second act. Caroline heard the clang of metal on metal as the musicians positioned themselves for their conductor. From beyond the curtains, she could hear the conversations of patrons returning to their seats.

"I'm okay," Caroline lied. She bit her lower lip to keep it from trembling and avoided Justine's inquiring eyes.

Justine cast her a suspicious look that told Caroline the woman knew something was awry. "If you're sure..."

At that moment Luke stepped out from the men's dressing room and gave Justine a questioning look. So he'd put Justine up to the inquiry, Caroline thought, probably because after dancing like a gangly adolescent in the first act, she'd refused to tell him why she wasn't her normal bubbly self.

Although in her heart she knew she loved him, she couldn't help feeling that her problems this afternoon—no, change that—most of her problems period, ever since that bed race, were connected in some way to Luke.

Ever since he'd come back to town, her life had been an emotional maelstrom. Just when she'd adjusted to the loss of her mother, to being alone in the world, he'd come along in his skintight jeans, threatening her equilibrium and with it the little town where she felt safe.

If he had stayed away, she wouldn't be working herself to death; she might not have taken that preservation job, and she might not have donated her mother's manuscript to the town.

The impact of those thoughts shot through her like lightning. What was it she'd just admitted to herself? That her motives for accepting the job, for donating the manuscript might not have been altruistic?

Denial chased the doubts from her mind. Those had surely been the thoughts of a distraught woman. But deep inside a niggling voice asked her if she hadn't sought the additional exposure the job afforded her because she doubted she could be as charismatic as her grandfather had been.

What about the manuscript? Subconsciously had she donated it to the town because she feared she'd fallen behind Luke in voter support? With her fingertips pressed to her throbbing temples, she forced the self-deprecating thoughts from her mind. She needed all her strength and self-confidence to save her home, to fight for what was right for Granbury.

The touch of Luke's hand at the back of her waist sent twin jolts of longing and resentment through her. "What are you—"

"Sshh," he said in a gentle, reassuring voice with a nod in the direction of the stage. "It's time to go on."

Caroline tried to hide her feelings, but the warmth of his touch shattered what composure she had left as she assumed her entry position in front of Luke at stage left. With him standing so close behind her, she found it difficult to disguise her gesture of wiping away her tears.

Suddenly Luke's warm breath was in her hair. "Listen to the music, sweet thing. Let it shut whatever's bothering you from your mind...for now. You can do it. You're a trooper. We'll go to Dad's and talk when this is over."

Desperate for anything to give her the strength to go back onstage, Caroline closed her eyes to the drumroll fanfare and let the crescendo of the lively Broadway music capture her being. The gentle pressure on her back propelled her onto the stage, and for one hour she shut out everything but the music, the performance...and the man she loved.

LUKE LEANED AGAINST A TREE in the alley behind the Opera House, hoping to catch Caroline sneaking out the back door. Her furtive glance at that door before she'd stepped into the dressing room after the final curtain call had signaled him she might try to avoid him by using the rear exit.

Whatever was bothering her was cutting so deeply that her normal stubborn resolve had all but crumbled. He hated to see her so unhappy, and it bothered him that she couldn't confide in him so he could help her.

A petite figure in red stuck her head out the door and darted in the opposite direction, but Luke's legs were longer, faster. He shot out his hand and clasped it around her wrist, almost knocking her off balance.

"Please, Luke, leave me alone," she said, struggling against his hold on her. She tilted her chin defiantly and looked down her nose at him in that haughty McAlester way again. Damn! He'd thought those days were over.

If she'd open up to him again, he'd love away any problems she had. Maybe she'd seen the results of the poll Carriker had shown him that morning. If so, she knew that he had gained on her and that his chances of winning the referendum on Dino-Land were almost even with hers.

Luke dismissed the poll as a source of her hostility. The subject of Dino-Land pumped Caroline into a frenzy, but it didn't make her cry. Besides, even though the local newspaper had come out in favor of his theme park, he still didn't think she doubted for a minute that she'd defeat him in the referendum. He sensed her anger was a mask to cover up a deep-seated hurt.

"Give me a chance, Caroline. Remember, I'm the man who loves you."

"I—I need to be alone right now," she said, but the tears told him she needed him more than she knew.

Cradling her in his arms, he stroked her head with one hand and her back with the other while her tears grew to deep, racking sobs.

A sudden breeze rustled the leaves on the branches overhead and whipped the dirt in the alley into little dust devils. Behind them Luke could hear voices, the opening and slamming of car doors, the starting of a car engine and the crunch of the tires on the street. The alley was no place to talk, not with Caroline in her state of distress. "What do you say we go for a ride?"

She crossed her arms over her chest and gripped her elbows, as if by doing so, she could plug the leak in her emotions. She looked pitiful standing there in the alley, red faced and puffy eyed and trying for all the world to pretend nothing was wrong. "No, I'd like to go home."

The tears started again. So did the sobs. There seemed to be no end to the tears. Tilting her chin upward, Luke thumbed the new ones away. "Talk to me. Tell me what's really wrong."

She hesitated for a moment, then leaned against his chest and sniffled. "I...feel...so...so all alone. I...need...somebody." She looked up at him and managed a thin smile. "I need...you."

Luke berated himself for not having seen the loneliness beneath that veneer of self-sufficiency Caroline had flaunted at the world for so long—her world, her safe little town of Granbury that he'd threatened with his plans.

He had a hunch. "Caroline, tell me, have you cried over your mother since she died? Really cried?"

A shake of her head against his chest gave him her answer. Her arms laced slowly about his waist, as if she needed the comfort of his body next to hers. "Then it's about time you grieved, sweetheart."

After a few moments of silence, she spoke in a soft voice he could barely hear. "Momma and I were never close. She worried too much about appearances, about what other people thought. When she died, I thought I handled it well—the funeral arrangements and all. But I miss her. I miss all of them, and now—" She heaved a sigh, moving a hand to trail her long, tapered fingers across the swells of his chest.

"Go on."

Caroline sniffled but said nothing.

"Here," he said, reaching into his hip pocket for a white handkerchief. "Come on, we're going to Dad's, and we're going to talk. Whatever is bothering you can't be as important as our love for each other."

THERE WAS SOMETHING about late-summer afternoons in north central Texas, when gusts of wind
whipped over the gently rolling hills and chased the
shimmering oven-hot heat from the road.

It was the time that marked the lapse of a hot day
into a balmy summer evening, a time Caroline loved.
With Luke driving, she was free to let the healing effect of the early evening soothe her as they headed toward his father's house.

She looked at the square set of Luke's jaw, the
shadow of his thick lashes on his cheek, and thanked
him in her heart for his patience. He was right. Their
love was more important than her misgivings about
that editorial, than her ill-conceived grudge against him
because she'd overextended herself in her efforts to
defeat him in the referendum. What was important was
the longing to be in his arms again, a longing reflected
in his eyes. She could think of a dozen things worse
than being alone with him tonight.

In reality, she wanted to get as far away from her
house as possible, so she could shut out the problem
with the loan. Luke wanted her to tell him what was
bothering her, but the best thing for her at the moment was to try to forget the quarter of a million dollars she had to scrounge up somewhere. If she told him
about it, he'd probably want to help. She couldn't allow that.

Once inside the house, Luke excused himself for a
few moments to check in with his answering service.
While he was gone, she studied his father's nutcrackers, lined up on a maple shelf on one wall of the living
room.

She was stroking the white fur plume of a toy sol-
dier nutcracker when he rejoined her. ''Your father

does beautiful work,'' she said, not looking up. ''There are few people in this country who make these well.''

He took the nutcracker from her hands and silently replaced it on the shelf. ''Tell me what's bothering you, Caroline. Who knows? I might be able to help.''

Please, Luke, not tonight. Be with me. Put your arms around me.

As if he'd read her thoughts, he drew her into his comforting arms. ''Don't you know it won't get better until you share the pain with someone else? I'd like that person to be me.''

Suddenly, there in his home where he'd grown up, she felt maybe she could tell him her problem. ''It's my house. I—I might lose it.''

''You might what?'' He lifted her chin until she was looking into his eyes, which at that moment were filled with love and empathy and a questioning she needed to answer.

''Mr. Wilson dropped by my house after church.''

''Wilson from the bank?''

She nodded. ''He's the executor of my mother's estate,'' she explained, then told Luke everything she knew about the action being taken by the Fort Worth bank.

''No wonder you're upset. You can't lose your house. It means too much to you.''

Thankful he understood how she felt, she watched while he pressed a finger to his lips.

''A quarter of a million dollars, you say?''

Following his line of thinking, she opened her mouth to protest, but Luke wouldn't hear of it. ''I'll go with you to the bank tomorrow. If they won't reconsider, I'll cover the loan myself.''

''I can't let you do that.''

"Why can't you? I have the money. There's nothing I'd rather do with it than help you."

"And how would you feel if the town votes against Dino-Land? I appreciate your offer, really I do, but I can't accept it. We already have too many things pulling at us. I'll have to find another way."

Luke didn't argue the point with her. "What bank is it that's calling your loan?"

"Columbia."

"Columbia?"

"Yes, why?"

"I—I'd heard they were having problems with their loan portfolio. I know some people there. Why don't you let me make a few calls, see what I can do to turn this around."

Caroline smiled. "Even though I can't accept your help, I appreciate your concern."

"But what will you do? You said yourself you don't know where you'll find that much money in thirty days."

"My grandfather had some friends in key positions at other banks. I remember seeing a directory of his personal business associates somewhere in his old office downstairs. Maybe one of them will help me."

The glow she'd seen earlier in Luke's eyes frosted over. "You'd rather take the money from one of your grandfather's good-ole-boy buddies than me? Don't you realize you'd be setting yourself up to do somebody a favor someday—a favor you might not want to do?"

"What are you trying to tell me? That my grandfather was a crook? If that's what you think, I wish you'd say it. I wish somebody would tell me if my grandfather was involved in something underhanded or illegal. The constant insinuations are driving me wild.''

Luke raked his fingers through his hair. ''I didn't say your grandfather was a crook.''

That's what he'd meant—she was sure of it. But she was ready to let it go tonight. She had too many emotions warring within her to add resentment to the mix.

Turning her back to Luke, she realized that by telling him about her house, she had released some of the pressure that had built up inside her. But it hadn't changed anything; she still had her problem.

Again she welcomed the feel of his body behind her, the touch of his hands at her waist. ''If you want to talk anymore, you'd better do it now,'' he said, turning her to face him.

The look of longing in his eyes swept thoughts of the loan from her mind. She turned her head slowly from side to side, but her gaze remained fixed on his eyes. ''I don't want to talk anymore.''

His dark eyes twinkled, and he took her hand. ''Good. Because, dear lady, I'm going to make you forget you ever had a problem in the world.''

CHAPTER THIRTEEN

"CLOSE YOUR EYES," Luke said, leading her down the hallway and through the door she knew had to put them in the bathroom.

"Now can I open my eyes?"

Tempted to look, she heard the strike of a match and wrinkled her nose at the smell of burning sulfur.

"Take a deep breath," he instructed her, "and tell me what you smell now, but keep your eyes closed."

Following his wishes, Caroline filled her lungs and smiled. "Peaches!" she said. "I smell peaches."

"I found some candles I thought you might like in a shop near my office in Fort Worth yesterday. If that scent does for you what it does for me..."

Her laughter echoed off the ceramic tile walls. "If you'll let me open my eyes, I'll show you what it does for me."

"So open them," he said.

Then Luke's lips, warm and insistent, quickly claimed hers, and her laughter became moans of pleasure. "Oh, Luke, I need you so."

"I'm here, sweet thing. I'll always be here for you."

Driven by her hunger for him, she quickly unbuttoned his shirt and slid his snug jeans over his tightly muscled hips, then watched his glazed eyes as he in turn disrobed her. While he reached into the shower and turned on the water, she ran her fingertips lightly over his body until he grabbed her hands and pulled her in with him beneath the pulsating spray.

He made a ritual of soaping her, from neck to toes, with a peach-scented bar, then watched the pleasure in her eyes while she lathered him, too.

Cleansed at last of the day's labors and problems, they came together there in the shower, Luke easily supporting her while she slid her legs about his trim waist and lost herself in water-drenched ecstasy.

Weak from loving, they scrubbed each other rosy with thick Turkish towels, then ran into the bedroom, threw back the comforter and slid between the sheets, unwilling to relinquish their intimacy.

Entwined in each other's arms, they listened to the call of a night bird, and stared resentfully at the telephone when it rang.

"Damn! That's what I get for letting my answering service know I'd be here."

Caroline wanted to shut the world away for a few more precious moments, but after the fifth ring she said, "You'd better answer it. It could be your father."

Luke grumbled a mild expletive and, stretching over her, swatted at the ivory phone on the nightstand on her side of the bed. The receiver fell to the floor. She could hear a man's imploring voice while Luke draped himself across her and dangled his arm over the side of the bed, straining to reach the receiver.

"Hello!" he barked into it. "Who is this?"

Luke braced himself on his elbow and let his eyes feast on Caroline. With the phone in one hand, his other was free to caress the satiny smooth skin above her navel. He could tell from her heavy-lidded expression and the way her body trembled beneath his weight that she wanted to make love again. It was a hell of a time to get a phone call.

"Is that you, Luke?"

"Conway, it's you."

The golden hair on Caroline's arms bristled when he said his partner's name. Luke sat up and winked at her, then patted her abdomen to tell her he'd get rid of his caller promptly.

He could tell the mere mention of Conway's name had upset her. Now that he knew it wasn't his father calling from Maryland, he wished he had let it ring. He'd waited too damn many years to make love to Caroline to waste precious minutes talking business while she lay beside him... wanting him as he wanted her.

"Did I catch you at a bad time?" Carriker asked.

"Yeah, well, I was... busy," Luke answered, smiling slyly at Caroline and gently circling a swollen nipple with his fingertips. Her eyes drifted shut as she drew his fingers to her lips, kissed the center of his palm and moved his hand to her other breast.

"This won't take a minute," Conway continued. "I want to talk to you about some investment property."

Luke felt Caroline's hand stroke the sensitive skin on the inside of his thigh, and resolved to get off that phone. "I'm, uh, tied up at the moment. Tell you what, I'll drive over in a day or two and we can discuss it."

"Don't wait too long. It's a hot property. When it goes on the market, I'd like to act on it first."

The gentle stroking of Caroline's fingers brought an abrupt end to the conversation. With his gaze fixed on her lazy smile, Luke slid the receiver into its cradle and pulled her into his arms.

Sometime later Caroline was thinking how nice it would be to have a world without telephones. Their unrestrained moments of caring had created in her an inner glow, a gift from the man she loved that made her feel she wasn't alone. Maybe his love for her would sustain her, keep her from losing her mind, if not her possessions, in the days to come.

Luke gently eased her head back onto her pillow and turned her to face him as he lay beside her. "You're beginning to get that look again."

"What look?"

"That look you had back at the Opera House. Not the mad one—the sad one. You're thinking about your house again, aren't you?"

"I guess it is on my mind."

A growling sound emanated from her stomach, and their laughter gave chase to her blue mood. Luke ran his hand over her lower abdomen. "Are you hungry? I think there's some tuna fish in the refrigerator."

"I'm hungry," she said, wiggling her brows. "But not for tuna fish."

Luke smiled at her knowingly. "How about a steak sandwich?"

She slid a shiny red nail beneath the swirls of dark hair on his chest. "Uh-uh."

"Does the lady want something more substantial?" he teased with a widening grin.

"Uh-huh." She let her gaze drift lazily over his face, a path she followed with her fingertips. One finger came to rest in the dimple on his chin. "Are you going to lie here and talk, or are you going to love me, mister?"

Chuckling, Luke gave a quick reply. "I think I'm equal to the task."

Two hours later Luke and Caroline finally dragged themselves from the bed to raid the refrigerator. Then, concerned about Amrod, she declined Luke's invitation to stay all night.

When they said good-night at her front door, he pressed a business card into her palm and insisted she put it by her phone.

"You'll never be alone again—promise. You can trust me to be here if you need me for anything. I don't care what time it is, if you can't reach me at the hotel, call the number on that card. It's my office in Fort Worth. When it comes to finding me, my secretary and my answering service are as good as private detectives."

Caroline glanced briefly at the card and smiled. "Thanks. It makes me feel better just knowing that."

"How about lunch tomorrow? I need to drive over to Fort Worth, but I could manage an early lunch."

Caroline felt her smile fade as she thought of all the calls she had to make in the morning—the bankers, her lawyer—calls that could take most of the day. "I'm sorry. I've got lots of work to do before I'm ready to meet with the banker."

"When do you think you'll be ready to see him?"

"Tuesday. Wednesday at the latest."

"I'll tell you what. I can postpone my meeting a day or two. Why don't you call me tomorrow after you make your appointment? I'll try to arrange mine for the same day. That way I'll be there if you need me."

Her gaze dropped to the tiny button at the tip of his collar. She remembered what had happened to her in Fort Worth, the night Jessie was killed, and she felt the familiar uneasiness return. "To tell the truth, I wasn't looking forward to making the trip alone."

"Maybe we could stay for dinner." He pulled her arms up around his neck. "Better yet, we could stay in my apartment."

Caroline slipped from his arms and avoided his gaze. "I'll have to get back home. I have . . . engagements every night this week."

"Oh" was his simple response. "It's back to that again, isn't it?"

She nodded. "I'm afraid so."

"I'll be glad when the damned referendum is over."

"OF COURSE, yes, I understand." Caroline dropped the receiver in its cradle and drew a thick, bold line through the last name on her list. Seated at her grandfather's old mahogany desk in what had been his office away from the mayor's office, she stared at the ten names, all gleaned from a personal directory she'd found in the bottom drawer.

Not one of the Texas bankers Barron McAlester had considered a personal friend would agree to meet with her to discuss lending the money she needed. Her fruitless efforts made her all the more aware of her mother's persuasive powers. How Meredith McAlester had gotten the bank in Fort Worth to loan her more than the house was worth, more than it would probably bring on the real estate market today, baffled Caroline and raised a sobering question.

What would she do if, forced to sell the house, she couldn't negotiate a price high enough to pay off the loan and cover the hefty real estate commission?

If the bank in Fort Worth insisted on the full repayment, she might have to mortgage the Emporium, something she could ill afford to do. The profits from her store, plus her meager preservation salary, simply wouldn't stretch far enough to cover a mortgage payment on her business and separate living quarters for her and Amrod.

Fortunately the Fort Worth bank president was out of town until Wednesday, giving her additional time to prepare for her early-afternoon appointment that day. But the more people she consulted about securing alternate financing for her house, the more depressed she got. Was this the strain that had caused her mother to have a stroke?

If it hadn't been for the sweet memory of Sunday evening, Caroline thought, the strain might have been unbearable for her, too. Since then Luke had been there for her when she needed him, phoning to tell her he loved her, showing up on her doorstep with a pizza Tuesday at lunch and—she closed her eyes—taking a few moments to run those glorious hands over her body. She had phoned to tell him about her Wednesday appointment, and he had arranged to conduct his business in Forth Worth the same afternoon. At least she wouldn't be alone.

By the time Luke arrived at noon Wednesday, dressed in a summer khaki suit, peach shirt and blue paisley tie, Caroline had worked herself into a dither. That morning her lawyer had advised her to cut her losses—put the house up for sale and pray someone would want a restored Victorian home badly enough to give her the inflated price necessary to pay off the loan.

One look at the caring expression on Luke's face and she immediately felt better. His presence helped ease the pain of anticipation as they drove northeast along Highway 377 toward Fort Worth. All her senses seemed tuned to him, and she felt a new bond between them created by their physical sharing.

The trip gave her the opportunity to learn more about his family. "What was your grandfather like?" she asked.

"He was plain folks, but he had a heart as big as Texas."

"What kinds of things did you do together?"

"Oh, we fished. He didn't care if he caught anything—he just liked to sink his line in the water and talk."

"It's a shame he didn't live long enough to see how successful you've become."

"Money, power—those things didn't mean anything to Grandpa. What did was a man's heart—the way he treated other people."

Caroline looked out the window at the scenery whipping by them. "I thought my grandfather was the most wonderful man in the world. I wanted to grow up to be just like him. I'm beginning to learn there was a side of him I never knew about. A side that hurt your grandfather."

"If Grandpa were alive, he'd tell us to put the past to rest, to live our own lives."

"Those are almost the same words Amrod used when I told him how I felt about you."

"You talked to him about me?"

"Yes. By the way, I think he and Ellie have been conspiring to get us together."

He squeezed her hand. "Worked, didn't it?"

She returned his smile and squeezed back.

"Speaking of Amrod, how's he doing?"

"Fine," she said. "He told me last night he's been going to A.A. meetings."

"That's great. Can you tell if it's doing any good?"

"He hasn't been on one of his binges in a while, if that's what you mean, but he's still struggling, Luke. He's been drinking to forget something. I think he needs professional therapy to help him come to grips with it."

"Have you suggested that to him?"

"Yes. I even told him I'd go with him and pay for the treatments. But when I mentioned it, he clammed up and wouldn't talk anymore. I think he'll have to handle his problem in his own way in his own time."

"At least it doesn't sound like you'll have to force him to move out."

"I hope not. I'm awfully fond of him."

After a few moments of silence, Luke said, "You don't talk much about your father. Were you close?"

"Since he died when I was only ten, we didn't have much time together, but he was a kind man with gentle ways. I used to wonder if he took that traveling job so he wouldn't have to listen to my mother's constant badgering about social proprieties and obligations.

"I remember the night we got the phone call that he'd died. Momma had a houseful of guests in for Granddaddy. She functioned more or less as Granddaddy's hostess. My Grandma Lydia never cared much for parties and big gatherings of people."

"There seemed to be enough of those in your house. More times than not, the place would be lit up like a Christmas tree when I'd ride by at night. I used to wonder what it would be like to be invited to a Mc-Alester party."

"And I used to wonder what it would be like to grow up with both my parents. Tell me about yours."

Luke smiled. "When I think of them together, I remember laughter. One time they decided to raise chickens to save money on groceries. Our backyard was full of the pecking devils until one day a whole batch of newly hatched chicks got drenched in a sudden rainstorm.

"They looked deader than mackerels. Mom and Dad scooped them up, brought them inside—we're talking four-dozen chicks—and stuck them in the oven. God, what a mess it was, and have you ever smelled wet chickens? It could have been a time when tempers flared, but they laughed together through the whole ordeal."

Caroline chuckled. "What a happy home yours must have been."

"Just simple folks with simple virtues. Mom and Dad said the secret of their happy marriage was a good sense of humor and trust in each other."

"Trust."

Luke glanced over at her, this time with a serious expression. "Trust. Faith. Confidence in each other. Not a bad foundation for a relationship, wouldn't you say?"

"Not bad at all," she replied.

For the next several miles she thought about the differences in their two families and couldn't help feeling she'd missed out on something. Then she spotted a building under construction on the side of the road and remembered that she'd promised herself she would admit something to Luke today. "Who did the plans for your theme park?"

"A firm in Houston Conway and I used for the Arkansas park. Why?"

"Oh, well, they did a good job. Except I still wish they'd find a way to tone down those fifty-foot dinosaurs."

Luke winked at her. "My goodness, Miss Caroline. Do you mean to say you studied those plans?"

"I know I was stubborn at first, but, yes, I did look them over—several times, in fact."

"But you still don't like them, do you?"

She sighed. "No, I don't."

Suddenly, in a dusty haze, skyscrapers loomed on the horizon. God, she was back in Fort Worth, and she hated it.

Soon thereafter they were sitting in Luke's car in the downtown area, boxed in briefly by some noon-hour traffic. The exhaust fumes from all the other cars threatened to turn Caroline's already queasy stomach into a wrenching mess. The odor reminded her of evenings she'd fought traffic on her way home to her apartment, and that uneasy feeling crept over her again.

"I wish you'd let me go with you."

"I told you. This is something you can't help me with. You know why. I'll meet you here in two hours." She hoped she'd need two. One to persuade the president to extend the loan, a second for the paperwork to be prepared and negotiated. If so, she'd dance her way back to Luke's car.

Luke pulled his car to the curb and put on the emergency brake. Turning in the seat to face her, he hooked one forearm over the steering wheel, one over the supple leather upholstery on the seat back.

Drawn to Luke, she pressed her lips to his, lingering until the driver in the car behind them leaned on his horn. "Wish me luck."

"Good luck, and remember, I love you."

She smiled, his love giving her the strength to face the president of the bank. "I love you, too."

A few minutes later she stepped off the elevator on the tenth floor and walked noiselessly over thick carpet to a receptionist dressed in a navy suit. That suit and the location of the woman's desk barring the entrance to the executive suite of offices told Caroline the striking brunette was probably the president's receptionist, dressing by the book for a climb up the office ladder.

Caroline paused to grip the back of a chair, memories of corporate politics, crowded parking garages, congested streets and rush-hour traffic swimming in her head. Visions of her apartment, of that horrible night, brought the taste of bile to her throat. *Calm down,* she told herself. *Get this appointment out of the way, and Luke will be waiting for you outside.*

The receptionist ushered her into an expansive office on the corner of the building. Floor-to-ceiling windows on two sides of the room and rosewood paneling on the others made Caroline feel inconsequential, and her earlier determination seemed to wilt.

On one paneled wall was a Picasso—a real one, she judged—and in the center of the table beneath it sat an exquisite piece of Steuben glass that filtered the bright rays of the August sun streaming through the windows. The room smelled of a fresh coat of paneling oil.

Against one wall of windows at an antique rosewood desk sat a tall, trim man with a bald pate. His attire of a gray, pin-striped suit, white shirt and conservative navy tie had "bank executive" written all over it.

As she approached his desk, he stood, shook her hand with the enthusiasm of an ailing octogenarian and motioned for her to sit in the straight-backed chair that faced him. Unsmiling, he clasped his hands and rested them on the desk before him, his gold Rolex watch barely visible beneath a stiffly starched cuff.

"Miss McAlester, I want you to know how it distressed us to place you in this untenable position with your family home." His gaze rested on a file folder on one side of his desktop. He picked up the folder and opened it, as if he were scanning its documents before making a decision.

"I'm prepared to mortgage my business to secure the loan on my house," Caroline announced before he had a chance to speak. Somehow she'd find a way to make the impossible payments.

"Miss McAlester," he said in a deprecating tone of voice, "surely you must know we've considered precisely that alternative and rejected it."

"But—"

"Our hands are tied," he interrupted her. "Our new auditor has taken the matter of your loan out of my control. The directors were so pleased with his discovery of your loan and several others with insufficient equity or collateral that they gave the man a promotion."

Bully for the auditor! The president was discussing her home as if it were a slab of concrete and a pile of boards, not the embodiment of four generations of family. Anger and panic flooded her; her pulse pounded so hard that she could hear it in her ears. "Are you saying there's no way I can keep my house? None whatsoever?"

The bank president stared at her for a long moment before speaking. "There is one possibility."

Caroline's heart leaped at the prospect, and with great effort she resisted the urge to jump to her feet.

"You should listen to the proposition before you pass judgment, Miss McAlester. It is, shall we say, unorthodox."

"Unorthodox?"

"Precisely."

Caroline had already tired of the man's condescending attitude. She wanted to write the word "precisely" on a thick piece of cardboard and cram it down his throat. Instead she asked in a civil tone, "Would you care to describe it?"

"One of the bank's biggest customers is an investment firm whose officers have a penchant for old homes. When your Mr. Wilson advised us of your distress over the matter, we contacted them. It appears they are willing to make a generous offer for your house."

Caroline's shoulders sagged. "An offer isn't what I want. I want to keep my home."

"Precisely. And that is what you shall do, if you accept this offer."

"But how can that be?"

"Your home would represent an investment. The restorations your mother effected are of great interest to our clients. But apparently they have no desire to live in the house, or to sell it anytime in the foreseeable future. They are rather concerned that, unoccupied, the house would deteriorate.

"If they purchase the property, they will do so on the condition that you continue to live in your house— forgive me, their house. They have instructed me to tender the offer of two hundred fifty-thousand dollars, net to you after any closing costs, registration of deed, et cetera. In return, they ask that you keep a watchful eye on their investment, care for it as you

would were it your own. It would enhance their investment and protect it as its value appreciates. Does this
offer interest you?"

She bolted from her chair and splayed her hands
across the top of his desk. "Would it? It's the perfect
answer!"

The balding man looked down his nose at her hands
until she removed them from his desk. "Do you wish
to think about the matter for a few days? I must warn
you, however," he added, "these gentlemen may, in
the meantime, find another property equally appealing and—"

"No!" Caroline interrupted him. "You get those
papers ready for my signature, and I'll sign them today. Right here. Right now!" Settling back in her chair,
she felt her heart pounding once more in her chest. She
could keep her house, or at least live in it, and maybe,
just maybe, by the time the investors got ready to sell
it she could buy it back.

"I rather imagined you would have that reaction,"
the president said. "I took the liberty of having my assistant prepare the appropriate papers. Because this
particular client has a considerable sum of money in
our institution, there is no need to await approval for
the purchase of your home. Oh, one more thing. The
new owners wish to inform you that, they will, in the
future, cover all costs of maintenance and repairs, as
is customary in such arrangements."

It was more than Caroline could have hoped for.
Amrod could stay on in his cottage, freed from the
maintenance chores he was getting too old to perform.
He could still garden. She could still run her store.
Nothing would change, except, she admitted with a
stab of melancholy, someday her own children might

not experience the joy of living in the McAlester family home as she had.

The man behind the desk picked up the phone and told his secretary to bring in the papers. Caroline carefully read line after line of fine print. She wondered if she should have an attorney check over the documents, but remembering what her lawyer in Granbury had advised her, she decided she had no choice but to sign.

With a pang of remorse, she placed the pen on the signature line. An idea popped into her head. She hid the smile it prompted behind a businesslike expression while she announced, "I want an option to buy." She placed the pen on the desktop beside the papers and sat back in her chair.

"Miss McAlester, I hardly think you're in a position—"

"Call them. Now. See what they say. Surely when they decide it's a good time to sell, they won't care if it's me who buys the house or somebody else."

The president pressed his lips into a thin line, lifted the phone and instructed his secretary to ring Conference Room C. So the buyers were somewhere in the bank, waiting to pounce on her house like vultures.

While the president talked into the telephone, she prayed the buyers would agree to her terms. Her prayer was rewarded. The document was changed, giving Caroline the first right to buy back her house if and when the new owner decided to sell it. The president and Caroline initialed the changes, and a notary came to finalize the procedure.

Her throat dry, she watched the president's secretary scoop up the documents and carry them from the office, apparently destined for Conference Room C and another series of signings.

It dawned on Caroline that she didn't know who had purchased her house beyond the name of a corporation. When she stood to shake the president's hand, she asked, "Will I have the opportunity to meet the new owner?"

"I don't think so. This firm prefers to keep a low profile on investments. However, they ask that you keep this card handy, in case you need repairs on their house." He handed the linen-weave business card to Caroline.

The term "*their house*" grated on her, but the prospect of being able to keep the house in top condition helped her overcome her irritation. She glanced at the card and read, "Equity Investments." The phone number on the card brought a frown to her face. Where had she seen that number?

"We'll send you a second copy of the papers after the buyer signs them," the president said by way of dismissing her. He slid a blue portfolio across the desk with the initial papers for her keeping. "Good day, Miss McAlester. I'm pleased we were able to work out an equitable arrangement of value to both parties."

Caroline was only too glad to leave his office. At the elevator she looked at the business card again and tried to remember where she'd seen that number. A television commercial maybe, or a billboard, or newspaper ad. The elevator door opened, and she stepped inside, turned and punched the button for the ground floor.

As the door slid shut, she spotted the president's secretary carrying papers from a narrow hallway across from the elevator and on to the receptionist's desk. On the wall beside the entrance to that hallway was a brass plate bearing an arrow and the designation Conference Room C.

Caroline noted the hour, punched the open button and stepped from the elevator. She still had fifteen minutes before she had to meet Luke. If those were the papers for the sale of her house, perhaps she could catch a glimpse of a representative of the company that had purchased her house. She wanted—no, she needed—to see who owned her home now.

With a confident stride, Caroline crossed the carpeted area and entered the hallway as if she belonged there. In a few steps she spotted two doors, one to the ladies' room and, opposite it, Conference Room C.

What luck! Smiling at her ingenuity, she darted into the ladies' room and held the door open a crack so she could see Conference Room C.

After what seemed like an interminable wait, her efforts were rewarded. She heard men's voices nearing the door to the conference room. She prayed that no one would need to go to the ladies' room before she could match faces with the voices.

While her heart beat in wild anticipation, the door to the conference room swung open. A secretary emerged first, obscuring her view. Behind her was one man dressed in navy and another she couldn't quite see.

Unable to contain her curiosity, Caroline opened the door to the ladies' room wider, as if she were about to step into the hallway. At that moment, the woman turned around, saw her and smiled.

Caroline managed a hesitant smile, but her gaze darted past her. She saw a tall man—a man with dark, wavy hair, a man dressed in a khaki suit and peach-colored shirt.

CHAPTER FOURTEEN

"LUKE, what are you doing here?" Still in the doorway to the ladies' room, Caroline waited for an explanation from the man she loved.

Luke's face had a hard look to it, and anger flashed from his eyes. He stepped forward and cradled her elbow in his hand. "Come on, let's get out of here."

Then she saw it. In his other hand, he held a blue folder identical to the one the bank president had given her with the sale papers on her house.

She felt the blood drain from her face as a sickening feeling collected in her stomach. He couldn't be the mysterious buyer of her home who had hidden behind the name of a business. Or could he?

While she searched his face for the answer, thoughts Luke had shared with her—thoughts of a lifetime of envy—gnawed at her mind: *"I used to watch you and wonder what it would be like to be a McAlester—to live in that big house of yours.... I guess I've always wanted to possess you.... I used to wonder what it would be like to be invited to a McAlester party."*

Unable to stop her suspicions from forming into words, she said, "You? You're the one who bought my house?"

"He didn't buy your house, Miss McAlester. We bought it—both of us."

She tore her attention from Luke's face and saw Conway Carriker step into the hallway, grinning like a cunning fox.

A seven-digit number flashed through her mind, the number on the card the president had given her to call for repairs on her house. The same number on the card Luke had pressed into her hand when he'd kissed her good-night after they'd made love Sunday—after he'd kissed away the tears she'd shed because she was afraid she'd lose her house. Equity Investments. Carriker and Luke. Did she feel duped!

Numb from disbelief, she backed away from Luke. "Why? Why did you do it?"

"I didn't," Luke said, spitting out the words as if they were venom. He jerked his head in the direction of his partner. "Carriker did. I just got here and found out about it myself."

"But he said—"

"We're partners. According to our agreement, he can negotiate a contract for both of us. And he did just that—before I got here."

"He'll do a good job managing your property for you, Miss McAlester," Carriker said. "If you have any problems, just give Luke a call, and he'll send a repairman right over. I trust you'll take care of our house for us. I've always been fond of it. That's why a few years back when I heard your mother was desperate for a loan, I persuaded the bank here it would be a good investment for them. Naturally I seized the opportunity to buy it when a business associate told me you needed to sell. Now if you'll excuse me, I have other business to attend to."

Carriker turned on his heel and retreated down the carpeted hallway. Caroline could swear she heard him chuckle under his breath, and he walked with a victorious spring to his step.

Caroline couldn't walk. All she could do was stumble another step away from Luke. The enormity of what had just happened hit her at once. "Why didn't you stop him? You must've known I'd never sell my house to that—that weasel!"

Luke stiffened and reached for her elbow again. "He may be an opportunist, but he's no weasel. Let's get out of here and go someplace where we can talk this over."

Talking was something Caroline didn't want to do. "I—I want to be alone," she said.

"This is one time you're going to listen to me, Caroline. We have to talk. You have to understand what just happened. Why it happened."

She tried to be patient, but anguish weakened her control. "How does it feel, Luke, after all these years, to own—what did you call it—the McAlester mansion? It's what you've always wanted above all else, isn't it?"

"That does it," he said. He tossed his blue folder onto the floor behind her, gripped her upper arms and backed her into the ladies' room. "I have a few things to say to you, and you're going to listen."

"You can't come in here."

"I'm in, aren't I?"

"Please, just leave me alone. I—I can't think. I have to sort it out. I have to—"

"Do you love me, Caroline?"

Confused and hurt and angry, she leaned against the wall for support. "I don't see how that has anything to do with—"

"I said, do you love me?"

She closed her eyes and swallowed over an ache in her throat. She couldn't lie to him, especially not about that. "Yes. You know I do."

"If you love me, you'll listen. You'll trust me enough to know I couldn't do what you think I did."

"Oh, Luke, I don't know. I have so many emotions warring inside me, I don't know what to think."

"Okay, don't think, just listen." Although the ladies' room afforded him little space, Luke paced back and forth before her while he explained how he'd come to be in that conference room, how he'd come to be the co-owner of her house.

"If I hadn't been in such a hurry to get off the phone Sunday night, Carriker probably would have explained that the property he wanted to discuss with me was your house. But with you lying beside me, all I could think about was making love to you again.

"Hell, Caroline, you were driving me wild with your hands. You remember that night! I told Conway I'd talk to him about the real estate later, because making love to you was more important than any business deal. Turns out, I should have listened to what he had to tell me."

"Luke, I—I'm sorry. I wanted to see who the mysterious people were who'd bought my house, and when I saw you, I naturally—"

"Assumed the worst," he finished for her. "Will you ever learn you can trust me?"

She shut her eyes for a moment and wondered that for herself. "It's Carriker I don't trust. I'll bet he engineered the foreclosure on my house."

It was her turn to pace. "He was probably afraid you were getting too close to me, afraid your feelings for me would diffuse your passion to build Dino-Land in

Granbury. So he discreetly arranged the foreclosure on my house to pit us against each other and keep me so busy right before the election that I wouldn't have time to campaign. I'll bet if you check around you'll find Carriker has a powerful friend here at the bank.''

Luke stared at her in silence. ''Then you don't know?''

''Know what?''

''That Conway is Columbia Bank's chairman of the board.''

''Chairman of the board? Now isn't that dandy!''

''But he had nothing to do with your loan foreclosure.''

''Surely you don't believe that.''

''Of course I believe it,'' Luke said. ''Conway's never lied to me. Some ambitious new bank auditor took a look at your loan and brought it to the attention of the board of directors. Called it an inordinate risk, a poor-quality loan, one that never should have been made because there isn't enough equity to justify the principal. The board voted not to renew it.

''Conway would never intentionally hurt you, Caroline—or anyone else. He's a fine, honorable man. I trust him. I have to trust him. I couldn't be his partner if I didn't.''

''Apparently you don't know the man that well. When I was in high school your partner wanted a ranch my granddaddy had bought for retirement. When Granddaddy wouldn't sell, Carriker bribed some agriculture department inspector to rule the herd on that ranch had some rare cattle disease.''

''That's a pretty serious accusation, Caroline.''

''Granddaddy had to shoot them,'' she continued, ''every last one of them, a big herd of fat Herefords ready for market. The government paid him to kill the cattle, but not nearly as much as he would've gotten from selling them. It nearly ruined him financially, and he had to sell the ranch. Do I have to tell you who bought it?''

"Conway."

"Good guess."

"That isn't the way I heard the story. I heard your grandfather got caught giving his cattle a drug to fatten them up—a drug that had been banned by the Food and Drug Administration from use in food animals a long time ago because it had been proven unsafe for humans."

Luke hesitated, running the fingers of one hand through his dark hair. "Maybe it's time you knew that your grandfather, the mayor, wasn't exactly lily white when it came to business ethics."

"Okay, so maybe my grandfather wasn't perfect. Lately you've made that abundantly clear. But he was good to me, and he was the best mayor Granbury has ever had."

It was time Luke learned something about himself. "You talk about motives. You know what I think? I think you let your envy of my family, of my grandfather, burn inside you until it became an obsession. I think you come back to Granbury as Conway Carriker's partner so you could shove it down everyone's throat that after all those years of being looked down on, George O'Connor's grandson was finally a someone!"

She paused, her voice and her limbs all trembling at once. "Oh, Luke, I know you think you love me. But is it possible that deep down you just *want* to love me so you can possess what you couldn't have early in life—my family's respect and social position? Luke, remember what you said before, that when you were growing up you didn't love me like you love me now? That's because you didn't really love me at all. You loved what I represented. Luke, are you sure your feelings have changed? That now you do love me? I don't think so.''

Luke gripped her arms tightly in his hands. ''How can you say those things after what we've shared? I love you, Caroline! It hurts to hear you say such ugly things.''

''They've needed saying—for a long time. And now that I've said them . . . please . . . let me go.''

Luke dropped his hands to his sides. ''Maybe you'd better go. I guess I was wrong, after all, when I thought you could learn to love me, that even though you grew up in that impossible family, you understood virtues that weren't even in their vocabularies.

''Do you remember me telling you how important trust is to a man and a woman? Without it, our love doesn't stand a chance. If it hadn't been for Mom's and Dad's complete trust and faith in each other, they never would have made it through all those tough times. We would have had tough times, too, Caroline. All couples do. If you can't believe I love you for yourself, not for the prestige you can bring me, it's over. I can't take the distrust any longer.''

As much as Luke's words stung her ears, Caroline had to say one more thing before she left him. ''Trust works both ways, Luke. You wouldn't trust me when I tried to tell you about Carriker. You defended him without a thought. You're so blinded by his power you can't see what he's done to us, to you. You want to tell me about trust, Luke? First you'd better learn who you can trust and who you can't."

She glanced over her shoulder as she left him in the ladies' room. "We were just kidding ourselves when we thought we could end the feud between our two families, weren't we?"

THERE WERE ONLY three passengers on the bus to Granbury. Caroline sat near the back and stared out the window, dabbing at her tears with a handful of paper napkins she'd grabbed at the bus station coffee shop. As the scenery whizzed by in a parched summer blur, the events of the past few weeks played over in her mind.

Luke's teasing, flirtatious words leaped from her memory and burned in her heart: *Hop in my bed, sweet thing, and I'll take you for a ride.*

Luke had taken her for a ride, all right, all because he couldn't overcome childhood hurts and dreams of envy. She wondered if things would have been different if she and Luke hadn't been McAlesters and O'Connors. If she hadn't been a member of Granbury's high-and-mighty McAlesters, maybe he wouldn't have been interested in her. Maybe if her grandfather hadn't done God-knows-what to Luke's, she and Luke might have had a chance to follow their hearts.

Damn her grandfather! For the first time in her life, she wanted to pummel his chest. She pictured him tumbling off that pedestal where she'd held him in such high regard.

But her anger was wasted. She and Luke were responsible for what had happened between them—or what hadn't happened.

The heat of the hundred-degree day rose from the road in waves as the bus crossed the small bridge over Lake Granbury. In the distance Caroline saw the riverboat, now empty, rocking against its moorings, its red-, white-and-blue trim brilliant in the late-afternoon sun. She tortured herself with the memory of Luke's hands on her body that night on the top deck and the way her heart had skyrocketed when he'd looked at her with longing in his eyes.

"Oh, Luke," she whispered. "We could have shared so much."

She talked the bus driver into letting her off at the Square, but everything she saw, or smelled, or felt reminded her of Luke. The scent of crape myrtles was almost sickening in the heat, a reminder of the bouquet Luke had given her the night he'd shown up at her house for chicken and peach pie.

Painfully she remembered it was also the night he'd secreted away on her veranda his plans for the theme park. From that moment the distrust had lurked beneath the surface of their relationship. She'd distrusted him, and he'd distrusted her, because she was a McAlester.

She spotted Ellie across the Square, pulling the heavy wooden door shut on the Emporium. Not ready to explain her red-rimmed eyes or endure Ellie's questions, she ducked behind a bushy crape myrtle and waited for her dear old friend to leave.

If Ellie was locking the store, it must be six o'clock, the closing time they'd agreed on for weekdays until Caroline returned as manager, until the *Pal Joey* run was over.

Caroline pressed her temples with her fingertips, hoping to silence the throbbing that had ensued when she remembered she'd have to dance with Luke the next night. She was, as he'd so aptly put it, a trooper, and she'd get through the last weekend of performances—if it killed her.

She had to get a grip on her emotions. Dino-Land. That's how she'd do it. Throw herself into the referendum battle. With only six more days until the election, she'd have to work double time to make up for neglecting the fight over the past couple of weeks. She was scheduled to speak to a church group that evening. Could she do it? She had to.

Now that Ellie was out of sight, the Emporium tugged at Caroline, an impulse she gave in to. But when she opened the front door, the scent of peaches hit her like week-old garbage.

Even if it had been one of her favorite elder ladies who'd provided the hand-packaged potpourri, it had to go if she was to keep her sanity. She found the cellophane packages tied with peach-colored satin ribbons, boxed them up and dumped them into the trash bin behind the store. Several spritzes with an air freshener did a fairly good job of obliterating the memory-evoking odor from the store.

But she couldn't spritz away the image of Luke in her back room in his cowboy hat, tight jeans and white shirt with the pearlized buttons. There was no escaping the man. He was the only man she'd ever really loved.

She glanced around the Emporium and forced herself to concentrate on practicalities. If Carriker or Luke ever exercised the right to force her out of her house, she'd have to make the store more profitable to cover her extra living expenses—and Amrod's.

It might take more advertising, some sophisticated marketing, but she could probably increase her sales substantially. Maybe if she let tourists experience more of the area's history when they were in her store, they'd spend more of their money there.

As she'd done as a child, she tried to imagine the store's ambience just after the turn of the century, when her great-grandparents had opened it. How lucky they had been to have each other, working side by side to make the store a success until their only child, Lydia, married Barron McAlester.

So great was their love for Lydia that they'd ensured the financial success of her marriage to Barron by making the Emporium her wedding present.

Thoughts of the days of her grandparents reminded her of the old dresses in her attic, and she recalled she'd never found the time to try them on. That was exactly what she needed to do today—crawl back into her family's world and hide from the pain of the present, from Luke.

Caroline walked home quickly. When she entered the front door and glanced up the staircase at the painting of her grandfather, she couldn't avoid the feeling that she'd somehow let down four generations of her family.

Her grandfather seemed to smile down at her. Whatever he'd done to hurt others, he was still there for her. She could almost feel his comforting arms about her as she gripped the balustrade and bit back the tears.

A shower helped. She scrubbed herself briskly, trying to wash away the hopes she'd had for her and Luke together...and the memory of his hands on her skin. But as she sat on a tufted stool in her powder room, patting herself dry, she found the telltale evidence of a love bite on her breast. The memory of Luke's adoring lips on her body flooded her with a sense of longing for the lovemaking she would forever remember.

She closed her eyes as a wave of loneliness settled over her. She had to forget that she loved Luke, but her heart told her it was too late. And her nipples hardened into tight buds as she thought of him. Her body refused to let her forget how she'd felt when he touched her . . . stroked her . . . everywhere.

She dusted herself with rose-scented powder and made two trips to the attic for the dresses. Most of them were a speck snug, especially in the waist, but she refused to harness herself into a corset. She'd had enough discomfort for one day, or for a lifetime.

How long would it take to feel alive again? Would she ever again be charged with the joy of living . . . and loving . . . as she'd been with Luke?

As she was about to slip out of a rose silk dress with a bustle, which had been her great-grandmother's, she heard Amrod's familiar voice call to her from the base of the stairs in the front hall. Scooping up the voluminous folds of antique fabric in her hands, she hiked the skirt to her knees so she wouldn't soil it. At the stairway she spotted Amrod in the entry hall, twisting his hat in his hands.

"Amrod, up here," she called to him.

He glanced up at her sheepishly. "I'm sorry, Missy. I knocked three times. Ellie insisted I check on you. Are you all right?" A soft smile creased his lined face. "You look mighty pretty in that dress you're wearin'."

She brushed her hands over the silky fabric, and the touch made her recall the texture of Luke's skin.

"Why, thank you, Amrod. I'm okay, I guess. Why did Ellie ask you to check on me?"

He looked down at his hat. "Said somethin' about a phone call from Luke." He glanced up at her again. "He's mighty worried about you, Missy."

Caroline almost choked over her answer. "If—if he calls again, tell him there's no need to worry."

Amrod shrugged and pinched the crown of his hat. "If you're sure you're doin' okay, I'll be goin'...."

The sweet old man was such a welcome sight, Caroline couldn't stand the thought of his leaving her...alone. "What are you doing right now?"

"Me? Nothin' much. Gardenin's finished for the day. I picked some roses for you."

Caroline bit her lip to keep it from trembling. "I'd sure appreciate your company." She glanced down at the old dress. "I've been trying on some dresses from the attic. Why don't you come up and keep me company while I finish? It won't take long. I have to speak at eight."

His eyes brightened. "Why don't I call Ellie? She could come over, and we could make it a party."

Caroline couldn't help smiling at Amrod's insistence on propriety. "Why don't you do that. There's an idea I'd like to run by both of you, anyway."

Ellie showed up in her bedroom so quickly that Caroline was sure her next-door neighbor had anticipated the invitation. With her, Ellie brought a large platter of sandwiches, and a smaller one of homemade chocolate chip cookies. Ellie and Amrod sat side by side on a settee in front of the window, noticeably quiet while Caroline tried on the dresses.

When only the two wedding gowns remained, Caroline plopped on her bed in a cotton robe. Bypassing the sandwiches, she ate three cookies. When she picked up the fourth, Ellie raised an eyebrow, glanced knowingly at Amrod and said, "You want to talk about it, child?"

How much did Ellie know? Caroline didn't think she could talk about Luke or about losing her house, not yet, especially in Amrod's presence. He didn't need to have the extra pressure of worrying that he might lose his home.

But it was Amrod who brought up the subject. "We know about the house, Missy."

She dropped her gaze to her lap. "He says we can stay as long as we want, but I don't trust Carriker."

Amazingly, at that moment she was reinfused with the strength of her McAlester upbringing. She lifted her chin confidently, and added, "I won't let you down, Amrod. You'll always have a place to live.

"I've decided to put more of myself into my store so it'll make more money. I'll do some extra promotions. Maybe a style show with these old dresses and a luncheon in the Nutt House on a Sunday. I could decorate the tables with some of those antiques Momma stuck away in the attic."

"You could sell them," Ellie suggested. "Especially if you had a commentator tell a story about each piece. People like to think they've bought a piece of history."

"Maybe you could get yourself on TV in Fort Worth and Dallas," Amrod said.

Caroline slid off the bed and wrapped one arm around Amrod, the other around Ellie, feeling a burning behind her eyes as they hugged her back and kissed her cheeks. She wasn't alone, after all. Ellie and Amrod were her family; they were all she had left.

The stirred-up emotions of the day made her voice quaver. "Will you help me? Both of you? We'll need to get moving on it soon."

Amrod patted her hand. "Make yourself a list of things for me and a list for Ellie. Maybe we could fix up some flowers from the gardens to make your store look prettylike. The crape myrtle smells mighty sweet, and there's plenty of it."

Crape myrtle again. Time, she decided. She needed lots of it before she could smell a crape myrtle blossom or eat a peach without feeling the pain.

Ellie gestured to the two wedding gowns that still lay on Caroline's four-poster. "There's your finale, and nobody but you should wear them."

Caroline reached for a tissue as she remembered her fantasy of marrying Luke, wearing one of those dresses.

"I'm an old fool," Ellie said. She rose from the settee to drape her generous arm around Caroline's shoulders. "Forgive me, child, but I know how much you love those dresses. And it looks to me like you're the only gal in these parts small enough to squeeze into them. Why, I'll bet they're close to size threes."

Caroline nodded. "The other dresses have been a bit snug. I'd have to diet—stay away from the cookies for a couple of weeks." She walked around her bed and unzipped the bag containing her Grandma Lydia's wedding gown. Could she bring herself to try it on?

A spark of her grandfather's feistiness flashed through her. She wouldn't let Luke destroy the special feelings she had about her grandparents' wedding.

"Come on," Ellie encouraged her. "I'll give you a hand."

Fifteen minutes later, Caroline emerged from the powder room, all the buttons but three at the waist fastened down the back. The satin gown with yards of pearl-appointed lace was heavier than it looked, smelled a bit musty and scratched her at the waist, but it wasn't a bad fit.

When she posed before Amrod and pivoted for his approval, he had the same strange look on his face he'd had Sunday morning when she'd shown him the wedding gowns in her parlor. Bending over, she patted his weathered hand. "What's the matter, Amrod? What is it about this dress that upsets you?"

"Better stand up, Missy, or you'll be gettin' it dirty. I haven't cleaned up yet from the gardenin'."

"Amrod—"

Ellie cleared her throat. "He's right, child. That lace is so old it's about to crumble. Why don't you slip out of the thing, and we'll put it on a hanger."

Caroline looked from Amrod to Ellie and sighed. Whatever secret they shared, they had no intention of letting her in on it. Reluctantly she acquiesced to their wishes to drop the subject and stepped into the powder room.

While Ellie unbuttoned the gown, Caroline leaned on the marble countertop to steady herself.

"You love him, don't you, child?"

Caroline hung her head. "Oh, Ellie, like no one I've loved in my life. But it could never work for us."

"No use trying on the other dress in your state. Plenty of time for that later. Slip into some shorts, and we'll sit on the veranda and drink lemonade and swat mosquitoes."

Caroline swiped at her tears, thankful for Ellie's gift of comforting. "I need to try on that dress if we're going to plan a style show. Will you . . . get it for me, please?''

''If you're sure . . .''

''I'm sure.''

When Ellie brought the second wedding gown to Caroline, there was a strange expression on the woman's face. Caroline could swear she stroked the dress lovingly as she smoothed out the wrinkles and undid the long row of satin-covered buttons that descended from a high, Victorian neckline down the front of the dress.

Remembering how much it had upset Ellie the last time she'd seen the gown, Caroline kept her questions to herself. The buttons took an eternity to fasten, and all the time Ellie was doing them up, Caroline remembered how she'd fantasized Luke undoing them, kissing each inch of bare skin as he went.

When the dress was in place, Caroline fingered a faded satin rosebud on the bodice. ''Oh, Ellie, it's exquisite, much prettier than the other one. Tell me why Grandma Lydia didn't wear this one when she married Granddaddy.''

Ellie avoided Caroline's eyes. ''You want to show it to Amrod?''

The old woman was hiding something. It showed in her face. ''Why won't you tell me, Ellie?''

Ellie shook her head. ''Some things, child, are best left unsaid.''

''I wish you and Amrod would tell me what it is about this dress that bothers you both.''

''We will . . . someday.''

Puzzled, Caroline scooped the full skirt of the hundred-year-old gown into her arms. As she did, a stiff, flat object rubbed against her forearm from inside the dress.

Her curiosity piqued, she sorted through the layers of fabric until she found a hidden opening at the side, at hip level. She carefully stuck her hand through the slit, sliding her fingers through layers of fine fabric in the attached petticoats, until her fingers closed over a crinkly object in a slick satin pocket.

She pulled out the treasure and stared at it. It was a faded, cream-colored envelope addressed in elaborate cursive. "Ellie!" she exclaimed. "Look at this."

Ellie's eyes widened as she looked at the envelope. The old woman covered her mouth with her fingers and stumbled backward, landing with a thud on a brass trimmed vanity seat, which slid back, banging against the wall to the bedroom.

CHAPTER FIFTEEN

"YOU LADIES doin' okay in there?"

"Amrod, come in. Hurry!" Caroline called to him as she rushed to Ellie. The poor woman's arms were flailing and her legs kicking in an effort to right the seat, which was wedged against the wall on its two back legs. From the wide-eyed expression on the woman's face, Caroline wasn't sure whether Ellie was okay or not.

Amrod stuck his head in the door and nearly tripped over the folds of Caroline's great-grandmother's wedding dress as he rushed to Ellie's side. "Lord, Ellie, are you hurtin'?" He turned to Caroline. "What happened, Missy?"

"Quit fussing, you two, and help me get this thing back on four legs," Ellie grumbled.

The look on Ellie's face as Amrod and Caroline pulled on the woman's outstretched arms told Caroline there was something in the letter to fuss over. Once the older woman was seated comfortably on the righted vanity seat, Caroline picked up the envelope and studied it more closely.

It was addressed to George O'Connor and had apparently never been opened. "What's a letter to Luke's grandfather doing here?" she wondered out loud.

Ellie reached for the letter. "I'll take care of that, child."

"No," Caroline said. "I want to know why a letter addressed to Luke's grandfather wound up in my great-grandmother's wedding gown."

She turned the envelope over in her hands and read the return address scrolled across the back flap. "Dear God," she said, her gaze darting to Ellie. "Grandma Lydia wrote this letter." She turned the envelope over again and examined the postmark carefully. "On June 13, 1930."

The date flashed in her mind—June 13, 1930, the day before her Grandma Lydia married Barron Mc-Alester. George. Lydia. Barron. Was her Grandma Lydia the woman Luke had spoken of—the one both George and Barron had loved? Had her Grandma Lydia been the reason the friendship between the two had dissolved into a feud?

She looked to Ellie for an answer. Not speaking, Ellie glanced at Amrod and shook her head.

"Amrod," Caroline said, "do you know why Grandma Lydia wrote George O'Connor a letter the day before she married Granddaddy?"

Amrod blanched, a look of terror in his blue eyes. "Don't read that, Missy." He stretched out a shaking hand. "Give it to me, please."

Amrod didn't look so good. Caroline put the letter on the marble vanity top and went to him. "Are you okay?" It was somewhat of a miracle he'd lived more than eighty years, considering how he'd abused his body. She'd never forgive herself if she precipitated a heart attack in the dear old man. "Perhaps you'd better lie down on my bed."

Ignoring her suggestion, he glanced furtively at the letter on the vanity. That he didn't want her to read what was in the envelope made her all the more anxious to do so. She retrieved the envelope and debated whether or not she should open it.

"Missy—"

"Amrod," Ellie interrupted him, gripping his forearm, "maybe it's time she read it. Maybe if she does, things will be different for her, better than they were for Lydia."

"But, Ellie…" The old man leaned back against the doorjamb, his forehead beaded with perspiration.

"We've got to think of her happiness—hers and that young man's."

Ellie's obvious reference to Luke confused Caroline even more. "Will you please tell me what this has to do with Luke?"

"Child, you'd best sit down," Ellie said. "What's in that letter's bound to confuse you. Hurt you, too. But it's time you knew. We'll be waiting outside in your bedroom when you finish. You'll have questions, I'm sure."

Caroline watched Ellie maneuver out of the powder room, with the assistance of a still-pale Amrod. Ellie paused and turned. "I'm trusting you to find it in your heart to be forgiving, child."

When the door clicked shut behind them, Caroline hastily removed her great-grandmother's wedding dress, slipped it over a padded hanger and hung it in the wardrobe against the wall. Then, seating herself on the vanity stool, she opened the brittle envelope.

A sense of foreboding came over her as she drew three pages of crinkly stationery from the envelope, along with a stiffer piece of paper folded into fourths. She opened the letter first. The salutation almost knocked her off her stool and confirmed her worst suspicions: "My beloved George." Caroline's heart pounded as she read the letter, penned almost sixty years ago by her grandmother:

> My beloved George,
> When I was a young girl playing with my dolls in my mother's garden, I pretended I was a bride and you, dear George, were my handsome, debonair groom. I think I fell in love with you the day you moved to town. I have loved you so many years that what I must do tomorrow breaks my heart, and, if you still love me, I fear will break yours, too; for at noon I will wed not you, but Barron.

Caroline's hands trembled. At last she would have her answers.

> I pray you have not by now discarded this letter without reading it through, for I may never again be afforded the opportunity to explain why I seem to have abandoned you, the man I will always love. These past weeks I have lain awake at night, wanting to explain why I broke our engagement by way of a messenger, without a single word from my lips.

Caroline paused, unwilling to admit that her grandparents' marriage had been other than her romantic, fairy-tale vision, yet aching at the thought that her dear grandmother had married her grandfather while she loved another man. Dabbing at her eyes with a tissue, Caroline forced herself to read on.

> Please know that I marry Barron against my will. If I do not, he vows he will report to the authori-

ties that your father was a deserter from the army during the war. Since your dear father, this day, lies stricken with an ailing heart, I know I must do as Barron bids, or I shall be responsible for killing your father as surely as if I pulled the trigger of the gun they would point at him on his arrest. How Barron secured the information about your father's desertion is a mystery, but he seems to have many sources of information. I have told no one. I would never betray your father for risking the rest of his life in a military prison so he could be at the side of your dear mother while she gave birth to your elder brother.

The letter fell from Caroline's shaking fingers to the marble vanity. Could her grandfather have done the terrible things her Grandma Lydia accused him of in the letter? Had he blackmailed her into marrying him instead of the man she loved? Denial raced through her like wildfire as she picked up the letter and read on:

I promise you this, my dear. I will never permit Barron into my bed, will never share with him the gift I have saved these many years for you. Though we are denied the pleasure of each other's arms, I can present you with what would have become ours had we been able to marry as planned; namely, my father's store. You must not reveal this conveyance until your father dies; for Barron would invoke his wrath and make good his promise to report the desertion to the authorities. Once your father has joined his Maker, Barron's threat will be empty, and you may register the change in ownership. At that time, I shall leave

Barron, and I only pray you will have found it in
your heart to understand and forgive me. If not,
you shall still be the rightful owner of Cain's Emporium, and always, my beloved, the keeper of my
heart.

Forgive me,
Lydia

The fluid writing swam before Caroline's eyes. On the
veranda outside her bedroom, a cat wailed a mournful
cry that echoed the pain in Caroline's heart.

Hardly aware of what she was doing, she unfolded
the remaining sheet of paper and read a legal document that transferred the ownership of the Emporium
to George O'Connor. A tear rolled down Caroline's
cheek and landed with an ugly splat on the aged paper, blurring the inked signature of her grandmother.

If the letter contained the truth, the hateful expression on Luke's father's face when he had met Caroline
in the Opera House, the long-standing abhorrence of
the McAlester family by the O'Connors was justified.
She guessed Luke's father had known of the heartache
his own father, George, had endured at Barron's
hands. And so did Luke; she was sure of it.

"You'll have . . . questions."

Somehow she made it into her bedroom, clutching
the letter in her hand. Ellie sat on the bed, twisting a
handkerchief in her lap, while Amrod, on the settee,
gazed out the window.

"Oh, Ellie!" Caroline glanced at the letter. "Can
this be true?"

Ellie's nod was the answer Caroline had dreaded.
Caroline eased herself onto the bed beside Ellie and let

the older woman envelop her in her generous arms. Oh, God, her world was falling apart around her!

After a moment, she found the strength to speak. "Grandma Lydia loved Luke's grandfather—loved George?"

"Yes, child, for as long as I can remember."

"And she and George never . . . ?"

"Never. She was afraid if she went to George, Barron would kill him."

"But why is the letter here? Why don't the O'Connors own the Emporium? Why didn't Grandma wind up with the man she loved? Why was the letter postmarked but never opened?" She turned to Amrod, remembering he'd been the postmaster years ago. Perhaps he had some answers. "Amrod?"

The old man looked at her, his eyes, too, glassy with tears. "George never got the letter, Missy. He never got it, because . . . because—"

"Let me finish," Ellie said, interrupting him. Shifting her weight on the mattress until she faced Caroline squarely, the woman tucked a curl behind Caroline's ear and sighed. "Lydia thought she could trust the lawyer in Glen Rose who made up that document. What she didn't know when she snuck away to Glen Rose the day before the wedding was that that snake of a lawyer was beholden to Barron. Of course, the polecat never told Lydia that. He waited until she left, then tipped Barron off about what your grandmother had done.

"Your grandfather was a good mayor, child—I'll give him that—but he was unprincipled when it came to getting what he wanted. From that desk of his downstairs, he wielded more power than this county had ever seen.

"At the time that letter was written, Amrod was the postmaster, and his dear mother worked by herself in a millinery shop on the Square. Barron prevailed on his friendship with Amrod, asking him to intercept that letter before it was delivered and bring it to him. When Amrod refused, Barron told him that if he didn't cooperate there might be a fire in the millinery shop one day when Amrod's mother was alone.

"After Amrod did as he was forced to do, Barron got Amrod fired from his job. Amrod was the youngest, most ambitious postmaster Granbury's ever had—on his way to a promising career.

"After the wedding, after poor Lydia suffered through the ceremony and a long reception, Barron brought her to this bedroom and stuck her letter to George in her face. He warned her if she ever spoke to George again, he'd kill him."

"Oh, Ellie! How could he do such things!"

"Barron McAlester may have been a good grandfather to you, child, but he was a dangerous man. He came from lean beginnings and was determined to marry your grandmother. He had it in his craw to acquire the old-time prestige and the respect that the Cain family had, not to mention the Emporium, the most lucrative store on the Square. It didn't matter that George and Lydia had promised themselves to each other and had already planned a wedding."

She paused, rubbing the back of Caroline's trembling hands between her fleshy ones. "I'm sorry, child. We—Amrod and I—hoped you'd never have to know about Barron. Now that you know, I expect it's a relief for both of us. I'm sorry you had to learn it today, after your breakup with Luke and all. Maybe now you'll understand what drives that young man. Maybe you'll be more understanding.''

Caroline wiped away the tears brimming on her lower lids. ''No wonder Mack O'Connor didn't trust me.'' Her gaze fell to her lap. ''And Luke. Dear Luke. He must know. That explains why he's envied me all these years—why he talked about this house with such emotion in his voice. If Grandma and George had married, Luke would've grown up here, instead of me. It would have been the O'Connor home, not ours.''

''There's one more thing you should know,'' Ellie said. ''Luke's grandfather wasn't always the town drunk. I think that without Lydia, George quit wanting to live, and found his courage in the bottle.''

Caroline's gaze darted to Amrod as she remembered his words: *''Guilt, blamin' yourself for things that happened a long time ago—things you did, things you didn't do—can eat away at you till you don't want to live.''*

''Is this what drove you to drink, Amrod? This business with my grandfather?''

One corner of Amrod's mouth turned up ruefully. ''I hated myself for what I'd done, like you must be hatin' me now, Missy. I'm sorry.'' He shook his head. ''I never wanted to hurt nobody, least of all Lydia . . . and now you. It feels like it's happenin' all over again.''

Caroline slipped off the bed and dropped to her knees before him. ''I don't hate you. Forgive me if it seems as if I do. I'm numb, that's all.'' She folded her arms over his legs and rested her cheek on them. ''It's been a horrible day. But not as terrible as Grandma's life with . . . with him must have been. No wonder she didn't want to wear her mother's wedding gown.''

"All those years she'd planned to wear it when she married George," Ellie said. "It seemed a sacrilege to marry Barron in it. She put it away in the attic and went there from time to time, tried it on and pretended she'd married the man she loved."

"So that's why she kept the attic locked."

"Yes, dear."

Amrod cleared his throat. "I'd best be leavin' you two alone. Expect you have some woman talkin' to do."

Ellie's voice, crisp, imploring, filled the room. "Aren't you going to tell her the rest?"

Amrod froze, his eyes seeming to plead with Ellie not to say more.

Caroline looked from one to the other. "There's more?"

The only sound was the grandfather clock ticking outside the bedroom door.

"Please, if there is, tell me now," Caroline pleaded. "Let me get it over with all at once."

Ellie stuck her hands on her hips and glared at Amrod. "She needs you. Can't you see that, you old fool?"

Amrod rose to his feet, looking from Caroline to Ellie. "I—I can't tell her."

The touch of Caroline's hand on Amrod's shoulder halted his retreat from the room. "What is it Ellie wants you to tell me?"

Amrod looked down at his scuffed-up gardening shoes. "There's more, Missy. Lots more."

Ellie ambled across the room to join them. With one hand on Caroline's shoulder and one on Amrod's, she turned them until they stood close, side by side, gazing into the beveled glass of the cheval mirror.

Caroline glanced at the two pitiful figures, victims, as her grandmother had been, of the man Caroline had looked up to all her life—her grandfather, the almighty mayor. She reached out and squeezed Amrod's hand, finding solace in sharing the pain. "I'm sorry my granddaddy hurt you."

"Child," Ellie's voice came from behind her. "What we're trying to tell you is Barron McAlester wasn't your grandfather. Your grandfather—" she paused "—is Amrod."

Caroline's jaw fell open, and her heart thudded in her chest. She turned to Amrod. "You're . . . you're my . . . grandfather?"

Amrod nodded, then let his gaze return to his feet. When he closed his eyes, tears spilled over the rims and followed the jagged lines down his cheeks.

"You and my grandmother . . . ?"

Again he nodded, still unable to look in her eyes.

"But—"

Ellie patted her shoulder. "Sit down, child, and listen, and I promise, this is the last of the secrets. After all these years, it'll all be out in the open, and you and Amrod can begin to share your lives with each other."

As if in a trance, Caroline backed up to her bed and sat down, her eyes focused on Amrod. She stared at the old man for a sign, a hint that she . . . her father . . . came from him. His bloodshot gaze finally met hers, and she saw it in the shape of his eyes, in the curve of his chin. He was her grandfather.

"The day after the wedding," Ellie began, "Lydia installed herself in a separate bedroom down the hall. At first Barron was satisfied with the prestige and money the marriage afforded him. He made frequent out-of-town trips to, uh, satisfy his masculine urges."

Ellie bit her lip; her voice quavered as she continued. "Then Barron began to threaten Lydia that he intended to exercise his marital rights. Although Lydia tried to avoid him, Barron had his way with her occasionally. Having been installed on the back of the property as a caretaker, Amrod heard Lydia's sobs of desperation through her back window on those occasions and offered her the sanctuary of his cottage whenever she could manage to escape Barron.

"Over the months their friendship grew, and they fell into each other's arms, a sad kind of affection for two love-starved people."

Caroline looked at Amrod and tried to picture him with her grandmother, a gentle woman, as he was a gentle man.

"When Lydia became pregnant with your father," Ellie continued, "Barron assumed he was the father. But Lydia knew better." She bent over and whispered to Caroline. "She kept a close watch on her cycle, because she was determined not to get pregnant by Barron."

"Barron never knew he wasn't the father?" Caroline asked.

"Not until fifteen years ago," Ellie said, "when your grandmother got her fill of Barron. In a fit of anger she told Barron he wasn't the father. He went into a rage, demanded to know who the father was, threatened to kill him. But Lydia, God bless her, wouldn't tell him. Barron decided it had to be poor old George, who by that time had married a woman who had secretly loved him for years."

Amrod broke into the conversation. "A week after Lydia told Barron, Luke found his granddaddy near dead by the lake."

Caroline gasped, remembering Luke's suspicions that his grandfather had been murdered. "He—Barron didn't—?"

"Not with his own hands," Amrod said. "Barron was too smart for that. He paid somebody to do it for him. I heard Barron talkin' about it out back late one night." He glanced away. "Barron had found out George couldn't take drinkin' gin. I tried to warn George, but I—I was so drunk I passed out before I got to him. I've had to live with that all these years."

Caroline's stomach heaved; she clamped her hand over her mouth and ran for the bathroom. Amrod came to her there, and with a cold washcloth he bathed her forehead until she rid her stomach of its contents. Then, helping her into bed, he pulled the covers under her chin, while Ellie phoned the church and canceled Caroline's speaking engagement.

Later, after Amrod and Ellie had spent a couple of hours answering Caroline's questions, Amrod squeezed her hand and looked at her with tears in his eyes. "I know what you're feelin'. I lived with the guilt all my life—that is, until you helped me see God can forgive a man his mistakes." The old man's voice trembled. "Oh, Missy, I'm hopin' you can, too."

Caroline was vaguely aware of Ellie slipping from the bedroom. The silence of the old house, the house that had harbored so many secrets, echoed the woman's retreating steps. The grandfather clock on the landing outside Caroline's door struck a resounding chime.

Caroline stared at Amrod for a long moment, thinking of all the years they'd been denied each other's affection. Of the two of them, he had surely suffered more.

There was so much love in his eyes. Denied the opportunity to share it with his son and granddaughter, he'd lavished it on a series of pets over the years. He stretched out his arms hesitantly in a circle of invitation. Raising up from the pillow, Caroline hugged her grandfather, and whispered into his ear, "I forgive you . . . Grandpa."

LUKE LEANED against a tree outside city hall and shoved his cowboy hat back on his head. Although it was almost seven-thirty in the evening, the heat was oppressive, there being little wind to stir the August humidity.

He took a swig of lemonade dispensed by young lovelies provided by Conway to care for their supporters. The leggy brunette who had made it her business to provide for his needs whispered an invitation into his ear to join her in her Dallas apartment after the victory party. She was nice, but she wasn't Caroline.

He fixed his eyes on Caroline, who had managed to position herself with her supporters as far away from him as possible while they waited for the election law judge and the clerks to count the paper ballots. Why the hell had she worn that red outfit! He remembered sliding it off her body, inch by inch, until he'd thought he'd explode with the need for her.

She glanced his way, and he tipped his hat, but she averted her gaze almost immediately. They had hardly spoken since that day at the bank, and in the meantime she had thrown herself with a vengeance into defeating him.

One of his campaign lieutenants, trained by Conway to interpret what he saw during the counting process, swaggered out of city hall and shot Luke the thumbs-up signal. They were still in the running.

Luke pictured in his mind the stretch of land south of the Square—the land he'd saved for, the one piece of commercial real estate he'd bought without Conway's assistance.

When he was five years old he'd dreamed of dinosaurs, not as the ugly prehistoric giants they were to others, but as imaginary friends he'd romped with in his mind. From that childhood fantasy had grown his dream of building a dinosaur theme park children would love. Hell, he'd ride the rides himself, something he'd been unable to do as the child of a poor working-class family.

Dino-Land would be a place that would make the townspeople sit up and say, "My, but hasn't that O'Connor boy made something of himself?"

Caroline had been right. His reasons for developing his theme park in Granbury had been rooted in his ego or in his pride—his family pride. And what the hell was wrong with that? Disney had slapped his name on his big parks, hadn't he?

Luke crumbled the paper cup in his hand and cursed, drawing the surprised attention of several around him.

Yeah, but Disney probably hadn't come strutting into town wearing five-hundred-dollar cowboy boots he didn't really like and driving an expensive car instead of the pickup he preferred to drive.

He glanced around at his crowd of supporters and shook his head. Well, it had worked, hadn't it? The townspeople were well aware of his material success, and he'd earned the respect of the people who'd made fun of him and his family all those years. Today they had decided whether he had a right to pour millions of dollars into their town. If the vote went his way, then in a few minutes he would realize his dream—success and respect for him and his family. He'd be able to walk through town with his chin in the air.

And what had he lost in the process? "Caroline." He said her name out loud, the sweet sound lingering in his ears.

Whenever he phoned, she wouldn't answer, and she had refused to see him when he went to the Emporium or to her house. Even Amrod appeared to be in on the conspiracy to keep them apart, although the old guy had seemed apologetic when he'd explained to Luke at the door to Caroline's house that she didn't want to see him.

He closed his eyes, savoring the sweet memory of her satiny thighs, the honeyed taste of her kisses, the gardenia scent that wafted from the pores of her heated skin. And yes, the feel of her hot flesh when it had parted in invitation and he'd become one with her. Only she could relieve the heat, but more than that, only she could cure the ache in his heart. What the hell was he going to do?

"Hey, buddy, you okay?" his lieutenant asked him.

Luke nodded, but he knew he was far from okay. In his mind he went over the report he had commissioned after he'd recovered from the sting of Caroline's words at the bank.

He didn't want to believe what the private detective had found out about Conway—the partner he had trusted as he'd trusted his own father.

Carriker, the wealthy developer. Carriker, the one who'd arranged the big bucks financing for Dino-Land, while he, Luke, provided the creative genius, the management skills, the ability to assemble contractors and subcontractors as he had in Arkansas to build a first-class theme park.

That same Carriker, the report said, had paid someone to impersonate an agriculture department inspector and a county agent to condemn Barron McAlester's herd.

Luke felt sick to his stomach. Carriker had wielded his power as the Fort Worth bank's chairman of the board to get his wife's nephew hired as an auditor. That nephew had been instructed to find some way to force Caroline out of her home—and fast.

Caroline had been right. She'd gotten in the man's way, and Carriker had dealt with her in the same underhanded manner his partner had accused Barron McAlester of using. Luke knotted his hand into a fist, wishing he could smash it in Carriker's face at that moment.

How could he go on with his dream, Luke wondered, knowing that the man who made it possible had shattered the other dream in his life—to have the woman he cherished. He recalled his promise to restore respect to his grandfather's name and said a quiet prayer. "Please, dear God, let me find a way to do both."

At that moment, an election official opened the door and stepped outside, waving a card over her head. Pushed forward by his supporters, Luke found himself standing beside Caroline, so close he could bend over and kiss her sweet lips.

She lifted her head and looked at him. There were shadows beneath her pretty blue eyes that smiled at him softly, as if longing, as he did, for earlier, happier days. What in God's name were they doing there, looking as if they were ready to sail to opposite ends of the earth?

"'Evening, Caroline. I—"

"Hello, Luke."

His heart lurched, for there had been a gentle quality in her voice, and yes, a measure of caring. He wanted to take her in his arms and the referendum results be damned!

"You folks look like you're about ready to wilt," the election secretary said, fanning herself with the vote tally. Someone handed her a cup of lemonade, and she paused to take a drink.

"Now," she said, "for the news you've all been waiting for. Three of us have counted the ballots three times and come up with the same results. If the unhappy side wishes to request a recount, we will oblige. However, I—"

"Oh, hell, Shirley, get on with it."

The crowd laughed at the remark made by the election secretary's husband. She shot him a withering look before clearing her throat and speaking. "Those for granting the zoning and permission to develop Luke's Dino-Land—seven hundred and forty-three votes."

Luke looked at Caroline and saw hope flicker in her eyes. The city had approximately two thousand registered voters. The vote could go either way.

"And," the secretary continued, seeming to enjoy the full attention of the crowd, "those against Dino-Land—seven hundred and forty-one votes."

The few cowboy hats still on heads sailed through the air, and a Sousa march boomed from a speaker mounted on top a car. Hands reached out of the crowd, pulling Luke to stand up on the city hall steps and deliver his victory speech. But he held back and, looking down into Caroline's eyes, said, "I'm sorry. I know how this hurts you, I—"

"Congratulations," she said simply. Then, standing on tiptoe, she brushed her lips to his cheek, turned around and disappeared into the crowd.

THE SUN had just risen Wednesday morning when Caroline shut the wooden lid on the freshly filled peanut butter cookie bin in her store and peeked into the next one. Only three chocolate chip cookies remained in the bottom. She'd restocked three days ago. They were probably stale, unsalable. So she could eat them. She did.

As she brushed the crumbs from her fingers onto the seat of her jeans, she sucked in the pooch in her stomach and berated herself. When would she quit drowning her misery in calories? Probably when she stopped remembering Luke. Memories. They were all she had left of the man she loved.

Well, she'd lost Luke—or Luke had lost her—but some good had come out of it all—she'd gained a grandfather.

Dear Amrod. She had to get him out of Granbury if he ever hoped to resolve his drinking problems. At eighty, he had few years left to enjoy sobriety, and he deserved to live somewhere that memories and mistakes, ghosts of the past, didn't haunt him and tempt him to drink, as they had for years.

She glanced at the legal-size envelope in her hand and sighed. Today was the day she had to do it. Her gaze drifted to the window, past the courthouse and the crape myrtles shimmering with delicate pink blossoms, to the Nutt House on the far side of the Square.

Was Luke up yet? Had he had breakfast? Surely he was in town. After winning the referendum, he must have a myriad of things to do.

Before she lost her nerve, she set out for the back room and the telephone. Her hands had just parted the blue gingham curtains, when she heard an insistent rapping on the door.

What inconsiderate soul wanted to shop at—she glanced at her watch—six-thirty? The rapping continued, but no face appeared above the gingham curtains on the door. Probably a child, an early riser, after a bit of candy before his mother awoke to feed him breakfast.

She steeled herself to be polite yet firm, but, being a sucker for kids, grabbed a peanut butter cookie on her way.

When she opened the door, a hand reached up from the side of the doorway and clamped around her wrist.

CHAPTER SIXTEEN

THE MAN who shot up from a hunkered-down position at the side of the doorway towered over Caroline with a familiar air. He doffed his cowboy hat with his free hand and offered a wide, lazy grin. "'Morning, Caroline."

"Luke." Her pulse, already racing from the shock of being grabbed in the near-dawn quiet, quickened as she felt the warmth of his eyes heat her face. Even now as they stood in the doorway, she could see his eyes glisten and knew hers, too, revealed her joy at his touch. She longed to wrap her arms around his neck, to tangle her hands in his hair, to feel his lean body hard and insistent against hers. Dear God, she couldn't.

Still gripping her wrist, he backed her into the store, kicked the door shut with the heel of his boot and bent his head to nibble at the peanut butter cookie in her hand. "Into the cookies already?"

"Why, I, yes," she stammered. Oh, God, she was going to miss the laughter in his eyes, the teasing tone in his voice. And why had he worn that skintight outfit that had dazzled her on the Fourth of July?

"Why are you here?" she asked him in all honesty.

With a mischievous smile, he looped his arms loosely around her waist. "Cost you a kiss to find out."

A kiss would be heaven. Tempted to respond to his teasing words, she pushed away from him and hugged her chest with her arms. "Luke, please, don't pretend it'll work for us. It hurts too much to say goodbye."

His smile faded, and a muscle twitched in his jaw. "I've missed you. I guess I was expecting too much when I hoped you'd show up at the victory party last night. I hoped I could corner you, tell you what's been on my mind, since you wouldn't take my phone calls or see me."

"I almost called you last night—to tell you I'm truly glad you'll get to see your dream become a reality. Yesterday morning I sat down and looked over your plans again and tried to think as the average voter might."

She shook her head. "No wonder you won the referendum. There's a lot of good in what you plan to do. I realize now that I let my emotions and insecurities get in the way of what was good for this town. The events of the past week have helped me see that quite clearly."

"I thought it would feel good to win," Luke confessed, "but when the secretary read those numbers all I could think of was the hope I'd seen in your eyes and how much you must be hurting. Are you okay?" he asked. "I appreciate the fact that you're being a good sport about this, but the park will make Granbury grow, and I'm worried about how you'll be able to handle that. I think that's what you were afraid of most."

Her gaze slid to her feet. "I don't think that'll be a problem. I should have gone for counseling a long time ago about the fears I developed after that robbery." She managed a thin smile. "My feelings about Fort Worth are pretty irrational, aren't they?"

"No, I wouldn't say so. I mean Fort Worth is really a pretty decent place to live, but after having your house broken into and your dog killed... Caroline, I didn't come here to discuss the merits of living in Fort Worth."

She had to give him the letter, had to tell him about Barron... and her Grandpa Amrod, before she left. Tonight she and Amrod would load the car, and tomorrow morning they'd leave all but the memories behind them. But they would also leave the truth in Luke's hands.

At the thought of leaving Luke, she felt like curling up in a corner and crying. But she was no longer that self-possessed woman who figured that just because she wanted something... someone... she should have it.

"I'm glad you dropped by," she said. "I want to apologize for being so ugly when I saw you there at the bank. And... I have something to tell you."

When she turned away, he snagged her arm with his hand and nodded toward the back room. "Can we go back there to talk?"

She lifted one shoulder in a shrug. "I suppose so."

"Good." Grabbing her hand, he ducked through the gingham curtains and drew her with him to the table. Suddenly one arm was at the back of her knees, the other at her back, as he scooped her up and held her close to his chest. Instinctively she circled his neck with one arm and rested the other over the swells of his chest. Beneath her fingers she felt the hammering beat of his heart.

"That's more like it," he said, planting a quick kiss on her lips and grinning devilishly. With one sharp-toed cowboy boot, he pulled a chair away from the table and sat in it with her in his lap. "Whooee! You've been eating a few cookies, haven't you?"

"I guess. These jeans seem awfully tight."

He flashed her an outrageous grin. "Want to slip them off? I'd be glad to help."

"Luke!"

A look of longing replaced the mischievous glint in his eyes. "Caroline, I won't let you down until you listen to me. I haven't been able to sleep, thinking I might never hold you like this, might never make love to you again. I was wrong when I said it was over between us. Caroline, with the love we have for each other, it'll never be over."

She concentrated on the smooth, pearlized button at the open neck of his shirt. "Love wasn't our problem. It was generations of mistrust, our families and upbringings, and Carriker. We had enough problems for three couples."

"I was wrong for giving you a hard time about not trusting me, when all along a part of me didn't trust you—simply because you were a McAlester. Trust builds on trust. Dad lectured me on that when I told him what I'd said to you at the bank. He said that if we're open with our feelings and dedicate ourselves to each other, we can make it. What do you say, Caroline? Will you give us another chance?"

Caroline closed her eyes, afraid to hope they might make it, yet hoping in spite of her fears. When she opened her eyes she saw Luke's adoring face through the sheen of her tears. "I—I want to, but there's so much you don't know. So much I have to tell you."

Luke's eyes sparkled with her encouraging words. "You didn't say no. That means yes, doesn't it?"

She smiled. "It means maybe."

"Come here, sweet thing." His lips brushed hers lightly at first, then crushed them with a bruising force. Joy raced through her like liquid silver, and she widened the kiss and whimpered into his mouth. Ah, there it was, his tongue, the texture of a peach, thrashing, as wild as the force that drew them together.

When he broke the kiss, his breathing was ragged and the blue of his eyes was like midnight. His breath warm on her skin, he bent over and kissed the flesh in the vee of her blouse.

But before she permitted herself to forget problems that could haunt them later, Caroline had to be sure, so she pressed her hands against his chest and said, "Luke, please, we have to talk."

Luke took a deep breath and lowered her feet to the floor so that she stood between his legs, facing him. "Okay, get it over with, because as soon as you do, I have a present for you and some news I think will make you happy."

He patted the curves of her hips with his palms. "Then I'm going to get that quilt that's strung across the wall out front, and I'm going to make love to you right here, sweet thing. Think about that while you talk, while I do this." His hands began a leisurely path over her body, lighting fires wherever they touched.

Caroline clasped her hands over his wandering fingers and stilled them, causing him enough confusion to permit her to back away from him, to pick up the envelope from her desk; she'd addressed it to Luke that afternoon after a trip to the courthouse.

"Maybe you'll understand my behavior the past few days when you read this." She thrust the envelope in his hands and readied herself for his reaction.

"I thought you were still upset with me over the foreclosure on your house. That wasn't it?"

"Open it."

From the envelope he pulled a copy of the deed to Cain's Emporium, which she'd registered that afternoon in Luke's name—Luke's and his father's. Luke held the document loosely in his hand and looked to her, confusion clouding his eyes. "Why did you do this? I know how much this place means to you."

"The store rightfully belongs to you and your family. But you know that, don't you?"

Because Luke's eyes did not register surprise and he asked no questions, Caroline knew that he did. "After I got back from the bank Wednesday, I went through a bunch of old dresses I found in the attic," she said, "including two wedding gowns I'd seen there a few weeks ago. Thanks to your call after I left the bank, Ellie and Amrod were with me, helping bolster my spirits, and they told me what brought my grandmother to write . . . this."

She gave him the letter her grandmother had written his grandfather so many years ago. "I found it in one of the wedding dresses, where Grandma Lydia had hidden it."

Luke propped his forearms on his thighs and read Lydia's letter to his grandfather. When he had finished it, he refolded the brittle sheets, tapped them lightly against the palm of his hand and gave his shoulders the slightest of shrugs. "So, now you know."

"And you knew all along what was in that letter, didn't you? That Barron blackmailed my grandmother into marrying him."

Luke pulled her back between his legs and hooked his fingertips into either side of her jeans waistband.

"Your grandmother came to my grandfather fifteen years ago and told him about that letter. By that time my grandfather was not only married and a father, but also a grandfather. He still loved Lydia, but too many people would have been hurt if he'd acted on the love still between them.

"Lydia tried to get him to take the Emporium, but he refused. He told her he had to think of what Barron might do to his wife and family if he accepted her gift."

"Why didn't you tell me all this when I asked you questions about Barron?"

"What good would it have done? It was too late for our grandparents, and Barron had already met his just reward. But there's a lesson here, sweet thing. Time together is a precious thing especially when two people love each other as we do. We shouldn't waste it on silly arguments and accusations."

She bit her lip and let her gaze drop to her fingers, which were smoothing the fuzzy hair on Luke's muscled forearms. His hands moved up and spread their heat over the sensitive skin above her waist. "Tell me what you know," she said.

"Grandpa George's father—my great-grandfather—lived on for a number of years," Luke said, "so Lydia couldn't go to George for fear Barron would kill him. Shortly after my great-grandfather died, Lydia showed up pregnant. That's when my grandfather gave up all hope. He married a good woman—my grandmother. Of course she knew he'd never love her in the same way he loved Lydia."

"And that's why your father has harbored a resentment against the McAlesters all these years," Caroline said. "Your grandfather must have told your dad about all this."

"When I was a boy and developed this fantasy about you, Grandpa warned Dad to keep me away from your family. It seems that after Barron and Lydia were married, Barron threatened Grandpa. Said if he ever caught Grandpa near Lydia, no telling what might happen. You can see why, when Grandpa...drowned and we suspected foul play, Dad figured..."

"He figured Barron had killed your grandfather."

"I'm afraid so."

"Luke," she said, feeling tears of shame well up in her eyes, "your father was right. Your grandfather didn't drink himself to death, and he didn't commit suicide. He was murdered. The person responsible was my grandfather...Barron, the man I looked up to all my life."

Luke's fingers slid from her waistband, and his hands fell to his knees. "How do you know? What kind of proof do you have?"

Caroline shrank back from him, worried for Amrod because of the anger she saw in Luke's eyes. "Amrod overheard Barron talk about killing your grandfather the night it happened. Amrod tried to warn George, but he was so drunk he passed out."

Luke leaned back and stared at the ceiling. "Barron took away the woman my grandfather loved. Why did he have to take his life, too?"

"Because...because my grandmother told Barron he wasn't the father of her child—of my father. Barron thought your grandfather had slept with my grandmother, so Barron fulfilled his promise to kill him."

Luke sat up straight in the chair. "Wait a minute. Are you saying—?"

"I'm saying that one day Grandma Lydia had her fill of living with Barron, and she finally had the nerve to tell him my father wasn't Barron's child. Barron acted like a madman, but he couldn't get my grandmother to tell him who the real father was. Barron decided it had to be your grandfather, and after hearing about your grandfather's intolerance for gin, he hired someone to—"

"Kill him," Luke said.

Chilled by his words, Caroline backed away and watched the muscles bunch up in Luke's shoulders.

After a moment, he stood and came to her. With his fingers at the back of her neck, he tilted up her chin with his thumb until their eyes met. "That means Barron isn't . . . wasn't your grandfather. You aren't—you never were a McAlester."

He paused and asked the question she knew would come. "If not Barron, who?"

"Amrod."

"Amrod." Luke whispered the name and for a long moment was silent. From the expression on his face, she could tell he was thinking of all the implications of the news she had given him.

After she'd explained how Amrod and Lydia had sought the comfort of each other's arms, she said, "So you see, Amrod is the man my grandfather would have killed had he known the truth, not your grandfather. Amrod kept the fact that he and my grandmother had . . . been together a secret all these years. He never went to the authorities with what he'd overheard Barron say. If he had, Barron and the others responsible would probably have been arrested, and people would have known your grandfather didn't die from alcoholic self-destruction.''

Luke shook his head. ''So all these years your real grandfather was living right in your backyard, and you never knew it. I wonder why Amrod never told you.''

''He thought I'd be happier thinking I was a McAlester than the grandchild of a...a drunk.'' Her lips trembled. ''Amrod needed me. I wish I could have been there for him. Knowing what I know now, I would rather have had his love than that of a terrible man like Barron McAlester.''

''I hate to give anything to the man, but you have to hand it to Barron. Once he found out you weren't his real granddaughter, he didn't treat you any differently, did he?''

She shook her head.

''They say even the worst scoundrel has a soft spot. I guess you were his. Can't blame him, though. Look at you.''

''That's generous of you, Luke. Do you think you could possibly be as generous toward Amrod? I know you must resent him for not reaching George in time to warn him.''

''Caroline, I—''

''Oh, Luke! He's paid for his mistakes a hundred times over. Please don't hate him! He was blackmailed, too—forced to intercept my grandmother's letter before it reached George so your grandfather didn't learn about it until years later. Amrod feels responsible for all the agony George suffered for years, for George not knowing why Lydia suddenly broke their engagement and wouldn't speak to him.''

''Caroline—''

"Please, Luke, try to forgive him. It's only natural for you to be angry with him, but he's my grandfather, and I want to protect him now. I want to take care of him."

She uttered a deep, shuddering sigh and turned away. "That's why I've decided to move. To take him away from all the everyday reminders of the mistakes he's made. I called my old boss, and he said the firm has openings in San Antonio and Austin. I plan to get a small house somewhere. Something like your dad's, someplace where Grandpa can garden. Maybe near a lake where he can fish. He isn't drinking, thanks to A.A. He deserves to live his last years away from this place and all the bad memories."

Luke turned her by her shoulders and forced her to look at him. "You can't leave me, Caroline. I won't let you. We almost lost what we have. I won't let it happen again."

"But I can't turn my back on Amrod."

"You won't have to. You're right. Amrod deserves some happiness after all these years, and he deserves it with you. With us. He doesn't want to leave here, you know. I stopped by your house this morning and told him I was coming to see you. He wouldn't give me any details, but he told me I had to see you today, and he wished I'd change your mind and tell you that's what he wanted, too.

"And that brings me to this." He reached into his back pocket, removed a folded sheath of papers and pressed them into her hand.

She glanced at the papers he'd given her—papers putting his share of the McAlester house back into her name. She looked to him for an explanation.

"You were right about me," he said. "I realized it after you told me you thought I merely wanted to love you. I spent a lot of time soul-searching. I realized I'd grown up envying you because you had everything I never could. Later, when I learned Barron had kept our grandparents from marrying, I became even more obsessed with having what would have been my family's had George been allowed to follow his heart and marry Lydia. Envy's a terrible thing, Caroline. It almost cost me you. I'm sorry I ever coveted that house."

Caroline smiled at his admission. "I can't blame you for envying me. Life would have been so different for you if your grandfather had married my grandmother."

"Your grandmother's the one who suffered, having to live with Barron all those years."

"She was a strong woman," Caroline said proudly.

"So are you," he said, taking her face in his hands and drawing her lips to a kiss. "And your grandfather is Amrod," he repeated, gathering her into his arms. "The poor man was as much a victim of Barron McAlester as your grandmother and my grandfather. So many people hurt by one selfish man.

"That leaves just one little complication between us. Carriker. But I've taken care of that problem. You were right about him, too."

She drew back and looked at him questioningly.

"He's everything you said he was—a first-class crook. After you left me at the bank I got to thinking over what you said. I didn't like the way that business with your loan was handled, so I checked it out, along with his version of the story about your grandfather's ranch. I hope you don't mind my saying this, but the man reminds me of Barron. The worst was what he put you through to get you out of the way so we could win the referendum.''

''It's turned out for the best. People around here seem to be looking forward to Dino-Land.''

''A two-vote margin isn't exactly a mandate. Maybe folks won't be too disappointed when they find out I'm dissolving my partnership with Carriker and I plan to build a much smaller theme park.'' He winked at her. ''Smaller and more tasteful. If the city council approves, I'd like to change my plans—construct a theme park that builds on Granbury's Western history. Maybe even run air-conditioned stage coaches from the park to the Square to the lake.''

Caroline regarded him carefully. ''Are you sure you want to sever your relationship with Carriker?''

''I can't do business with a man who manipulates people like chess pieces, and I won't tolerate anyone who hurts you.''

''Oh, Luke,'' she said. ''At one point I thought you'd be furious when you heard everything I had to tell you. You're a good, forgiving man.''

He gripped her forearms and set her back from him. ''I'm only furious about one thing, sweet thing.''

''What's that?''

''That we've wasted all these weeks, let the mistakes of our relatives interfere with the love we have for each other. We have to put a stop to that.''

She was so full of love for him, for his tenderness, she thought she would burst. ''I'm willing if you are.''

''Willing?'' he said, his eyes dancing. ''Wait right here.'' He turned on the heel of his boot and disappeared into the front of the store. In a moment he returned with the quilt, which he spread out with a flourish on the floor.

Tipping up the rim of his cowboy hat with his thumb, he grinned at her. "Hop in my bed, sweet thing, and I'll take you for a ride."

She chuckled and placed her hand in his. "That has a nice ring to it."

"I hope you'll like a real ring a lot better."

Hardly able to contain her enthusiasm, she asked the leading question. "What ring?"

"The ring I'll buy tomorrow if you say you'll be my wife. I love you, Caroline. Share my bed and my life with me. We could stay here. It's what Amrod wants, and I know you love this town."

"Oh, Luke," she said, coming into his arms. "Of course I'll marry you. I love you so much I was prepared to spend the rest of my life living on my memories of you. But now we can share our love as our grandparents never could."

They sealed their vows with a kiss, while the birds outside the door heralded the start of a new day.

"I wrote a letter to the editor," Caroline murmured into Luke's chest. "I wrote down the whole story. I want everyone to know your grandfather died an honorable death." She kissed his chest and smiled up at him. "And I want everyone to know Amrod is my grandfather."

"You didn't have to do that."

"Yes, I did. I've never been one to lie. I'm not about to start now. Luke...what do you say we sell our share of the house. That place has so many unhappy memories."

"Sounds good to me. It doesn't hold the same fascination it once had for me."

"But I want Amrod to keep his cottage."

"He might not need that place for long. When I stopped by your house, he and Ellie were sitting on the swing in the first light of morning. He had his arm around her, and he was holding her hand."

A smile played across Caroline's lips. "I should have known. Those two have been close lately."

"Ellie could wind up being your grandmother."

"In many ways, she has been for a long time."

"You remember those ghosts you talked about—the ones the folks around here say haunt the Square?" Luke said. "Those ghosts may have been our relatives—George, Lydia and Barron—sticking around to settle old differences. I think we've finally put them to rest."

Caroline slipped her thumb under the top button on Luke's shirt and snapped it open. "Since I'm going to be your wife, do you think you can tell me a secret?"

"What's that?"

"What was the last word your grandfather said when he died in your arms?"

Luke smiled. "The word was a name, actually—Lydia."

"Oh, Luke."

"He loved her to the very end. They say you never forget your first love. Lydia was his. You're mine."

"You'd better not forget me, darling."

"Then come here and give me something to remember."

Harlequin
Superromance®

COMING NEXT MONTH

#362 WORD OF HONOR • Evelyn A. Crowe
As a child, Honor Marshall had witnessed her
mother's death in an air disaster. Years later, when
she found out it was murder, she vowed to seek
revenge. Special agent Travis Gentry agreed to help.
But his price was high.

#363 OUT OF THE BLUE • Elise Title
When a wounded Jonathan Madden showed up in
Courtney Blue's bookstore, it was like a scene from a
thriller—and Courtney had read plenty of those!
Jonathan was no mere professor, as he claimed to be.
But he was definitely hero material....

#364 WHEN I SEE YOUR FACE • Connie Bennett
Mystery writer Ryanne Kirkland couldn't allow
herself to think of a future with Hugh MacKenna,
the charismatic private investigator from Los
Angeles. Firstly she was blind, and secondly there
was a possibility she'd have to live her life
on the run. Hugh only wished he could make her
understand that his life was worthless
without her....

#365 SPRING THAW • Sally Bradford
When Adam Campbell returned to her after a
twenty-year absence, Cecilia Mahoney learned the
meaning of heaven and hell. Heaven was the bliss of
love regained, hell the torment of being unable to
find the only child Adam would ever have—the one
she'd given away.

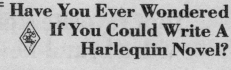

Have You Ever Wondered If You Could Write A Harlequin Novel?

Here's great news—Harlequin is offering a series of cassette tapes to help you do just that. Written by Harlequin editors, these tapes give practical advice on how to make your characters—and your story—come alive. There's a tape for each contemporary romance series Harlequin publishes.

Mail order only

All sales final

- -

TO: ***Harlequin Reader Service***
Audiocassette Tape Offer
P.O. Box 1396
Buffalo, NY 14269-1396

I enclose a check/money order payable to HARLEQUIN READER SERVICE® for $9.70 ($8.95 plus 75¢ postage and handling) for EACH tape ordered for the total sum of $_____*
Please send:

- ☐ Romance and Presents
- ☐ American Romance
- ☐ Superromance
- ☐ Intrigue
- ☐ Temptation
- ☐ All five tapes ($38.80 total)

Signature_____

Name:_____ (please print clearly)

Address:_____

State:_____ Zip:_____

*Iowa and New York residents add appropriate sales tax.

AUDIO-H

Your favorite stories with a brand-new look!!

Beginning next month, the four American Romance titles will feature a new, contemporary and sophisticated cover design. As always, each story will be a terrific romance with mature characters and a realistic plot that is uniquely North American in flavor and appeal.

Watch your bookshelves for a **bold** look!